THE NEXT THING ON MY LIST

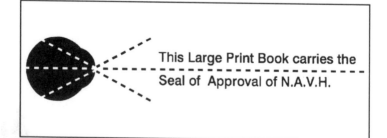

This Large Print Book carries the
Seal of Approval of N.A.V.H.

THE NEXT THING ON MY LIST

JILL SMOLINSKI

THORNDIKE PRESS
A part of Gale, Cengage Learning

GALE
CENGAGE Learning™

Detroit • New York • San Francisco • New Haven, Conn • Waterville, Maine • London

GALE
CENGAGE Learning™

LIBRARY OF CONGRESS CATALOGING-IN-PUBLICATION DATA

Smolinski, Jill.
   The next thing on my list / by Jill Smolinski.
      p. cm. — (Thorndike Press large print laugh lines)
   ISBN-13: 978-1-4104-0783-2 (alk. paper)
   ISBN-10: 1-4104-0783-7 (alk. paper)
      1. Overweight women — Fiction. 2. Large type books.
   I. Title.
   PS3619.M65N48 2008
   813'.6—dc22   2008010995

Published in 2008 by arrangement with Crown Publishers, a division of Random House, Inc.

Printed in the United States of America
1 2 3 4 5 6 7 12 11 10 09 08

For my son, Danny Elder

CHAPTER 1

Next on the list: *Kiss a stranger.*

"How about him?" Susan pointed to a guy so rakishly handsome, it was odd to see him in a downtown Los Angeles bar wearing a shirt and tie instead of modeling underwear in front of a camera, where he clearly belonged.

"Let's be realistic."

"Why? It's just a kiss."

Easy for her to say — she wasn't the one doing the kissing.

It was Thursday after work, and the Brass Monkey was hopping. Susan and I had already been at the bar for an hour, casing the joint and sipping two-dollar margaritas that were, sadly, much too weak to help me muster my courage.

"What do you think — on the lips?" I asked.

"Definitely, but tongue is up to you."

After much debate, I settled on three guys

at a cocktail table across the bar. Mid- to late thirties and dressed in casual business attire, they seemed harmless, which was their primary appeal. *Here goes.* I hoisted myself bravely from my chair as if I were about to march forth into battle. My plan was to go up to their table, explain my predicament, and hope one of them would take pity on me and volunteer for the job.

In the event that that didn't work — well, I didn't want to think about what would happen if it didn't work. I suppose it would involve skulking away in humiliation.

I swigged down the last of my drink, took a breath, and strode to the table. The three guys looked at me with open curiosity. A woman approaching who wasn't a waitress was an interesting sight indeed. Plus I'd sort of slutted up for the occasion. I wore a snug suit over a camisole, and I'd gone to town with the eyeliner. My hair was doing its usual insane tumble of waves and curls to my shoulders.

"Hi! I'm June!" I said perkily.

After a moment, perhaps debating if I was going to try to sell them something, one of them said, "I'm Frank, and this is Ted, and Alfonso."

"Nice to meet you!" And then I plunged in. "I came over here because I was wondering if you could help me? I have this list of things I need to do." I held up the list, Exhibit A, which was handwritten on a sheet of ordinary notebook paper. "One of the things on it is that I need to kiss a stranger. So I was wondering —"

"You want to kiss one of us?" Alfonso asked eagerly.

Frank chimed in, "What — you on a scavenger hunt?"

"Not exactly," I answered.

"So would this kiss be on the mouth?"

"Yes."

"Tongue?"

"Optional."

Three sets of eyes gave me a once-over, but — bonus points for them — they tried to make it appear as if they weren't.

"Aw, Christ," Alfonso said with what appeared to be genuine regret, "we're all married."

"I'm not *that* married," Ted added. "I mean, if it'll help the girl out . . ."

"That's okay," I said, starting to back away. *Why hadn't I thought to check for rings?*

"No, we want to help you. None of us can do it, but we got a buddy here from work who might be able to. Hey, Marco!" Frank shouted across the bar, and who should turn around but the underwear model. Terrific. "There's a girl here needs a hand!"

Marco trotted over. Well, he seemed eager enough. Trying not to blush — and knowing Susan was probably bursting a spleen laughing — I repeated my story. Before I could finish, he snatched the paper from my hand and started reading it aloud.

"Let's see what this list is about," he boomed. " 'Twenty Things to Do by My Twenty-fifth Birthday.' " Then he paused to look at me and smirk. "*Twenty-fifth* birthday?"

Oh, real nice!

I'll have him know that I may be thirty-four, but in certain lighting I still get carded.

"Give me that." I made a grab for the list.

He blocked me with his shoulder and kept reading. "Let's see what it says, shall we? Ah, yes, here it is: *Kiss a stranger. . . .*"

Afraid the list might get ripped if I grabbed for it again, I stood still, arms crossed, fuming.

Ted attempted to defend me. "Dude, don't be an a-hole."

"*Run a 5K. . . . Get on TV. . . .* Oh, wait, here's the best one: *Lose one hundred pounds.* Used to be a fatty, huh? Well, you're looking mighty fine now, sweetheart, so I can see why that one's got a line through it."

"Look," I snapped, "it's not even my list."

"Yeah, right."

"It's not. But it so happens I need to do the things on it."

Alfonso asked innocently enough, "Why's that?"

I sighed. "Long story. Please . . ." I held my hand out. "Give it back."

It was true. The list wasn't mine.

It belonged to Marissa Jones.

Even though there was no signature on it, I'm certain it's hers. I know because I discovered it myself in the days after I killed her. I'd been washing the blood off her purse so I could return it to her parents, and there it was. Folded and tucked inside her wallet.

Of course, I gave everything of hers back — even a pair of sunglasses found near the scene that I thought might possibly be mine.

But I kept the list. Didn't say a word about it to them. After all, how heartbreaking would it be to see your twenty-four-year-old daughter's list of dreams that would never be fulfilled?

Out of twenty items, she'd completed only two: *Lose 100 pounds* and *Wear sexy shoes*. The first one was already crossed off. The second I had to mark off for her myself —

and seeing it written there sure explained those silver stilettos she was wearing when she died.

Naturally, everyone insisted that it wasn't my fault.

They nearly fell over one another at the funeral offering assurances and hugs — which I accepted as part of my penance. My body was one big bruise. Even the gentlest touch was agony.

And here's the worst part: She'd been thin less than a month. One lousy month. After a lifetime of knowing nothing but being fat.

As if to rub it in, staring at me from the front of the church had been a blown-up photo of Marissa standing in a pair of size twenty-eight pants — her body fitting in one leg while she held the waist out to its side. The smile on her face clearly said, *Okay, world, here I come!*

Well.

The whole time the minister was at the podium, I barely heard a thing he said. Instead, I devoted my thoughts to concocting the lie I would tell Marissa's family about her final words. They were going to want to know, after all. And there was no way I was going to tell them the truth: that she'd been giving me a recipe for taco soup.

Turned out I didn't need to worry. My

entire interaction with them was limited to a handshake and an "I'm so sorry for your loss." I skipped the wake, feeling that my presence there — with my bruised collarbone and big shiner — would be nothing short of vulgar. Besides, it's not as if Marissa and I were friends. I'd only met her the night she died.

She and I had been at the same Weight Watchers meeting. I'd just joined, hoping to lose the ten pounds that had managed to creep up from the *last* time I lost ten pounds. She'd received her lifetime pin for being at her weight goal (the irony of that word *lifetime* not lost on me now). Offering a ride to a stranger is something I wouldn't normally do, but I saw her teetering toward the bus stop on those "sexy shoes." I thought about how amazing it was she'd dropped so much weight and said to myself, *What the heck. Maybe her success will rub off on me.*

So there we were, zipping along Centinela Boulevard and chatting about dieting. I said to her something along the lines of "I'm worried I'll fail because I get so hungry when I go on a diet."

Then she said, "I have a recipe for a soup that's super filling."

And I said, "I'm not much of a cook."

And she said, "This is totally easy."

And I said, "Really?"

And she said, "I have the recipe right here with me. I swear, it's so simple — nothing but opening a bunch of cans."

And I said, "Well, great, let's see it!"

And she reached into the backseat of my car to grab her purse, which was the reason her seat belt was unbuckled at the moment of impact.

MARISSA JONES'S TACO SOUP

4 cans navy or northern beans
1 can Mexican-spiced tomatoes
1 can diced tomatoes
1 can corn
1 package taco seasoning
1 package fat-free ranch dressing mix

Mix ingredients in large saucepan. Heat and serve.

MAKES 8 SERVINGS.

As best I can recall (my head took quite a whack, so my memory is dodgy), a dresser toppled off a truck in front of us, and I'd jerked the steering wheel to avoid it. The rest is unclear. Witnesses reported that we skimmed the curb at an angle, which sent us rolling.

"Landed ass over teakettle," I heard one paramedic say to another as they slid my stretcher into the ambulance.

Another thing I overheard: "No hurry on that one, she's dead."

Dead? My hands felt around on my body. I wasn't sure which one of us he referring to.

It wasn't me.

Which meant . . .

Oh shit.

Shit, shit, *shit*.

After the accident, I tried to go back to life as usual, without success. Seemed I'd failed to account for one simple yet irrefutable fact, which is as follows: Knowing that you killed somebody is really depressing. Honestly, I can't fathom how people like Scott Peterson can pick themselves up afterward and go fishing. I barely had the energy to report to the office and perform a job I've been doing so long that I suspect I could do it in a coma.

The weeks ticked by. The bruises faded, and yet, unable to shake the despair that clung to me like a fog, I was left to conclude that there are two types of horrible events: the type that shake you up and cause you to grab life by the throat and never again take it for granted, and the type that make you lie in bed and watch a lot of reality TV.

Mine fell into the latter category.

With no one close enough to witness my downward spiral, I was free to fall. No husband or kids. No roommate. My boyfriend Robert made his break in late August, a month after the accident. We'd been on the brink of splitting anyway, lingering at that stage where we both knew things were over and yet, like a car we weren't quite ready to sell, we kept patching and paying for small repairs, waiting for something huge like the transmission to blow. As it turned out, the relationship was totaled. Robert could barely stand to look at the wreckage I'd become, and frankly, it was a relief when he left. I barely noticed him packing his toothbrush and the extra set of shoes he kept under my bed, what with the new fall TV season starting up.

If only Marissa hadn't written that list . . . or if hers had been more like *my* to-do lists: a bunch of nothing that nevertheless had occupied my time for the past three-plus decades. Pick up the dry cleaning. Run to the gym. Meet a friend for lunch. Some of the tasks got crossed off . . . others were transferred from paper to paper until I'd either finally get around to doing them or decide they weren't as important as I

16

thought they were.

If I died, what could my obituary possibly even say? *June Parker, on- and off-again girlfriend, midlevel employee, and lifelong underachiever, died waiting for something to happen. She is survived by a new pack of socks, the purchase of which was the greatest achievement crossed off her to-do list.*

I'd read Marissa's list only once before hiding it away in my dresser drawer. I wasn't even sure why I'd kept it. Sure, I told myself it would be sad for the family — but still, why did it bother *me* so much?

It was only when bathed in the forgiving light of the TV that I could bear to admit the truth to myself: Horrible as it was that I'd killed someone, I was relieved I hadn't died. For whatever reason, I'd been given a second chance.

Which is why I felt so guilty about squandering it. The gods who spared me were probably sitting around in the clouds, scratching their heads, and saying things like "You'd assume rescuing her from a pile of destroyed metal was enough! What do we need to get through to this woman? Plague? Locusts?!"

Problem was, I had no idea how to change. I wasn't and had never been that person who could sit down and write a list of things

I wanted to do and then actually do them. Marissa Jones needed to rub off on me all right. Not so much the part of her that could lose weight, but the part that seemed to at least have a clue about what she wanted once she did.

It seemed it would require a miracle to pry me from my malaise and set me on a new course. As it turned out, all it took was a guy at the intersection of Pico Boulevard and Eleventh Street selling ten-dollar bouquets of roses.

It was January 20, exactly six months from the day Marissa died. My stomach had twisted when I noticed the date on my calendar and realized half a year had passed. It felt like both yesterday and a lifetime ago. My original plans to honor the occasion involved going home after work and . . . well, I had no plans. But then I stopped at a traffic light next to the man selling roses, and an idea instantly formulated in my head. I'd visit her grave. I'd apologize, and in doing so, maybe I'd be set free.

Flowers resting on my passenger seat, I stopped by a booth at the cemetery's entrance for directions. A woman gave me a photocopied map, using a Sharpie to mark the route to Marissa's grave site. I parked and then walked the rest of the way to where she was buried. Her tombstone, a tastefully simple marker, read, *Marissa Jones, loving daughter, sister, and friend,* and gave her birth and death dates.

"Sorry," I whispered, and set down the flowers.

I stood there for a while, waiting for a sense of peace that didn't come, when someone behind me said, "June?"

I turned around to find myself in that situation everybody hates: I didn't recognize the guy. Easy on the eyes, though. Had that surfer-dude grown-up look. Thirtyish. Tall but not too tall, sun-kissed blond hair, a strong nose, and a jaw that worked well with it. Jeans and a Billabong T-shirt. "Oh, hi there," I said, trying to pass off that I knew who he was.

"You probably don't remember me. I'm Troy Jones. Marissa's brother."

"Of course I remember you."

Okay, maybe not right away. He'd been dressed more formally at the funeral. And his hair had been shorter. Plus I'd met him only long enough to shake his hand.

"I thought it might be you, but I wasn't sure. Do you come here often?" As soon as he said it, he shook his head. "Boy, did that ever sound like a pickup line. Next thing

19

you know, I'm going to ask what a nice girl like you is doing in a place like this."

Avoiding the obvious response — visiting your sister who is dead because of me — I said, "If you're working your way through the lines, I'll save you time. I'm a Scorpio."

"Good to know."

"And to answer your question, no, I don't come here often. But since today was six months . . ."

"Yeah," he said. "Me too."

Apparently we then decided to observe a moment of silence, because we stood there not speaking, and just when I was about to make an excuse to leave, he said, "Care to walk around a bit?"

If only I'd dumped the flowers and run when I had the chance. "Sure," I said, not wanting to be rude. "That'd be nice."

We headed up a dirt path that wound through the grounds, taking a leisurely pace.

"You're looking well," he said, gazing over at me. "You were pretty banged up last time I saw you."

"Yeah," I said noncommittally, and to my relief, from there we chatted about nothing of significance — how we'd gotten so much rainfall lately and how dogs bark before earthquakes. He so resembled his sister. It stirred up what I'd tried to stuff deep inside

— the shame I wore that was as ugly as if I still had the shiner. I feared if I said too much, he'd be able to see what I'd been able to hide from others for months. That I might look okay on the outside, but inside I was still tender and purple and swollen.

We eventually wound our way back to where we'd started, a short distance from my car. "I'm parked right here," I said.

He walked me the rest of the way. I had my keys in one hand, my other reaching for the door handle, when he said, "Do you mind if I ask you a question?"

Rats. So close, and yet . . .

"Of course not."

"It's just that . . . you were the last person with Marissa."

Alarms sounded in my head as he continued, "My parents and I have the details on the accident, but the one thing we can't figure out is . . . why wasn't she buckled? She *always* wore her seat belt. It didn't make any sense. I hate to bother you with it, but it's been driving us crazy."

There you had it. I was going to have to reveal her final moments. Granted, I could say I didn't know, but that seemed crueler than the truth.

"She was getting a recipe for me from her purse."

"A recipe?"

"For a taco soup."

"A recipe." He ran a hand along the back of his neck. "That'd be my sister."

His expression was so disappointed that I added, "It sounded quite tasty."

"I'm sure it did."

Oh, why didn't I lie? Tell him that she'd been telling me how she adored her family — especially that brother of hers?

"Sorry it wasn't something better," I said lamely.

"It's okay. I'm not sure what I was expecting. It's only that . . ." He stuffed his hands in his pockets, leaning against my car. "There's so much I don't know — that I never will. That's what keeps you up at night. It's not only that you miss them. It's the regret that you didn't ask the big questions while they were still here." He looked over toward where her grave sat and then continued. "A few weeks before she died, Marissa and I were at my parents' house for dinner. We were outside, goofing around, playing a little one-on-one. I asked her how her life was different since she'd lost the weight — besides the fact that she could now whup my ass at basketball. She told me she had so many things she wanted to do. And she sounded so excited that I'd

22

asked her what kinds of things. But then my mom called us for dinner, one thing led to another, and I never got around to following up. I mean, what was the big hurry, you know? We had all the time in the world."

Oh God. My insides bubbled and frothed as he spoke.

Returning the list wouldn't have been unkind. It was wrong to keep it, especially now that this perfectly nice guy standing in front of me had been grieving all the more because of my selfishness.

"Um . . . actually . . . ," I ventured, not sure what to say, but feeling I had to say something. "There was one more thing. She had a list." When he didn't respond right away, I blurted, "Your sister had written a list of things she wanted to do by her twenty-fifth birthday. I have it."

His eyes shifted to meet mine, and — brrrr — did the temperature just drop fifty degrees? Because the look in them was icier than I could have ever imagined. "You kept it? There was a list . . . *and you kept it?*"

Well, when he put it *that* way . . .

"I had to," I said defensively.

"Why?"

Why indeed? Panic was setting in when, luckily, I thought of a lie so brilliant that it felt as if it were the truth.

"Because I'm completing the list for her."

The change in his face was like one of those square puzzles where you can move the pieces around to form a picture — it hadn't settled yet, and since I didn't know what it was going to be, I kept talking. "I figured since Marissa couldn't do it for herself, well . . . it's only right that it be me. I was the one driving when the accident happened. I feel responsible."

And there it was: The coldness had melted and was replaced with an expression I couldn't quite read but I knew that I liked. It lifted me up and floated me skyward. I was no longer June Parker, accidental murderess and borderline slacker. I was the sort of woman who'd find a list of uncompleted dreams and take it upon herself to get the job done. I fucking *rocked*.

"That's so . . . amazing," he managed to say, and then to my horror he added, "Do you have the list with you? Can you show it to me?"

"It's at home," I replied hurriedly. "And I'm afraid you'd be disappointed to see it. There's not much crossed off . . . what with her birthday still being months away." July 12, I remembered from her tombstone. Less than six months left to go. "In fact, if we could not make a big deal out of this, I'd be grateful. I'm nervous enough about it. I'd rather keep things to myself right now, if you don't mind."

"I understand." He nodded. "No problem."

I made a show of glancing at my watch and then said, "I'd better get going."

"Sure."

As I got into my car, he pulled out his wallet and fished through it. He handed me a business card. "Call me if there's anything I can do to help. Anything at all."

It occurred to me there was something he could do. "It'd probably be helpful for me to know more about Marissa. I don't want to bother you too much. Maybe you could send me her old yearbooks or photo albums? Anything that might shed light on what might have motivated her to write the things on the list that she did."

He agreed without hesitation, and I gave him my business card before driving away, the blood pumping through my veins so wildly that I suspected I must be visibly throbbing.

I was going to do this. I was going to complete the items on Marissa Jones's list. If I couldn't make something out of my own life, at least I'd make something out of hers.

For the first time in a long time — since

the accident and even before — I felt a surge of an emotion so unfamiliar, it took me the entire drive home to figure out what it was.

Hope.

I felt hope.

Which brought me to where I was: at a bar, realizing there was no way I was going to kiss this jerk, no matter how bad I wanted to cross something off a list.

"So," he said, flashing a gleaming white grin as he handed me back my paper (and, may I add, there is such a thing as *too* much whitening), "what kind of kiss?"

His friend Frank filled him in: "Mouth . . . tongue optional."

"Never mind," I said, "I'll just —"

Before I could finish, his mouth was on mine, his tongue thrust between my lips. It wasn't awful. My first attempts with Grant Smith back in high school were certainly a whole lot sloppier. But I'd experienced significantly more zing with Grant. This kiss, frankly, left me feeling as if I might as well be paralyzed from the waist down.

As he pulled away, he said a glib, "You're welcome."

Oh, *please*. I wish he'd said it while he was kissing me, because then I could have thrown up in his mouth.

"Unfortunately," I said, feigning regret, "the list specifically states that *I* have to do this kissing — you know, be the kiss*er*, not the kiss*ee*. I'm afraid this doesn't qualify. But hey" — I winked at the guys at the table before turning to go — "I appreciate the effort."

On my way, I nearly bumped into a busboy. Hmm. He appeared to be about seventeen years old and was conveniently just my height. "Mind indulging me?" I asked. I took hold of his collar to pull him closer and — pausing for a few seconds to give him a chance to run for the hills if he wanted — planted a kiss on his mouth. No tongue, but plenty warm and moist, and — yes! — there was that zing I was talking about.

Then, over the sound of the guys at the table having quite a guffaw about the whole thing, I grabbed Susan. "Let's get out of here," I said. After all, I still had plenty more things I needed to cross off the list. And as my grandma used to say, there's no rest for the wicked.

CHAPTER 2

20 THINGS TO DO BY MY 25TH BIRTHDAY

1. ~~Lose 100 pounds~~
2. ~~Kiss a stranger~~
3. Change someone's life
4. ~~Wear sexy shoes~~
5. Run a 5K
6. Dare to go braless
7. Make Buddy Fitch pay
8. Be the hottest girl at Oasis
9. Get on TV
10. Ride in a helicopter
11. Pitch an idea at work
12. Try boogie boarding
13. Eat ice cream in public
14. Go on a blind date
15. Take Mom and Grandma to see Wayne Newton
16. Get a massage
17. Throw away my bathroom scale
18. Watch a sunrise

19. *Show my brother how grateful I am for him*
20. *Make a big donation to charity*

"Skydiving is at the top of my list," Susan said, taking a bite of her ice-cream cone.

"You have a list?"

"Not anything written. But sure, there are things I want to do before I die."

"Well, I for one can't imagine anything worse than skydiving — hurtling through the air, no control over how fast you're falling or where you might land. Why people find that fun is beyond me."

We sat at an outdoor café taking a break from work, slurping on double-scoop ice-cream cones. The offices of Los Angeles Rideshare — where Susan is client services director and supervises a staff of twenty and I work as a writer and am more, say, in the worker bee category — are located in one of the older downtown business districts. Ornate buildings line the narrow streets, making it seem unusually old for Los Angeles. On this particular afternoon, with the sun blazing warm on our shoulders, we watched pouring rain across the street where a Visa commercial was being filmed. Huge machines sprayed water on faux New York taxis. Tourists stood at the periphery in tank tops and shorts, holding pens and paper for autographs in case that guy grinning at the camera was a real celebrity.

As much as I was riding high from the success of kissing the busboy, I knew there was much more to do.

The list sat on the table between us so Susan could help me establish the rules — the dos and don'ts, as it were, for completing it. For example, we decided that I didn't have to do the tasks in order. Also, I had to obey, as Susan put it, "the spirit of the law" — a result of my saying that to do #8, *Be the hottest girl at Oasis,* I could merely walk into the bar and set myself on fire.

"So what's your plan to get this done on time?" Susan asked as she used a napkin to dab at ice cream that had spilled onto her blouse. She looked amazing as always, wearing a simple silk pantsuit, no makeup except for red lipstick, and her black hair knotted into an effortless updo. It was the sort of look that made me regard my flowered skirt and blouse from the Everything $15 Store a little less charitably than I had when the cashier had been ringing it up.

"My plan?" My brow furrowed. "I figured I'd wing it."

"I don't know, June. Some of these seem time-consuming. Like this one: *Change someone's life.* That's hardly the sort of thing you can handle on your lunch break."

"Oh, don't worry — I did that already. In fact, do you have a pen? I'll cross it off." I sounded so gloomy that Susan looked at me perplexed until I elaborated. "Marissa was alive. Now she's dead. That's quite a change, don't you think?"

"Ugh. How long do you intend to beat yourself up over this?"

"Until this list is done, that's how long."

"All the more reason to take it seriously."

"I sure hope I finish."

I didn't need to say anything more than that. Susan and I have been best friends since we met as students at UC Santa Barbara — she's been around long enough to know that it won't be easy for me. She's seen it all. The vacations I planned but never got around to booking. The half-completed master's degree in marketing I thought would jump-start my career. For that matter, the poncho I recently tried to crochet that took so long, ponchos went back out of style.

"You know that anything I can do to help I will."

"Thanks." I glanced at my watch. "I'd better get back to the office. Lizbeth's having one of her famous late afternoon meetings

31

to make sure none of us tries to sneak out early. But hey, at least I'm getting one task accomplished today." I held up my ice-cream cone in the gesture of a toast. "Number thirteen: *Eat ice cream in public*."

"About this one . . . I don't get it. What's the big deal about eating ice cream?"

"Fat people aren't allowed to eat in public."

"What are you talking about?" she said, a bit snobbily in my opinion. "I notice them eating all the time."

"Exactly."

"You lost me."

"It's hard to enjoy the eating experience when you feel everyone's staring at you, thinking, *No wonder she's such a fat cow. Look how she eats*."

"I don't think that!"

"Sure." Although I'd never carried the sort of weight Marissa had, I was no stranger to how feeling fat can affect things. I've gone up and down the same ten or twenty pounds my whole life. I have one of those body types that lean in that direction: all curves and boobs and butt. Currently, thanks to being too miserable to eat after the accident, I was the lowest weight I've been in a long time — a diet strategy, by the way, that I don't recommend. Logically I know that

I'm not overweight, but I fear that one wrong move — one taco or burrito too many — and I could burst into fat without a moment's notice.

Susan tipped her chin toward my cone. I'd worked my way through the rocky road and was well into the cookie dough. "*Are* you enjoying that?"

"To be honest, I'm not a big fan of ice cream."

"How can anybody not like ice cream?"

"Too big a commitment."

"That makes no sense."

"Think about it. Once you buy ice cream, you have to finish it right then and there. Either eat it or lose it forever. I mean, look at this. It's already drippy. You can't tuck it away to finish later like you can, say, a cookie."

"Oh, come on! Have you ever once in your life put a cookie away to finish later?"

"That's not the point. It's that I could if I wanted to."

"Seems to me that if you're going to do this task justice, you *need* to enjoy that ice cream. No guilt. No worries. Let yourself get into the moment." When I looked at her skeptically, she said, "That's what Marissa would have done."

She was right, of course, darn it. So I

closed my eyes and slid my tongue over the ice cream. I let its cool sweetness wash over me. Let myself taste it. Feel it. When I finally let down my guard, I had to say it was incredible. Soft and creamy. I enthusiastically licked it down to the cone, sighing and letting out an *mmmm* of pure pleasure.

And then I opened my eyes.

Peter from the accounting department stood at the edge of my table, breathing heavily with a big grin on his face. "Hey, I hear there are Krispy Kremes in the break room. Any chance you'll let me know if you decide to eat one? I want to be there if you do." His eyes moved longingly between Susan and me. "Even better, maybe the two of you could *share* one."

"Hi guys," I said, grabbing a chair at a gleaming conference table that could accommodate a family of twelve for Thanksgiving dinner. It was almost the size of my entire cubicle. I set down my Diet Coke and watched happily as it formed a fat wet ring.

Lizbeth Austin Adams's office reminded me more of a living room than a place of business. She'd brought in plants and lamps and other homey touches — each new addition a knife in my heart, as it meant she was setting down roots.

"Her Majesty will be here in a few," Lizbeth's assistant, Brie, informed me, barely glancing up from her issue of *Us* magazine. "Dang, I can't believe that Beyoncé acts like she invented the whole bootylicious thing." She crossed an ample thigh, exposing the control-top line of her panty hose. "I had a booty when that girl was still running around in diapers."

"Wait a minute — you can't be any older than she is," I countered. "Wouldn't that mean you were in diapers, too?"

"Yeah, but I had a booty."

It was three o'clock on the dot, and the marketing department, such as we were, was assembled. Gazing around at my co-workers, I almost had to feel sorry for Lizbeth. After she'd joined as director of marketing for L.A. Rideshare two years ago, unexpected budget cuts brought a wave of layoffs. The empire she'd moved from Texas to lead dwindled to the four of us. Like strangers thrown together in a lifeboat, we seemed to have only one thing in common: an instinct for survival. Besides Brie and me, there was Greg, the designer, and Dominic Martucci, known only as Martucci, whose job it was to drive the "Rideshare Mobile." Martucci had a thin-lipped smile and a habit of fondling the tiny braided rattail that he'd let grow like a hairy tadpole from the nape of his neck. Sometimes I shuddered to think he had his hands all over my brochures.

"Good afternoon," Lizbeth said as she breezed in. Martucci and Greg straightened in their seats. She had that effect on men. I half expected them to chant like schoolboys, "Good afternoon, Miss Austin Adams."

She tossed a manila folder in front of me. "Nice work on this brochure. I made a few comments." I thumbed through the draft copy I'd given her to review. There was so much red ink, I thought perhaps she'd opened a vein over it. As if I'd be so lucky. "Overall I'd prefer that you make it less" — she gave me a patronizing smile — *"Jane Fonda."*

"Jane Fonda . . . ?"

"You know," she said, wrinkling her nose and whispering as if saying a dirty word, "strident."

"All it says is that cars cause pollution."

"Right."

"But isn't that the —"

"All right, people, we've got quite a bit to cover today," she said, ignoring me as she always did and addressing the group instead. "Let's get started."

I tucked the brochure away. I'd make the

36

changes she wanted — what was the point in arguing?

As at every department meeting, Lizbeth went around the table having each of us report the status of the projects we were working on. When it was my turn, I mentioned a brochure on carpool lanes I was writing and a press release announcing a new bus pass. I bored even myself as I talked about it.

When people discover I work as a writer, I'm quick to point out that I'm not a *real* writer. I see their eyes light up — ooh, a writer?! — so I try to squelch it before it goes any further. While I'm not exactly ashamed, let's face it: My job lacks glamour on a level almost impossible to comprehend. Carpooling isn't exactly sexy stuff.

That's why it baffles me how someone like Lizbeth Austin Adams wound up working here. Well . . . besides the fact that Lou Bigwood, our agency president, "discovered" her at a conference she'd put together — a tale passed around the office with the same reverence as the one about Lana Turner getting discovered at Schwab's. That was Lizbeth's forte: event planning. At our first department meeting two years ago, she'd boasted that she'd planned the Bush twins' coming-out party, to which Brie had slapped her ever exposed thigh and exclaimed, "I *knew* they was gay!" Bigwood, apparently impressed with Lizbeth's credentials — or impressed with something, at any rate — had offered her a job on the spot.

Not just any job.

My job.

Granted, it wasn't mine *technically.* But my old supervisor had groomed me for the position. I would have been managing a staff of twelve, in charge of ad campaigns and publications, plus running promotional events — big parties where we'd feed people hot dogs and, once their mouths were full, talk to them about how very fun sharing the ride could be.

Instead, I'd had to force a smile and applaud as Lou Bigwood had trotted Lizbeth out at a staff meeting and introduced her as the new director of marketing.

I suppose it shouldn't have been such a shock. He was notorious for finding stunning women and — to the endless frustration of the human resources manager — offering them hefty salaries and the plum jobs at the agency without consulting with anyone else. He was a maverick that way. Lizbeth, blond and in her late thirties, was conventionally attractive in a TV-weathergirl sort of way. That in itself was a surprise.

Bigwood's tastes usually leaned more toward the exotic — dark-haired beauties like my friend Susan. In fact, not only *like* Susan, but Susan herself had at one time been the object of his interest, much to my horror.

"You mean *you're* one of Charlie's Angels?" I remember exclaiming after Susan had casually mentioned that Bigwood had hired her after they'd met at (where else?) a conference. I believe I'd been working at L.A. Rideshare for only a few weeks at the time, Susan having recommended me for the copywriter position.

"At least I'm the smart Angel," she'd replied.

"But that's horrible! He hired you based on your looks!"

She'd shrugged.

"Doesn't that bother you?"

"Not particularly."

I must have gotten puffed up and judgmental and *strident* looking because she'd said, "Look, I know Bigwood's an ass, but that goes for anyone who runs a company. I get the job done. People respect me. What do I care why he hired me? Besides, turnabout's fair play — do you have any idea how many men get the job over a woman for the sole reason that they are the proud owner of a penis?"

She had a point.

And now, I realized with a sigh — watching Lizbeth slice Greg's web designs to ribbons in her cool but impossible to contradict manner — that I had a female boss who had balls of steel.

"I spoke with three reporters today," she said briskly when it came to her turn to talk. "I have nibbles but no bites."

She was talking about the Friends of Rideshare project. It was one thing that made me cringe as much as the memory of that typo I'd let slip through in a newsletter back in 2002. (I'd accidentally put "pubic transit" instead of "public transit.")

Friends of Rideshare was an idea that I'd pitched as part of my failed job proposal. I suggested that we ask local traffic reporters to mention carpooling when they did their on-air traffic reports. They might say things along the lines of "Rubbernecking is causing slowdowns on the 405 . . . don't you wish you were ridesharing?" My old boss had marveled at the simple brilliance of the plan. Except when Lizbeth came on, she'd claimed the project as her own and started going after big-name celebrities. I heard she'd spent months calling Brad Pitt's people, trying to get him as a spokesman.

She couldn't even get through to his people's people. The project was tanking, and Lizbeth made sure everyone knew it had been my idea. "I'm doing the best I can to make a silk purse out of a sow's ear," I'd overheard her complaining to another director.

So now, she told us, she was giving up on movie stars and musicians and had an idea — and how novel! — about approaching on-air reporters who specialized in traffic. Although . . . and she gave a woeful sigh . . . she wasn't certain there was any salvaging things.

"No offense," she said.

None taken. Bitch.

We wrapped up the meeting and were gathering to go when Martucci said, "Maybe June could talk to Troy Jones."

Uh . . . er . . . what? Why was he mentioning Troy Jones?

Lizbeth wondered the same thing. "What about Troy Jones?"

"You didn't hear? June ran over his sister back in July."

"I didn't run her over!" I protested.

Martucci snapped a folder shut. "Fine, then. She didn't run her over. But that girl in her car was Troy Jones's sister. Right, Parker?"

41

Lizbeth looked at me with interest. "Is that true? That's who was in the accident with you? Why didn't you say anything?"

A cold finger of dread wormed its way up my spine.

Everyone obviously knew who Troy Jones was — besides his being Marissa's brother. I sure wished I did, but I wasn't about to ask.

Luckily, Greg came to my rescue. "Who's Troy Jones?"

"Traffic reporter," Lizbeth said. "Recently started on K-JAM morning radio. Very up-and-coming . . . gets a lot of airtime."

So Troy was a traffic reporter. I supposed I should have known, but I'd let my interest in the industry slip right around the time I lost out on the promotion. There was no point in being in the loop if they weren't going to pay me for it.

Lizbeth leaned forward. "So will you be talking to Troy soon?"

"For what?"

"Oh, the usual. Memorials. Ashes scattering. That sort of thing. I'd love to get him to work with us. Now that we have you as a personal contact . . ."

I gaped at her, my jaw dropping on its hinge. Was she serious? "I met him at a *funeral.*"

Martucci, ever the kiss-ass, said, "Now this sounds to me like an *opportunity.* What's that old saying?" He snapped his fingers. "Ah, yes . . . when a door closes, a window opens."

My brows shot down in a scowl. How dare he attempt to quote *The Sound of Music* against me!

"That's right, you never know," Lizbeth said. "Sad as his sister's passing is" — she held her hands out across the table . . . and fortunately I was sitting too far away, or I suspected she might have tried to clasp mine — "from these sorts of tragedies, bonds can form."

"Yeah, it's not as if you ran over his sister on purpose," Martucci said, almost kindly.

"Ooh, you know who you shoulda run over?" Brie interjected. "Rick Hernandez on Channel Five. That man is *fine.* I wouldn't mind sharing a ride with him, if you know what I'm talking about."

"*I . . . didn't . . . run . . . anyone . . . over,*" I hissed.

Martucci leaned back, his arms crossed. "No need to get yourself all in a twist, Parker. We're just brainstorming."

"Maybe we should drop this," Greg said, which was lucky because Martucci deserved a snappy comeback, and since I was struggling unsuccessfully to come up with one, *someone* needed to defend me. "This guy isn't the only traffic reporter in the world. I have a feeling that June would prefer to put the accident behind her."

I gave Greg a watery smile in gratitude. He'd managed to shut Martucci up, but alas, Lizbeth wasn't giving up so easily. She turned to me. "I want you to consider it." Her voice was crisp . . . back to business. "Getting Troy Jones on board would mean more funding for this department. It would be a feather in your cap."

A better woman than I would have leapt to her feet and shouted, "How dare you ask that I exploit a situation as horrible as this!" For the fun of it, I also pictured myself slapping Lizbeth across the face. Stomping on her foot. Giving her arm an Indian burn. Making her eat a really hot pepper.

Truth was, however, I rather enjoyed the notoriety. Suddenly I was the school geek who had an extra ticket to the hottest concert of the year.

In a strange way, it felt good.

Not that I planned to do anything about it. Hell would be a skating rink before I'd cash in on any connection I might have to Marissa's brother to further my own career. Or, more realistically, Lizbeth's. The very thought was appalling.

Yet I couldn't make myself say no. Instead, I did what I do so well.

I procrastinated.

And when it comes to that sort of thing, they had no idea who they were dealing with.

"If you think it will help," I said, gathering up my notes. "Let me see what I can do."

CHAPTER 3

A few days later, I bustled home in a cheery mood. I'd stopped by Susan's after work to watch the twins. Her husband, Chase, was out of town, the baby-sitter needed to leave, and Susan had to work late on a proposal. Glad to do it, I told her. There's nothing that lifts the spirits like spending a few hours with two guys who think you're the bomb — even if they are five.

It was almost ten o'clock by the time I got home, and I couldn't wait to crawl into bed. The kids were cute, but I was beat.

Santa Monica, where I live, is a bustling city that nestles the beach — liberal when it comes to aiding the homeless, yet welcoming yuppies with equally open arms. It is perhaps most famous for being both the home of the O. J. Simpson civil trial and the place where Jack, Janet, and Chrissy caused all that wacky mischief in *Three's Company*. My apartment building is a couple of miles from the beach, hugging the border of West L.A. It has twelve units, stacked two floors and arranged in a U-shape surrounding a pool that hardly anyone uses. I have an upper two-bedroom apartment. I've lived there for twelve years — Susan and I were roommates before she moved out to marry Chase. I may die here, because thanks to rent control, I pay only $550 for an apartment that's worth several thousand. Desperately hoping I'll leave so he can hike the rent, my landlord refuses to do any repairs that he can even remotely call cosmetic. There was quite the debate a few years back over whether fixing my falling-in ceiling was "necessary." So the carpet's pretty ratty, and the counters have seen better days, but it's roomy and bright.

I dropped my keys on the counter and hit "play" on my answering machine before heading to the refrigerator to see if I had any leftovers.

I had two messages, both from my mom.

"Junie, this is Mom . . . give me a call when you get a chance."

I'd call her first thing in the morning — it'd been a while since I'd checked in. My parents live in the San Fernando Valley in the same house where I grew up. I typically talk to my mom every week or so — and my dad for the five seconds it takes for him to say, "Here's your mother!" should he pick up when I call.

On the second message — I don't know what time she left it because I never bothered setting the clock on my phone, so the digital voice always announces these arbitrary times — she sounded odd. Sort of breathless and confused.

"Hi, sweetie. I was hoping you'd be home . . . oh, well, this isn't the kind of thing I want to leave in a message. I wanted to . . . Oh, dear. Well, call me back. . . ." Her voice trailed off. "Right away . . . ?"

My heart clattered in my chest. *God, now what?*

It had to be horrible. What could be so bad that she wouldn't say it in a message? Somebody died. My dad . . . or my brother . . .

I dialed with shaking hands, and it seemed as if the phone rang forever. *Pick up . . . pick up . . . pick up . . .*

"Hello?" It was my mom.

"I got your message. What's going on? What happened?"

She caught my urgent tone. "Goodness, I didn't mean to worry you. Everything's fine. I'd called to see if you knew who got voted off the island last night. Your dad had his bowling banquet, and I thought I set the VCR, but I must have messed up. Anyway, I'd have asked Pat Shepic, but —"

"I thought Dad was dead!"

"Sorry," she said sheepishly.

"Or he'd had a heart attack."

"No . . . although" — she raised her voice, apparently for my dad's benefit — "if he keeps getting into those potato chips, he certainly *could* have a heart attack!"

I heard him in the background. "It's my first handful!"

"So . . . ?" she said.

Still a little shaky, I gave her the information grudgingly. "They voted off the German guy," I said. "The one with the gap in his teeth."

"Oh, good. I didn't care for him. He seemed phony."

After a bit of catching up on who was screwing who on the island, we chatted about Marissa's list, which I'd finally told her about after running into Troy Jones at the cemetery. Mom had been disappointed there'd been no swimming with the dolphins on it but otherwise was enthusiastic about the project. She thought it might be a good way for me to get back on the dating horse after my breakup with Robert and refused to believe there wasn't anything on the list about finding a man. "There's the one about going on a blind date," she'd said. To which I'd countered, "But that's more about the thrill of meeting someone new than the torment of picking up their socks from the floor for the rest of your life." To which she'd then replied, "You wind up picking up their dirty underwear, too." Which, as it turned out, was a real conversation stopper.

The microwave bell dinged, and I said I needed to go. My dinner was ready. I'd composed an "international sampler" consisting of leftover spaghetti (Italy), a fish taco from Rubio's (Mexico), two California sushi rolls (Japan), and a slice of Kraft fat-free cheese (France).

Before hanging up, my mom said, "Again, honey, sorry for scaring you."

"Don't worry about it. Guess I have death on my mind these days."

She snorted a laugh. "This is nothing. Wait till you get to be my age."

Leaning over Susan's shoulder to see the computer screen in front of her, I marveled, "This feels strangely like shopping."

She scrolled through a row of men's photos. "How about this one: *Hot Lover Seeks Wild and Free Lady*."

"*Ew.* He might as well just say, *Horny Guy*

Seeks Slut, as Whore Too Expensive."

"Oh, come on," she taunted in the superior way that only the happily married can. "Where's your spirit of adventure?"

"It's home wearing bunny slippers and watching *Entertainment Tonight.*"

"You need a life."

"Isn't that what we're trying to do here?"

Most of the office was deserted. Susan and I stayed after hours so we could find a man for me on the Internet without fear of anyone finding out. Task #14, *Go on a blind date,* might as well be next to check off the list. My mom had been dropping hints that she might be able to set me up. She'd told me that several of her friends' sons were getting divorced and were ripe for the plucking . . . and who's to say for how long? In situations such as this, I figure, the best defense is a good offense.

We couldn't use my cubicle. Not only does my computer screen face out so that anyone walking by can see exactly what's on it, but for people at my level, the company programs in all sorts of blocks limiting where we can go on the Internet. Apparently only upper management is welcome to online date and view porn all day.

"He looks nice." I pointed to a photo of a guy who . . . well, I'd describe him, but he

51

had the sort of face you don't remember. His intro line said, *Nice Regular Guy.*

"What do you want a nice regular guy for?"

I scowled. "What's wrong with a nice regular guy?"

"Nothing."

"Okay, then."

"But . . . remember how you asked me to keep you honest about this?"

"Yes," I said hesitantly.

"If I'm being honest, I think you're being a coward."

"Terrific."

"Seriously! The whole idea of this is to take a risk — to put yourself out there. I'm sorry, but I happen to believe that you're funny and smart and very pretty. A guy like that is beneath you. You can do better."

It's hard to argue with someone complimenting you while they bawl you out. That's probably why Susan's employees love her so much. She's slippery that way. "Are you coming on to me?" I asked jokingly, hoping to change the subject.

"I mean it. Remember those photos from C.J. and Joey's birthday party last month? I e-mailed them to a few people, and Chase's friend Kevin e-mailed back to ask who the babe was in the red shirt."

52

"Really?" Even I have to admit I look piping hot in that shirt. "Well then, why don't we skip this and you can set me up with this Kevin fellow?"

"For starters, he's in Zimbabwe. Secondly, he's beneath you."

I sighed. With all these men beneath me, you'd think I'd have a more exciting love life.

"All I'm saying," she continued, "is that you have an opportunity here to take a risk. Aim high. Go for someone who seems out of your league. Isn't that the whole point? For example . . ." She scrolled down until she found a man who resembled Fabio. "Him. *Personal Trainer Seeks Fit and Funny Lady.*"

"He doesn't want me. I'm no lady."

"Who cares what *he* wants?"

"I don't know. He's almost *too* good-looking. Besides, it says here his favorite book is *Likes movies better.*"

Susan kept searching and then stopped on what looked like a Calvin Klein ad. Dark hair, a graze of stubble along the jaw, intelligent but smoldering eyes . . . hands casually in pants pockets of what appeared to be a very expensive suit.

"Forget it," I said, cringing from the memory of the jerk at the bar. I was done with underwear model look-alikes.

"He's a writer!" She clicked open his profile. "His name's Sebastian, and he works as an advertising copywriter. Thirty-three . . . never married . . . nonsmoker . . . ooh, and look, he's man enough to check the 'any age' box rather than saying he wants the woman to be younger than him. We should e-mail him. He's perfect!"

Exactly. That was the problem. It was one thing to put myself out there, but this guy wasn't simply out of my league . . . we weren't even playing the same sport. "He vacations regularly in St. Croix. I don't even know where that is!"

"Oh, come on."

"I'm willing to go on a blind date, but the list didn't say anything about being humiliated and rejected. Thanks, but no thanks."

She told me I was being silly but finally moved on. Not much later we gave up for the night, and I left for the gym. The down side of getting over my funk was that my appetite had sprung back to its full glory.

Susan stayed behind to finish up a report, exhibiting the sort of work ethic that is the reason she gets a door and full Internet access and I don't.

The next morning, Brie came into my

cubicle. She wore a yellow top that clung to her generous bosom, along with a leopard-print mini. Her hair — a never-ending source of entertainment for me and often nothing short of a work of art — was in a flip reminiscent of Diana Ross in her Supremes days. All in all, on the demure side for Brie.

"I found this in the printer," she said, waving a piece of paper at me, "but I'm not sure if it's for you or for Susan. It's from her computer, but the note is addressed to you."

I'd been deep in thought — trying to come up with a good rhyme for "transit" for a headline I was working on — so I barely glanced up. "Thanks. . . ."

"It's from some guy named Sebastian," she continued just as I was dismissing "rancid" as being too negative. When I heard the name, little fingers of worry starting to worm their way up my spine.

"Sebastian?"

"Yeah. It's strange because he's asking one of you . . . I think *you* . . . on a date . . . and I figure Susan's married, but as I said, it was from her computer, so . . ."

I snatched the paper from her hands.

Her face got excited. "He's inviting you to a book signing. Sounds like the kind of thing you'd be into, huh? All intellectual and whatnot. Me, I prefer a date with a little action in it, where I can dress up real nice. You know, like going to a club — ooh, there's that new one in Hollywood I went to last weekend, and let me tell you, it was off the chain! I wore my new pink leather skirt, and —"

"Brie?" I interrupted. "You said you found this in the printer?"

"Yeah. You and Robert break up?" When I didn't answer right away, she narrowed her eyes at me. "You're stepping out on him?"

"We split, back in August. Give me a sec, will you?" I paused to read what she'd brought in, which was a printout of an e-mail. It was from Sebastian all right. He thanked me for writing him, said how excited he was to hear from a fellow copywriter and that he loved the photo I sent him. And then he invited me to a book reading and signing at seven o'clock on Thursday at Book Soup. *There'll be wine and cheese there, and we can go out for dinner afterward,* the note read. *I know that it's last minute, but let me know if you can make it. Love to get together and find out more about you.*

"Susan must have written him," I said, and realized it was the wrong thing to say when Brie put up both hands and started to edge away.

"You know what? This is none of my business. Whatever kinky kind of things y'all are into, that's for you to know and me to never find out."

Great. Now Brie was going to tell everyone in the office how Susan and I were into some sort of swinging lifestyle.

"Come with me." I grabbed Brie's arm and dragged her to Susan's office, where I marched in and shut the door behind us.

Susan looked up from her desk. Without saying a word, I waved the printout in the air.

"Oh, dear," she said. "It did print out."

"Yeah. Oh, *dear*," I mocked.

"I couldn't get the printer to work right last night," she went on to explain. "I was going to bring it in to you this morning and talk to you about it. Anyway, I thought I canceled the job —"

"You wrote him pretending to be me!" I cut in.

"Yes, and he asked us for a date!" And then she corrected, "Well, *you*. I told you that picture of you from the party was gorgeous. He e-mailed me back within minutes. We had a couple back-and-forth e-mails. I'm no writer, and we know it's been forever since I've had to flirt . . . but obviously I've still got it. A date! A *blind* date, if you catch my drift."

"Brie here," I said pointedly, "found it."

Susan pulled the corners of her mouth down in an *oops* face, but just for a second before moving on to berate me. "It's ridiculous you're being so private about this whole thing anyway. If I were doing something this nice, I'd sing it from the rooftops."

I blew out a breath and looked at Brie. For some reason, I didn't want her to think badly of me. I admired her "take no bullshit" style. No one else could handle Lizbeth the way she did.

Brie knew about the accident, of course, so I proceeded to fill her in about Marissa's list and how I was completing it for her.

When I was done, Brie gushed, "I saw something like that on *The Guiding Light*! This lady had a rare blood disease and only had six weeks to live, so she was trying to do everything real fast before she died. Oh, and if you ever want to watch it, I usually book Lizbeth into meetings in the conference room at two o'clock so I can use that portable TV she keeps on her side table."

"Brie, this is between us, though. Okay?"

"Sure. So's that thing about watching the *Light*."

Before I left, they made me e-mail Sebastian and accept his invitation. What the heck. It wasn't as if I had any other offers.

Then Susan picked up a phone call, and Brie walked with me back to my office. "So, what kind of stuff is on this list, anyway?" she asked.

I rattled off a few of the items, then realized maybe it wasn't so bad that Brie found out. Being Lizbeth's assistant, she could prove helpful. "That reminds me," I said after a moment. "One of the things I have to do is pitch an idea at work. I have an idea for a gas giveaway, but Lizbeth seems so hell-bent on this traffic reporter project, I don't know if she'll even listen to anything new. Any suggestions?"

Brie paused to consider my question. "The woman's a bulldog. If she can't get what she wants one way, she'll get it another. It'll be tough, but don't you worry about a thing," she said as we parted ways in the hallway, "I got your back."

CHAPTER 4

I've had eight boyfriends so far in my life, with the average length of relationship being 9.8 months. The mean is 14.4 months. Two out of the eight — a full 25 percent of all of my romantic entanglements — were named Scott.

I came up with these statistics on a girls' weekend in Palm Springs a while back, when rain kept us indoors with nothing else to do but play cards and calculate our romantic affairs. Linda, a friend of mine from high school, brought a laptop, so we were able to put the whole thing on a spreadsheet.

My track record seemed reasonable until Linda started playing with the numbers a bit more. "Check this out," she said. "Your average span of time between boyfriends is 13.4 months. That means . . ." She clattered away until she pulled up a new report. "You've been single as an adult 150 percent more than you've been with someone."

Well.

Isn't that something?

I cringed to think how almost half a year had already passed since Robert dumped me and yet I'd made no progress at all toward finding someone new. Granted, I'd been busy. First, there was all that TV to watch. Then the list to do. But still, I read all the time about celebrities walking down the aisle when the ink is barely dry on reports of how their last affair ended. It just wasn't fair.

I want marriage! I want kids! I thought bitterly as I showered the morning of my blind date. Other people seemed to tumble into husbands and children as if they were God-given rights and not the Herculean achievements I seemed to find them to be. It's not as if I were being greedy — I wanted only one husband. Some people my age had already had two or three. Probably one of them was supposed to be mine. They probably had my kids, too.

There were times among my eight men (numbers three and seven) I thought I might have found the right guy. Provided we could work out a few kinks. If only he could manage to be more (a) committed, (b) employed, (c) willing to stop that habit of picking his toenail and flicking it on the carpet. If only I could manage to be more of whatever that mystery thing is that men want that apparently — at least for the long haul — I don't have.

Ah, well, this shower sure feels like heaven. Nothing like steamy water on a rainy January morning to take the chill out of the bones. Even though I'd pay for it later. My apartment has only the one hot-water tank. When it's out, it's out.

Please let him like me. I'd been on plenty of setup dates before, but they were usually less deliberate than tonight's affair. A friend would have a party or a get-together at a bar and invite me as well as the potential love interest. There might be a bit of prodding on the part of the hostess to generate enthusiasm, but overall we were free to pretend we didn't know it was a setup if we didn't click.

Please let us click tonight.

There'd be no problem with the clicking on my side. I was clicking all over the place just thinking about that photo of him.

Which was why I was fretting. Sebastian seemed the sort of man who had women hanging over him. He probably had to beat them off with sticks. He certainly didn't have on average 13.4 months between lovers as I did. More like 13.4 minutes, I'd guess. Lucky for me there wasn't an interview process to dating — that I didn't have to bring a résumé outlining my pitiful love life. Imagine Sebastian getting a peek at that!

"So, June," he'd no doubt say, peering at me from across the dinner table, "this looks good. But tell me, what were you doing with that time between Jason and Mark? It shows here that you broke it off with Jason in August 1999 — finally accepted that he was all talk and no action — yet I show a three-year gap before you took up with another man."

"Was it three years? Gosh, I hadn't realized it was so long. . . ."

"Yes, you see that big hole right here on your résumé?"

"Now that you mention it, that *is* quite a long break."

"Maybe you were focusing on your career at the time?" he might supply helpfully. "Or traveling the globe? Learning a new skill?"

I'd shake my head woefully.

"Being selective, then? Going on date after date to make sure you found someone deserving of your love?"

Ooh, that one sounded good — and worth an enthusiastic nod. Even if it was a lie.

Truth was . . . I had no idea what the truth was. Only that I had a habit of burrowing like a groundhog any time a relationship failed. I didn't have that ability to dust myself off and try, try again. The only thing that brought me out of the hole was a soul brave enough to reach in and grab me.

It was crazy to expect that a man Susan found on the Internet might be the one to do that. For crying out loud, I was only going on this blind date to fulfill another person's wish list. I knew nothing about him other than what he wrote in his profile.

Yet that morning in the shower, as if guided by forces outside of me, I found myself digging through my pile of abandoned beauty products to find a loofah. If by chance things did click, I decided, there was no sense in scaring him off with rough elbows and knees.

I was ten minutes late getting to Book Soup and far more frazzled than I'd expected to be.

Besides the time I'd spent primping and fretting over what was proper attire for a book signing, there was Lizbeth's department meeting that ran over.

The meeting had been ready to wrap at five o'clock. Usually we'd be bolting for the door, but then Brie said leadingly, "Hey, June, why don't you tell us about that great idea you had for an event?"

I held back a scowl. Brie's notion of "having my back" apparently meant throwing me unprepared to the wolves, the first to my carcass being Martucci. "This ought to be good," he stage-whispered to Greg, and then grandly set the papers he'd gathered back down to enjoy the show.

The rest of them looked my way. *June is going to trot out another idea even as her Friends of Rideshare program lies flopping and gasping for air like a dying fish?*

It would have been nice if Brie had warned me she was going to do this. I'd have preferred to have charts or stats or a write-up or *something* besides me. Still . . . the idea of completing two tasks in one day spurred me on.

"My idea," I said, trying to put some punch in my delivery, "is that we do a gas giveaway. Gas prices are hitting record levels everywhere. So I thought we could let people know that L.A. Rideshare is rewarding people who carpool by paying for their gas when they fill up. The media would eat it up."

"Interesting. The problem," Lizbeth said slowly, "is the same one we always have.

Funding. Who'd pay for this gas?"

"A sponsor. It wouldn't cost that much. We wouldn't give gas to every carpooler. We'd let them know we were out there . . . then sneak up on them at the pumps. Say, 'Surprise! We're paying for your gas!' "

"If we're sneaking, then how would the media know?" Martucci asked.

"We'd tip them off ahead of time," I replied smugly, pleased that I had an answer and therefore wasn't giving him the pleasure of tripping me up. "We'd just tell them to keep the locations a secret from the public."

"It certainly sounds . . . interesting," Lizbeth said. "And I admire your initiative in bringing it up here today. Unfortunately, I don't believe that's the direction we should be going. No, we should be putting our energies behind partnering with a traffic reporter. By the way," she purred, "have you contacted Troy Jones?"

My mind flashed to the box sitting on my desk filled with Marissa's yearbooks, along with a note from the traffic reporter in question: *Hope this helps.* I hadn't worked up the stomach to dig through them yet, although I needed to. One of the items I was particularly worried about (besides #3, *Change someone's life,* which did seem to be quite the tall order) was #7: *Make Buddy*

Fitch pay. Who on earth was Buddy Fitch, and what had he done to her that was so awful? I suspected I'd find a clue in those yearbooks — maybe a jock who tormented her for being fat. A bully who knew Marissa Jones would be easy prey. The very thought made my insides lurch.

Of course, Lizbeth didn't need to know any of that.

"Gee, I left one message," I lied sweetly. "I'll try to follow up."

Lizbeth nodded and then addressed the group. "People, we have plenty of work here and not enough budget to move through the projects already on our plates. Let's stay focused, okay? Have a good evening."

As I left the meeting, Brie whistled and made a gesture with her hand of a plane flying downward. "Shot down in flames," she said, shaking her head.

I limped away in defeat.

After freshening my makeup and trying to get my hair to recapture the self-control it had hinted at achieving earlier, I met Susan at a boutique down the street. She'd agreed to help me shop for an outfit that seemed sexy yet bookish after nixing the red shirt I was wearing — pointing out all too correctly that Sebastian had already seen it.

An hour and two hundred dollars later, I

was dressed in a pinstripe jacket over a rock 'n' roll T-shirt and a pair of jeans cut low enough that I had to bunch my underwear down to keep it from showing. I left for my date a new woman.

Book soup is a small independent bookstore on a trendy section of Sunset Boulevard in West Hollywood. When I arrived, a line was already forming to get into the store.

I'd arranged to meet Sebastian at the adjacent coffee shop. As I walked in, I was nervous that he'd be disappointed when he saw me. Brie had warned that my biggest fear should be the other way around, adding grimly, "The guys I met online looked like their pictures all right. If their picture had been taken twenty years earlier and fifty pounds lighter."

I saw Sebastian right away. He was an exact replica of his photo, except now in full color and 3-D. Holy cripes, he was gorgeous, dressed in another suit that seemed to scream "money." When he came up to say hello, I noticed he smelled good, too.

"Are you June Parker?"

"Yes, hi," I said, extending my hand to shake his.

He gripped my hand so firmly, it nearly fused my fingers together. "Great to meet you. Your photo doesn't do you justice." Before I could say anything else or blush prettily, he added, "Do you mind if we get going to the bookstore? I don't want to be late."

We walked outside, and he bypassed the crowd to head straight for the entrance. The bouncer — or whatever one would call him — let us into the room. Folding chairs were set up in an open section of the store. A podium and microphone faced the chairs. People filled some of the seats, while others milled around, thumbing through books and drinking wine.

"Wow. Do you know the author?" I asked.

"Actually," he replied sheepishly, "I am the author."

"Excuse me?!"

He picked up a book and held it out to me. *One-Woman Man,* a novel by Sebastian Forbes. "This is mine. I'm doing the reading tonight." He flipped to the back to show me the author's photo — the same one he'd posted on the dating website.

"You wrote this?"

"Guilty."

"I can't believe you wrote this."

What I really meant was, I can't believe you wrote this *and invited me here sight unseen to your reading.*

69

"I can't say it's exactly Shakespeare. More of a romantic comedy. But I'm proud of it."

"But why . . . ," I began.

"Why did I invite you?" he finished for me. When I shrugged a yes, he grinned. "Can you blame a guy for wanting to impress a girl? My other idea was to fly you to Paris for dinner, but I decided against it. Too showy."

I'd have come back with equally flirtatious banter, but I was too busy thinking, *He likes me!* which was seriously impeding my ability to formulate clever retorts. Instead I gazed coolly around the room.

(He likes me!)

(He's a published author and he likes me!)

(Me!)

"Drink?" he asked.

"Sure. Thanks."

"By the way," he said as he handed me a glass of wine, "I'm all for keeping the fact that this is our first date on the QT."

I smiled agreeably and took a sip.

(Oh no, he's ashamed of me.)

Attempting to check my insecurities, I harkened back to the advice I used to read in *Teen* magazine. I asked him about himself. Once I did, I relaxed. Sebastian Forbes put on his Armani slacks one leg at a time like anyone else.

Turned out he worked as a copywriter for DDB advertising agency and had written this book in his spare time over the past two years. That meant giving up any semblance of a social life, he told me, cashing in the evenings he used to spend clubbing by banging away on his computer. (And I wasn't sure what I envied more, the fact that he gave up clubbing to write or the fact that he'd been clubbing in the first place.) He wasn't sure if he was writing anything people would care about. "I had a story I had to tell, that's all I knew," he said. "Corny as that sounds." After he found an agent and he started shopping the manuscript, he found himself in a bidding war, a rare occurrence for a first-time author. Only once he made it through the grueling editing process did he realize how much of his life he'd let slide, and — pardon me while my ears perked — he was eager to get things back on track.

So the guy set my hormones in motion. Even more amazing was how comfortable I felt talking to Sebastian. Like talking to one of my girlfriends — only a handsome girlfriend who was starting to get the faintest shadow of stubble along her strong, masculine jaw.

"Aren't you nervous?" I asked.

"A bit. I can't believe this turnout. And the *L.A. Times* book reviewer is supposed to show up."

"That seems like a pretty big deal."

"It could make me or break me."

The room filled, and I was taking up the attention of the man of honor. "I feel like I'm hogging the bride and groom at a wedding," I confessed to him.

"I'm grateful for the distraction, but you're right. I should be mingling. Here, let me introduce you around." He took my arm, then hesitated before saying, "June . . . you have any nicknames?"

"My mom calls me June Bug. My brother had a few that don't bear repeating. Why?"

"You don't strike me as a June. I see you as having a spunkier name. Like, oh, I don't know, *JJ.*"

Then he led me into the crowd. "Come on, JJ, I need you with me to face the firing squad."

I met his agent and his publicist, each one shaking my hand and saying things along the lines of "It is *so* wonderful to meet you" and, even more strangely, "JJ, you're everything I imagined."

I'd heard movie people were a bunch of phonies. Maybe publishing people were the same — lots of air kissing and pretending to be fabulous friends. It was baffling, however, how many congratulated me. I could understand Sebastian . . . but me? After the third time it happened — the woman had even grabbed my hand and said, "Sebastian, you bad boy . . . why is this still bare?" I turned to Sebastian.

"What the heck was that all —"

"Sorry to interrupt," he said, "but we're ready to get under way."

He escorted me to a chair in the front of the room. "I saved this seat for you," he said, and he kissed my cheek before heading to the podium.

Sebastian read several excerpts from his novel, which was quite good. It was the story of a man who met the love of his life in the 1960s at a Peter, Paul & Mary concert and followed their courtship against the backdrop of the folk music era. It was quirky and smart — a romance novel, only from the man's point of view.

After reading, he answered questions from the audience. Then he introduced and thanked the agent and publicist I'd met earlier. Before finishing, he said, "And lastly, allow me to introduce my beloved JJ." Everyone applauded, and he motioned for me to stand, which I did, waving around to the people while confusion and dread formed a stew in my stomach. *My beloved JJ?*

Psycho. The guy was clearly a psycho. *Oh, why did I ever let Susan talk me into the Internet? Everyone knows it's crawling with loonies.*

As I entertained thoughts of being held captive in a cellar later while Sebastian decided which part of me he'd use to make his coat of human flesh, the guy who'd served as bouncer earlier announced that we'd be taking a brief break, after which Mr. Forbes would sign books.

Sebastian came over and this time kissed my forehead. "How'd I do?"

Be calm . . . be cool . . . don't aggravate the crazy man. . . .

"Great! But you know what I realized? I need to go."

His face fell. "You're leaving?"

"I forgot I have this big meeting tomorrow." I faked a yawn. "But I loved your book. Thanks so much for inviting me."

"Can't you stick around a while longer?"

No sudden movements that might startle him. . . . "It was lovely, really. But I need to get going."

"Give me a few more minutes, please. Let me explain." He pleaded so earnestly — and even though he was a psychopath, his face still seemed sweet — I let him lead me behind a bookshelf, where I figured my screams could be heard. "The *L.A. Times* book reviewer isn't here yet, and my publicist says he's due any minute. Can't you stay for that, at least?"

"To be honest, Sebastian, I don't understand what's going on here."

"Going on?"

"Everybody acts as if they know me, and they keep congratulating me. Then you introduce me as your beloved JJ."

"What, people can't be friendly?"

"Thank you, I'll be leaving now."

"Wait!" he whispered urgently, grabbing my arm. "There's something else."

"I'm listening."

"I may have let it get around that we were engaged."

"Engaged?! Why!?"

"Think about it. I'm writing about a lifelong romance between a man and a woman, but I'm coming to my own event stag? No one would take me seriously."

"You couldn't get a friend to pretend for you?"

He released my arm. "I didn't want to be that . . . devious. I was hoping you wouldn't catch on, the press would write it up — and by the time anyone was the wiser, my book would already be at the top of the best-seller list."

"Weren't you scared people might see your personal ad?"

"It was a chance I had to take."

"Sebastian, I wish you luck. I do. But —"

"No buts, please! I'm begging you! Just for another hour or so, pretend to be my fiancée. Please . . . as a favor to a fellow writer. I hate to ask this of you, but when I got your letter and photo, you seemed so *nice*."

"I'm not comfortable with this. I'm sorry. . . ." And I turned to go.

He slumped against the shelf. "You think I'm a lunatic, right?"

"I . . . uh . . ." *Yes?!!?*

"Would it ease your mind if I mention to you that, lovely as you are, you're not exactly my type?"

"What —" I bristled, finally fed up and not afraid to let him know. Now the psycho was going to insult me as well? "You mean *sane?*"

"No. Female."

I stared at him, he shrugged, and after a second a light bulb went on over my head. "Oh."

No wonder he was so good-looking.

"I'm not in the closet, but for this first

book, I thought it would be best if I appeared to be straight. The book has received good buzz. If the press found out I was gay, no matter how glowing the reviews, it would still be a gay man's account of a romance. I didn't want to see it limited that way. Believe me, once this hits it big, I won't care what anyone thinks. I'll hand out free copies at the Gay fucking Pride parade."

"I don't claim to know anything about writing books," I said, neglecting to mention the *Carpoolers Guide to Road Safety* I'd authored, "but don't they say 'Write about what you know'? Shouldn't you have written about a gay relationship?"

"This *is* what I know. It's the story of my parents' courtship — and it's a love story, but it's also a story about drug addiction and wife swapping and other things they grew out of and would be humiliated to have anyone know they used to do. They're dead. I wrote this to honor their memory in my heart, but to publicize it to the world as their story would have them spinning in their graves."

There it was.

How could I not help a man trying to tell his dead parents' story of romance?

"Oh, crud . . ."

He saw his opening. "Sit next to me while

I sign. Emit estrogen. That's it."

"Fine," I huffed. "But you'd better really be gay."

"Please. Would a straight man wear shoes this expensive?"

Afterward over dinner, I got the whole story. JJ was his boyfriend, to whom the book was dedicated and who — along with the rest of Sebastian's friends — boycotted the reading. That's how disgusted they were about his playing straight. But one friend — a Latvian model-trying-to-turn-actress named Mjorka, who had a tendency to be game for anything — had volunteered to play his fiancée. When she canceled on Sebastian for a last-minute shoot in Bolivia, in desperation he posted a profile online to see if he could find someone. Then along came my e-mail.

"JJ's probably dumped me for good," he lamented. "So maybe I'll switch my profile over to a gay site. How do you like Internet dating?"

I explained what I was doing with Marissa's list and decided to cross off *Go on a blind date* right there at the table. He made me feel the evening was worth it, applauding so wildly that the waitress came by to ask if champagne was in order.

CHAPTER 5

Rose Morales peered at me over thick red reading glasses. "So," she said, straightening papers on the desk between us, "why do you want to be a Big Sister?"

"I love kids, and I feel I have so much to offer," I replied, delivering the line I'd spent ten minutes rehearsing outside the Big Sister offices. "It's been a lifelong dream of mine to be a mentor to a girl — to share with her all I have to give."

Rose nodded.

She seemed to be buying it.

As director of the Los Angeles Big Sister program, she was in charge of interviewing potential Big Sisters — weeding out the felons and any weirdos who were in it for the wrong reasons. While she went over the particulars of being a Big Sister — a "Big," was how she put it — I sat smugly, congratulating myself on my clever plan. Susan had said I couldn't handle the task *Change*

someone's life on my lunch hour, but here I
was, noon on a Thursday, doing just that.
Or at least getting it started.

The idea had come to me as I'd ridden
the bus home the week before. Gazing out
the window and listening to Whitney Hous-
ton on my iPod — volume low so the hip-
looking guy sitting next to me couldn't
overhear — we passed a billboard for the
Big Sisters program. In huge type, it announced: "Change Someone's Life — Be a
Big Sister!"

Talk about your signs from above, literally.

I filled out an application online as soon
as I got home. Okay, after eating dinner and
browsing on eBay for new sunglasses. Still,
the speed at which I pushed the idea forward amazed me, considering that changing
someone's life struck me as the most difficult task. It'd take time. Perseverance. The
type of thing I'd usually put off — avoiding
the hard things until it's too late to do them
right, or to do them at all.

And yet.

If all went well — and Rose had seemed
mighty impressed that I worked as a writer,
even if it was brochures — I'd soon have a
Little Sister of my own. The idea of a sweet,
freckled little piece of clay, eager to be

shaped and molded, made me giddy. I'd buy her balloons and take her to pet ponies. She'd gaze up at me, her tiny hand clutched in mine, and say, "Gee, you're so much cooler than my mom." True, my motives for signing up weren't entirely sincere. I wanted to change someone more than bond. But as I listened to Rose talk about how vital role models were in the lives of these girls, I remembered how I *do* believe that children are our future. Teach them well. Let them lead the —

"How often would you want to see a Little?" she asked abruptly.

"How often?"

"Yes. Most people do outings once a week. Or every other week."

"Weekly," I said, amazed that that was all they were asking. Why hadn't I thought to do this before? Why didn't more people? "Definitely weekly." Excitedly, I added, "It'll be so fun! Taking a girl shopping for cute little outfits, and —"

"We frown on shopping sprees," Rose chided. "It's not to spoil them so much as to be a positive influence. We suggest sporting events or going to the beach or museums. Even cooking together can be lots of fun and very rewarding for both of you."

"Of course," I said, reddening.

Now I knew why more people didn't do this. It sucks enough to not get a job you want — it's downright humiliating to be rejected for a volunteer position. How big a loser would you have to be for that? I didn't care to find out. There was a matter of a July 12 deadline, and if I didn't get a Little Sister, odds were I wouldn't encounter any more billboards providing instructions on what to do from there.

Rose must have sensed my worry, because she said, "A little shopping is fine."

She went on to explain that they'd need to follow up on my references and do a background check, which typically took a few days. "If it pans out, hopefully we'll have a match for you soon," she said, packing up my file. "Anything you want to add before I let you go?"

I thought about the five months remaining before my deadline. It didn't seem like much time to change a life, but it was all I had. "Only that I'm eager to get started," I said heartily.

February 14. Valentine's Day. The day started on a sour note by *being* Valentine's Day. It then went from bad to worse before I even changed out of my pajamas. I'd stepped on the scale to discover that I'd gained five pounds. I didn't need Linda and her spreadsheet-making abilities to know that that constituted half of my total weight loss regained — and that every one of those pounds had gone straight to my ass.

No chocolates for me, I realized, sighing. No nibbling at the heart-shaped cookies people would bring into the office. No celebrating the holiday in the way I'd come to know it: as an excuse to consume mass quantities of sugar with joyous abandon. Not after seeing how much I weighed.

Then again . . .

I leaned over to pick up the scale. Then I placed it directly into the trash.

#17: *Throw away my bathroom scale.*

That Marissa was a genius, I thought as I scrambled an egg for breakfast — compensation for the damage I'd be doing later to my blood sugar. Getting rid of that scale had been positively liberating. So much so that I'd have tossed away my body shaper underwear, too, if it weren't for that one blue dress that I look lumpy in without it.

Shortly after lunch — I'd had a chicken salad to make up for the damage I in fact did to my blood sugar — I popped into Susan's office. "Am I still on to baby-sit tonight?"

She peered around a bouquet big enough to be mistaken for shrubbery. That was her husband, Chase. More is always more. "If you don't mind — I'd be forever grateful. We've got reservations at Nic's. Chase's mother offered to watch the boys, but she had that toe surgery the other day. I hate to ask her to run after a couple of five-year-olds so soon."

"It's no problem," I assured her.

I knew it was a special holiday for them since — and only Susan could pull this off — they'd met on Valentine's Day. It was back in college, when she and I were at a bar refusing to feel like losers because we were stag. At one point, a drunk guy the size of an army tank bumped into Susan, making her spill her drink over herself. Then he lumbered on without an apology. Chase — who stands six feet two and at the time probably weighed 120 pounds dripping wet — came running over. He tipped his chin in the lunk's direction and said, "You want me to kick his ass?" We gaped at him for a moment, stunned, and he said, "I'm kidding. The guy'd smash me like a bug." Susan was instantly smitten, and I'm pleased to report that Chase has since filled out nicely.

They live a few miles from me in Brentwood, in a three-bedroom ranch-style house that they bought for a song at an auction and that — thanks to California's ridiculous real estate market — was recently appraised at more than a million dollars. I call it the palace even though it's only about 1,600 square feet.

I arrived at the palace at seven o'clock. Susan had already fed and bathed C.J. and Joey and dressed them in their pajamas. "Hey, beasts!" I called to them in the living room, where they played with Legos.

C.J. and Joey — identical twins — were dark and gangly like their father. The only way I could tell them apart is by the scar Joey got when he fell off a table as a toddler. Joey squeaked an excited, "What's that?" when he noticed I held a big box, hopeful it was a treat of some kind. He and his brother went back to their Legos when I showed them it was only a bunch of Marissa's yearbooks.

"I figured tonight might be a good time to look through them," I explained to Susan as she and Chase tossed on their coats.

"Good luck . . . hope you find what you're looking for. And thanks again for doing this," Susan said. "We won't be long."

"No later than ten," Chase added. "I plan to be home in time to get my Valentine's Day booty."

Susan grinned at him. "Then that chore is out of the way until Easter."

"Ah, I'll wear you down before that. Besides" — he grabbed his keys and pulled on the door — "you're forgetting about Presidents' Day."

"Shut up with your boasting about your sex life!" I cried as they waved good-bye to me and the boys.

Once they left, I warmed up pizza for myself and proceeded to do what I always did when watching C.J. and Joey: let them run wild. Allowed them to pull out toys and games and balls and never made them put the old toy away before bringing out something new. Eat whatever they wanted. It was okay, the way I figured it, since I didn't baby-sit that often. It has occurred to me that that may be the reason I don't baby-sit that often.

The only time I scolded them at all the entire evening was when I noticed they'd left the door open to the cage of their guinea pig, Aunt June, named after yours truly. (Susan said it was proof of the boys' affection for me; I suspect there may have been prompting on her part.)

"We always keep it open," C.J. explained when I showed him the unhooked latch.

"Doesn't she escape?"

"Nope."

Joey then grabbed a sprig of parsley from the refrigerator to demonstrate. Even when he held the treat just outside her reach, she merely leaned on the base of the door and squealed. He tossed the parsley into the cage. "We asked for a dog."

It was a little after nine o'clock when the boys finally passed out on the living room floor. I had to step over C.J., curled up at my feet, to get the box filled with yearbooks.

Wrenching as it was, I made myself thumb through every one in search of Buddy Fitch. But there wasn't a trace of him. No one named Fitch at all.

So he wasn't a high school classmate. Although it meant that the search continued, I felt a degree of relief. I'd been weaned on teen movies where the basic principle is survival of the fittest, so I feared the worst. I'd concocted all sorts of scenarios regarding who Buddy Fitch might be. Most involved him starring as a wealthy, popular jock — think Steff, the head "richie" in *Pretty in Pink* — a boy who would have gotten his jollies from abusing Marissa for being fat.

And she was, too. Fat, that is. Poor kid. Her yearbooks showed the progression as she started out chubby in junior high and got heavier and heavier over the years. As if that weren't tough enough, there were photos of her in the marching band, in the glee club, and as a member of the chess team. Why didn't she just have a "Kick Me" sign sewn permanently to her back?

Marissa had a pretty smile in her senior picture, though, and it seemed genuine. Maybe her thought bubble would read, *Thank God I'm almost out of here!* Or — who knows? — maybe she enjoyed high school. After all, when I was in school, I thought I had a good time. It was only after I graduated and got out into the world that I realized how miserable I'd actually been.

One thing was certain: I was going to have to do some serious legwork to find Buddy Fitch. I'd need to know who he was and what he did before I could determine what sort of payback he had coming.

And I'd better get a move on. A month had already ticked by, and I'd completed only four of the tasks. (I'd have claimed five, but when I mentioned to Brie about how I pitched my idea to Lizbeth at the staff meeting, she'd exclaimed, "You call *that* pitching?" and I didn't dare cross it off.)

After setting aside the last yearbook, I pulled the list from my purse.

20 Things to Do by My 25th Birthday

1. ~~Lose 100 pounds~~
2. ~~Kiss a stranger~~
3. Change someone's life
4. ~~Wear sexy shoes~~
5. Run a 5K
6. Dare to go braless
7. Make Buddy Fitch pay
8. Be the hottest girl at Oasis
9. Get on TV
10. Ride in a helicopter
11. Pitch an idea at work
12. Try boogie boarding
13. ~~Eat ice cream in public~~
14. ~~Go on a blind date~~
15. Take Mom and Grandma to see Wayne Newton
16. Get a massage
17. ~~Throw away my bathroom scale~~
18. Watch a sunrise
19. Show my brother how grateful I am for him
20. Make a big donation to charity

I'd made a start, I knew, but there was so much left to do. If I was going to succeed, I needed to hunker down and stay on track. Next Tuesday I'd handle #6, *Dare to go braless*. Most of the staff would be off at a rideshare fair. I'd be able to go the whole day without encountering many people.

Maybe that was the easy way out, but I was willing to take any break I could get.

As I dressed for work Tuesday morning, I couldn't help but think how it wasn't fair. After all, Marissa was, to put it delicately . . . *petite.* As in flat-chested. A-cup at best, I'd reckon. Not that I'd spent a lot of time staring at her chest, but I have a distinct memory of her being quite unendowed. Therefore, the ceremonial relinquishing of her bra would have been a feeling akin to the tossing of her scale: freeing.

For me, it was bordering on obscene.

It's not that I'm huge — a C-cup usually, although depending on the bra occasionally a D. By Los Angeles standards, that's nothing. Problem is, unlike many of my contemporaries here in La-la-land, mine are real. Which is to say, they *move.* They bounce, they *boing,* they have minds of their own.

In an attempt to contain the potential damage, I searched my closet for my most conservative apparel and settled on a gray blouse over black slacks. Checking myself out in the mirror, I jumped up and down.

Good grief, I could put an eye out.

I took off the blouse, tugged on a black

stretchy pullover, and then buttoned the blouse over the top of that. I jumped up and down again.

Better.

The office, as I'd anticipated, was nearly empty when I got there. I spent the morning catching up on months of filing and was about to head to the break room to get the salad I'd brought for lunch when my phone rang. It was Rose Morales from the Big Sister program.

"I have wonderful news," she gushed. "We don't often have a match so quickly, but I've found the perfect girl for you. I remember you said that you were eager to get started."

"I am!"

"Her name is Deedee, and she's a real doll. I know you'll adore her. The reason I thought of you for Deedee is that she has dreams of being a writer when she grows up. Isn't that perfect? Let's see," she continued. "What else can I tell you about her? She's Hispanic on the mother's side. The father's not been in the picture since she was little. She lives not far from you in the Mar Vista area, and she's a freshman at —"

"Freshman!" I exclaimed. "How old is she?"

"Fourteen."

And with that my bubble burst. How was I going to mold and shape a teenager? As clay goes, they're already pretty hardened by that point. I couldn't hide my disappointment. "I was hoping for someone . . . younger."

Rose was silent for a moment and then said, "She's still a girl. A good kid, too. Her mother is legally blind. Deedee helps take care of her and her little brother as well. We thought she deserved some fun time."

"It's just that . . . fourteen? What do I do with a fourteen-year-old?"

"You could still take her to movies. Play with makeup. Do that Rollerblading you love so much," she said, and I cringed remembering that I'd put that on my application. "You may find you have more in common with an older girl than you would have with a younger one." When I didn't respond right away, she added, "I'm not trying to talk you into anything."

"I know."

"She's a sweet girl who could use a break."

"Can I think about it?"

"Of course. If you're not comfortable with this, we can always find you another match, although to be honest, I don't know when that will be. We tend to be more stringent about matching younger girls within their ethnic culture. It could be months. But it's important that you feel you can bond with your Little, so it may be worth waiting."

Months! I didn't have months! "I'd imagine it's tough having a mom who's legally blind," I ventured.

"Deedee shoulders much more responsibility than a fourteen-year-old should have to," Rose agreed. "She's spunky, though." Then she asked, "How old are you again?"

"Thirty-four."

"Here's something else to consider. I'm guessing you'll want to be starting a family soon." I tried not to snort into the phone as she continued, "Would you be able to balance the needs of a Little with your new family? Sadly, that's when many girls get set aside. A teenager, on the other hand — she's only going to need a Big for a few years at the most."

A few minutes later I hung up, having agreed to take the next step, which was to go with Rose Morales to meet Deedee and her mother at their home. We could check each other out, with absolutely no obligation to buy.

It was after one o'clock when I returned from the lunchroom, kicking myself for putting Rollerblading on my application. They'd had so many lines under "Hobbies."

I was embarrassed to leave them all blank.

Lost in thought, I didn't hear Bubba bound up.

Bubba was the CEO's black Labrador that he sometimes brought to the office. He immediately buried his nose in my crotch. Like owner, like dog.

Which meant, I realized with dread, that Lou Bigwood wasn't far behind.

"Hey, Bubba," I bleated, attempting to pull his face away in a gesture of friendly dog petting rather than the heavy petting that Bubba was aiming for.

Bubba clearly hadn't seen HR's sexual harassment video that talked about inappropriate touching. My attempts to push him away only excited him further. He lunged for me, sending me reeling back — stumbling and bouncing and *boing*ing and grabbing for the wall to catch my balance.

"Bubba!" It was Lou Bigwood. "Come back here, boy."

In all the time I'd worked at L.A. Rideshare, I'd seen Bigwood only from a distance at staff meetings. I was far too lowly for direct interaction. Bigwood was in his late fifties, I'd guess — graying at the temples, but hearty and hale. He could as easily be captaining a ship at sea as leading a traffic agency.

"Hi, Mr. Bigwood."

He held Bubba by the collar, squinting at me. "It's June, right?"

"Yes."

"How are things going in . . . publications, right?"

"That's right. Great, thanks."

I thought about saying "Have a nice day" and making a run for it, but he was staring at me curiously, stroking his chin in that way people do to show how very deep in thought they are. "There's something different about you," he said. "What is it?"

"Pardon me?"

"Is it your hair? Did you change your hair? I've got three daughters, I'm usually good at figuring out this sort of thing."

I shook my head noncommittally and he said, "Nice work on the annual report, by the way."

Stunned that he had noticed my work, I could only say, "Thank you."

He kept me standing there in the hall, chatting about ideas for future brochures. No one came by. It occurred to me he must be talking to me out of boredom, but he seemed genuinely interested in what I had to say. I wondered if he could see my nipples through my shirt. The hallway was a tad chilly — the sort of thing that tends to bring

out the high beams. I used my mental pow-
ers to will my nipples to stay put.

Bubba bumped into me again, sending me
bouncing.

Bigwood snapped his fingers. "I've got it!
You're wearing flat shoes. So you look
shorter."

Since I was, as always, wearing flats, I nodded.

"See," he boasted, "I told you I'm good at
figuring this sort of thing out."

Bigwood's gaze then shifted to something
behind me, and he suddenly looked
alarmed. "Is that clock right?"

I turned around. One-fifteen. "Maybe a
minute or two fast," I said.

"June, I need your help," he said urgently.
"I'm due at a meeting in Long Beach in
thirty minutes. I can't be late. I need you to
come with me so I can use the carpool
lane." He turned without giving me a
chance to reply and nearly sprinted down
the hall. Bubba barreled after him. "At the
elevators in two minutes!"

Talk about being wanted for your body.

The meeting, he explained as we climbed
into his convertible, was at S.C. Electric,
whom he hoped to bring on as a corporate
funder. "It's a long shot — those cheap
bastards. But I'll do what I can to squeeze a

few bucks out of them."

I held a notebook I'd grabbed off my desk clutched to my chest — why hadn't I brought a backup bra? This would surely qualify as an undergarment emergency. I could've tried another day for my task.

We cruised along in the carpool lane at speeds reaching a hundred miles per hour. "Look at that!" Bigwood exclaimed, tipping his head toward the regular freeway lanes. Even in the middle of the day, they were packed with traffic. "This is why we do the good work we do!"

I'd sort of taken it as a sign that we weren't doing such good work.

We arrived in one piece and parked. Bigwood led me into the offices of S.C. Electric with seconds to spare. I expected him to deposit me in the lobby to wait, but instead he insisted I join him. "This is how you learn," he said in a tone that I suspected he often used with his daughters.

Two women and two men already sat at a conference table. Bigwood introduced me as his associate in charge of marketing — a lovely, albeit temporary, promotion to Lizbeth's job — and went on to bluntly explain why S.C. Electric should give us money.

The proposition, for all its snappy delivery, went down in flames from the beginning.

And then, surprisingly, came my moment. Even looking back, I couldn't say if it was Bigwood wanting to give me an opportunity to prove myself or him deciding, as long as he was leaping from the plane, that he'd grab me to cushion the fall.

The S.C. Electric people had responded plainly that they couldn't fund us because they had limited dollars. Bigwood thanked them, and I expected we were going to leave. But then he turned to me and said, "June, do you have anything to add?"

In real life — that is, my old life, in which I wouldn't even be here because I wouldn't have been jiggling down the hall and attracting Bigwood's notice — I would have made a benign remark such as "I'm good to go."

Instead, I set down the notebook I'd been clinging to. Lizbeth was never going to listen to my pitch. This was my chance. If I blew it, what was the worst that could happen? I'd never see these people again, and Bigwood could hardly fault me for failing when he'd done exactly the same thing moments before.

"I do have a way we may be able to partner that would be low-cost," I said, aiming to keep my voice steady. "It'll help you get your feet wet. Once you see the good work we can do, I'm confident you'll want to continue the association at a higher level."

Then I pitched the hell out of my free gas idea. I was so focused on what I was saying that I didn't even worry that I was braless. Without the graphs and charts I'd been working on, I knew I was the main show, so I did my best to make giving away free gas sound like the next step in reality TV. I painted a mental picture of happy motorists screaming with glee as we told them they'd won free gas — of how they would surely thank their generous sponsors for this honor, perhaps even wipe away tears of gratitude. All on TV. And all for the low, low price of, say, a few thousand?

They loved it — they loved me! Although they couldn't commit on the spot — they first had to run it by the powers-that-be — they assured us they'd do everything they could to make the project happen.

Later, as we walked back to his car, Lou Bigwood gave my shoulder a squeeze and told me I did a great job.

"Thank you, Mr. Bigwood."

"Call me Lou."

That was when it hit me: I was now one of Charlie's Angels. Susan was going to keel over laughing.

I suspected that Lizbeth, however, would be less amused — leaving me to fret the entire way back to the office over how much she'd try to make my job a living hell.

CHAPTER 6

I woke to the phone ringing. *Seven forty-five on a Saturday. Who'd be calling this early?*

I let the machine pick up, but when I heard it was my mom, I grabbed it. "It's not even eight o'clock!"

"It isn't? Oh, sorry. Go back to sleep."

"No . . ." I rolled out of bed and ambled to the kitchen to start the coffee. "I needed to get up anyway. What's up?"

"I wanted to let you know that Vons has those bags of frozen shrimp on sale for $8.99 a pound."

As if I knew how to cook shrimp? "Okay . . . thanks . . . don't think I need any."

"I know, but your father wanted me to call you and tell you to pick some up. They have a limit of five bags. He's already been to the store twice, and he's afraid if he goes back again, they might catch on."

I smiled — my dad loved to find the

bargains. "Okay. No problem." After my mom warned me that the sale ended Wednesday, she and I were free to catch up. While I made toast and peanut butter for breakfast, my mom gave me what I've come to refer to as the floral report — that is, the state of various flowers in her garden. "So why did you need to get up early today?" she asked after sharing her haunting story about how the delphinium were at death's door.

"I'm meeting that girl who might be my Little Sister," I reminded her. "The one who's fourteen?"

"That's right. You told me that. But I guess I'm confused. I don't remember the list saying you had to get a Little Sister."

"It doesn't. This is for the one about how I'm supposed to change someone's life."

She gave a derisive grunt. "With a teenager? Good luck."

Exactly what I was worried about. "What did I get myself into?"

"I'm joking. Sweetie, when you were that age, I'd have loved it if a caring adult took you out to do fun activities. Maybe you would have been open to that. Lord knows I tried to get you to try new things."

"You did? I don't remember that. Like what?"

"Oh, you know, learning to play an instrument or taking up a sport."

"Bob did enough of that for both of us," I grumbled jealously. My brother — eleven months older than me — had so many activities on his college applications that he had to cut a few for space.

"He did always prefer to keep busy," my mom agreed, as usual turning a deaf ear to the sibling rivalry brewing. "But you know what I always appreciated about you?"

"What?"

"I loved how you seemed content being who you were. Didn't always have to go running around proving things. Of course, you could have watched less TV. But —"

"You thought I was content?"

"Absolutely. From the day you were born. Your brother cried and fussed so much as a baby. I had to entertain him almost every minute of the day. But you — we hardly ever had to pick you up. You'd lie there in your crib for hours at a time, gurgling away. Staring at the ceiling . . . happy as can be."

The afternoon haze refused to lift. Even at five o'clock when Rose Morales and I pulled up to Deedee's house, the sky continued to cast its gloomy spell. Luckily, the homes in the neighborhood were painted in intense yellows, pinks, and blues, so they practically generated their own light.

Where Deedee lived was almost tiny enough — yard and all — to fit inside my apartment. It sat mere yards from the entrance to the Marina Freeway. Even though cars roared by, a group of boys attempted to play a game of soccer on the street. I felt a twinge of rent-controlled guilt knowing that they probably paid twice what I did.

Rose put her Honda Civic in park and rolled up her window. The plan was to visit with Deedee and her mother for a few minutes. The mother didn't speak any English, so Rose would serve as interpreter. Then Rose and I would take Deedee to the Sizzler for dinner.

"Anything else I should know?" I asked before getting out of the car. Frankly, I was nervous about meeting a blind woman who didn't speak the same language as me. What were we going to do — *feel* each other hello? I supposed we could chat about burritos or *huevos con queso,* my command of Spanish being limited to food words.

Reading my worries, Rose assured me, "It'll be fine. Maria is a kind woman, and you and Deedee are going to hit it off. If for any reason you don't, you'll let me know.

We'll find you another match. It's that simple."

We walked to the house, and Rose rang the doorbell. After a moment, a boy answered the door. He was about ten years old, with a wide mouth and a haircut that looked as if it might have been self-inflicted. He left us there, shouting in Spanish. A bit later, a girl I assumed was Deedee came to the door and told us to come in.

The house was sparse and neat, and as soon as Deedee's mom came bustling up to meet us — short, broad, and dressed in a pink terry sweat-suit — I understood why neatness mattered. I'd have never known she couldn't see if Rose hadn't tipped me off. She clearly knew the lay of the land. If my own mom had been relying on Bob and me to pick up our things so she wouldn't trip, she'd have been falling and breaking a hip every other day.

Rose did introductions all around, and we took a seat in the living room. Deedee's actual name was Deanna Garcia Alvarez. The boy who'd met us at the door was her brother, Ricky. And I hadn't needed to worry about an uncomfortable silence. Rose chattered away happily in English and Spanish, expertly soliciting answers from the rest of us about a series of benign topics from home decorating to taking the bus to the fact that Deedee has made honor roll every semester so far in high school.

All the talking gave me a chance to steal a look at Deedee. She was about my height of five feet four and had large, almond-shaped eyes — and if I thought I'd been generous with the eyeliner the day I gave a kiss to the busboy, I was naive about the eye's ability to bear the weight of makeup. It suited her, though, in a cat-girl sort of way. She was a fourteen-year-old girl trying to look older. In other words, typical. Her hair was pulled back from a round face, and there was a mole above her right eyebrow that I thought was adorable but that I'd bet for sure she hated. She wore boys' big hip-hop-style shorts and an oversize Raiders jersey — her attire at one point being the topic of conversation, I suspected, because I saw Maria gesturing at her in that disapproving way moms do, and it was the only time Deedee appeared to get an attitude. Plus Rose opted not to translate that part.

Reflecting back on the dinner that followed, I can't pinpoint the exact moment I decided I'd agree to be a Big Sister to Deedee.

It might have been when she announced at the Sizzler that she loved salad and then loaded up on potato salad, macaroni salad, Jell-O salad, and ambrosia without a clue of the irony.

Or even before that, when we went to cross the street to get to the restaurant and — out of habit, I'll assume — she started to take my arm before dropping it and stepping away in embarrassment.

Who knows? I may have been drawn to a lively and willing disposition that gave promise of a certain . . . shall we say . . . malleability?

Plus I felt sorry for the poor kid. Rose whispered to me over the all-you-can-eat taco bar that Deedee had never been to a movie at the theater. Guess when your mom can't see, you might as well wait until it comes out on DVD.

Still, if I had all the girls in the world to choose from, I wondered if I'd pick Deedee. Hard to say. She was definitely a far cry from the dimpled, wide-eyed girl I'd envisioned. But I consoled myself with the thought that it doesn't work that way in life with kids anyway. You get what you get.

Lizbeth cornered me by the reception area first thing Monday morning. "Did you follow up on that call?"

"What call?" I asked, knowing exactly

what she was referring to. If she's going to keep giving me only the minimum merit increase every year, I want to earn it.

"Troy."

"Troy . . . ?"

"Troy Jones."

My brows furrowed as if I were trying to place the name.

"Troy Jones the traffic reporter for K-JAM radio," she snipped. "You said you called him and that you were going to follow up because he hadn't called you back."

This was another one of those times that I felt sorry for her. I couldn't imagine trying to supervise an employee who was so pathologically passive-aggressive. But that's what she gets for getting to me before I had my first Diet Coke of the day. And for being Lizbeth.

"As a matter of fact, I did. He said he needed to look into it, and he'd get back to me."

Her face lit up. "Did it sound hopeful? Maybe I'll call, too. Give him a bit of a —"

"He has to check with his boss," I said hurriedly. "He likes the idea, but it's a sticky situation . . . office politics and whatnot. I got the definite impression that he would have a problem with it if we applied pressure."

Lizbeth nodded, told me to keep her posted, and left to do whatever nefarious bidding was next on her agenda.

As soon as she was gone, I collapsed with relief. That'd teach me to try to be clever. Because fact was, everything I'd told her was true: I had called him, and he'd said he needed to check into it and get back to me. Only the "it" had nothing to do with being a spokesman for L.A. Rideshare. I hadn't even brought up the subject.

"It" was trying to find out who Buddy Fitch was . . . and what he might have done to Marissa.

That alone required supreme finesse. I had called Troy to thank him for sending the yearbooks. Then, while I had him on the line, I asked nonchalantly if he knew of a Buddy Fitch. Of course he asked why. Although I tried to stall him off by alluding vaguely to the list, I could tell the curiosity was eating him alive.

"One of the items on the list says, *Make Buddy Fitch pay,*" I finally admitted. "But I don't know who he was or what he did."

"It says to make him pay?"

"Yeah."

"Boy, it's weird to think my sister would write something so vengeful. It doesn't sound like her at all."

"It doesn't?"

"Not Marissa. If she was *that* pissed off, then this guy must really have it coming. He must have —"

"Troy, I'm sure it was nothing bad," I interrupted, hoping to shift his train of thought, at least for now. If the idea that Marissa was the victim of any sort of cruelty was going to get planted in his head, it wasn't going to be me with a shovel in my hand and dirt under my fingernails. "Maybe he played a friendly practical joke on her and she wanted to do something funny back."

"Yeah . . . maybe," Troy said, his voice skeptical. "So he wasn't in any of the year-books?"

"Nope. That's why I was hoping you might be able to ask around for me. I thought he could be a family friend or someone she worked with."

"Okay. I'll ask my parents, and I'll try calling her old boss. I'll let you know as soon as I find anything out." Then he added apologetically, "It could take a while, though. I'm swamped at work right now — the station's got some big fair coming up, and I've been roped into helping out. How fast do you need this?"

"No hurry. I just need to have everything

done before her birthday, so we've got time."

"Not that much time. Just over four months left."

I understood the warning underlying Troy's words. As far as he knew, I'd been working diligently on completing the list since the accident last July and not merely since I'd seen him at the cemetery six weeks ago. By his calculations, then, my time was half-over rather than only just beginning.

"Well, I didn't want to pressure you," I said by way of explanation.

"I just don't know how long it's going to take to find this guy. But I really meant what I told you before. Anything I can do to help I'm glad to."

If ever there was an opening for me to make Lizbeth happy and ask Troy to sign on as a spokesman for my company, this was it. Yet I couldn't make myself do it — not after he'd just told me he was so busy. Not while I was already asking him for another favor.

Instead, I merely thanked him, and even when he asked me directly if there was anything else he could do . . . *anything at all,* I demurely declined.

It didn't matter anyway, I assured myself. The traffic reporter project was yesterday's news. I sat at my desk, having escaped Lizbeth's scrutiny earlier that morning, and was secretly making plans for the gas giveaway. Granted, I still hadn't gotten a go-ahead from Bigwood — which meant S.C. Electric hadn't yet said yes — but I felt certain it was going to happen. I was in the midst of pondering whether I'd have the nerve to call them myself when Bigwood's secretary, Phyllis, strode into my office.

"You're late," she said in her road-gravel voice.

"Late? For what?"

She crossed her arms, which were twisted with muscle. Phyllis terrified me. Between her leathery skin, broad frame, and salt-and-pepper hair that she kept pulled back in a bun, she gave every indication that the rumors that she used to ride with the Hell's Angels were true. "The directors meeting started at ten. Everybody's already there."

I was invited to a directors meeting? *Me?* This sort of thing never happened to *anyone* here, much less me. If any of my predecessors went to a directors meeting, they never made it out alive because I'd sure never heard about it.

"Nobody told me," I attempted to explain as I followed Phyllis's confident stride. Then I added nervously, "Any idea why they want me there?"

"Beats me," she replied before depositing me in Bigwood's office without further comment.

I squinted to let my eyes adjust to the dimness. Even though he had a corner office with spectacular views, Bigwood had every curtain drawn, giving the place, for all its size, a cavelike feel. He was there along with Lizbeth, Susan, the head of finance, and Ivan Cohen, aka Dr. Death (no one knew what he did, but pack your bags if he ever called you to his office, because you were headed for either unemployment or some sort of career Siberia).

"Nice of you to join us," Lizbeth sneered.

Susan cleared off a space next to her, and I mouthed a "Thanks" in her direction.

Bigwood regarded me curiously. "You look different. What's different about you?"

I'm wearing a bra, perhaps? When I shrugged, Susan widened her eyes at me, as if to say, *Give an answer.* I quickly understood why: He wasn't going to drop it until I did.

"Glasses — did you use to wear glasses?" My mind raced — what could I say? Nail polish color? A brow wax? "Wait —" He snapped his fingers. "You've gained a few pounds!"

Lizbeth tittered. "You guessed it," I replied as gaily as I could manage, given the fact that I *had* gained a couple of pounds.

"Good for you," he said. "You look healthy. I admire a woman who isn't afraid to eat." To delight him further, I took a cookie from a tray in the center of the table.

My interest in being summoned to the inner sanctum soon turned into mind-numbing boredom. How did Susan stand this week after week? Bubba sat at my feet, probably because I was the one who kept feeding him pieces of cookie. They discussed strategies and funding and I don't even remember what else, because eventually there weren't even any more cookies to keep Bubba interested and me entertained, and as I wondered if winter had yet turned to spring and contemplated crawling across the conference table and begging Dr. Death to put me out of my misery, Bigwood turned to me.

"June, I'm putting you in charge of the gas giveaway promotion. I'd like to see it happen within the month."

At last . . . the reason I was here. Apparently, not only was my project approved, but I'd been given the lead on it. Over Lizbeth, no less! As delighted as I was, I was smart enough to squelch any show of emotion. "Great," I said, trying to sound casual. I dared not look directly at Lizbeth for fear I'd be turned into a salt pillar on the spot.

"Gas giveaway?" I heard her say. Clearly this was the first she'd heard about it, and she sounded none too happy to be out of the loop. "Gee, Lou, I don't believe that I —"

Bigwood cut her off. "June will fill you in."

And that was that. He stood to leave, and everyone else followed suit, including Lizbeth — who either respected Bigwood as the final word or was too busy plotting my murder to say anything further.

Cautiously, as one might approach a feral cat, I edged my way over to her. "Let me know when you want me to give you the details. I'd be happy to," I said.

Without so much as glancing at me, she replied frostily, "Oh, I'm sure you would."

CHAPTER 7

The problem with having a list of things to accomplish like Marissa's, I soon discovered, is that you become loath to expend energy on anything that isn't directly related to the challenge. It's about payoff. Like in high school when a teacher, eyes shining, would tell us about an exciting educational opportunity — a play we could attend or a museum exhibit related to our studies. It may have even sounded remotely interesting. But it came down to what one brave soul would eventually voice for the rest of us: Will we get credit for it?

That's how I felt when Sebastian Forbes called to ask me to a party he was throwing for himself. It was to celebrate the success of his book — which currently topped the *Los Angeles Times* best-seller list and was number five on the *New York Times* list. *Publishers Weekly* called it "a darkly comic tour de force." "I owe almost none of it to you," he chirped happily, "but I want you to come to the party and behold the rat bastards who abandoned me in my time of need."

"So they came back?"

"Like moths to the flame."

He hinted there might be fellow writers and a few actors there as well — there was already talk about turning his novel into a movie. Still, I had to force myself to accept the invitation. All I could think was, *Will anyone be giving massages? Will I get on TV?* I thought back to the list for other tasks I needed to accomplish: *Any chance there'll be boogie boarding? Is Buddy Fitch invited?*

I eventually caved and took down directions to his home. Before we hung up, he said, "I suppose I should tell you, I've been seeing my doctor."

"Oh . . ." I wasn't sure what to say. It seemed such an intimate thing to confide in me considering we'd met only recently. Besides, he'd seemed so healthy.

He caught my hesitation. "No, I'm *seeing* my doctor. His name's Kip, and he's smart and gorgeous, and he'll be at the party, so be on your best behavior."

I breathed a sigh of relief. "So I take it that JJ's gone for good?"

"JJ who?"

■ ■ ■ ■

Sebastian lived in a Mediterranean-style house in the Hollywood Hills — although a case could be made for calling it a mansion. I let out a whistle of appreciation as I walked into the vast foyer with Susan. (She'd begged to come along after I mentioned the party to her — she'd borrowed my copy of *One-Woman Man* and couldn't stop talking about it.) Painted in gold hues, the walls were covered with abstract paintings. I'm sure they were all of naked people.

"So these are the spoils of a best-selling author, eh?" I said to Sebastian as he collected our coats.

"This, the spoils? Hardly," he scoffed. "My advance was minuscule. The home is thanks to Grandmum, who died several years ago."

"I'm sorry. . . ."

"Don't be. She was an evil, bitter hag who made everyone miserable."

"I loved your book!" Susan gushed out of nowhere, making me start.

Sebastian beamed. "And June, who is your lovely friend?"

I made introductions as he escorted us into the main living area. Susan launched into a breathless swoon about how the earthquake metaphor he used to parallel his tumultuous relationship with his mother had brought her to tears.

About a dozen people milled around the room, which had high ceilings, minimal furniture, and — instead of walls — massive windows opening to a sparkling, twinkling city below. The night was clear but nippy. We'd seen a sky full of stars on the drive over, which — because of the perpetual haze and smog and city lights — is a rare treat around here. From my apartment, I can usually spot only a handful on any given night. It's ironic: Los Angeles is the city of stars, but only the kind that are on the ground, attending premieres and getting the best tables at fancy restaurants.

"It's still early, so you're among the first here," Sebastian said.

"Early? It's ten-thirty!" I cried.

"I know — a pretty good crowd so far, don't you think?"

I hoped Susan and I didn't stand out. We both wore black on black, although she had a classic silk sort of thing going. My outfit looked as if it were off the rack from Express — which it was, but it had seemed a whole lot more sophisticated in the dressing room than it did here.

I was helping myself to a crab puff off a passing tray when a swarthy, well-built man walked by in what appeared to be standard men's trousers, only cut so low in the back that his crack showed. He wasn't "sagging" the way the kids do — that is, wearing them low with his underwear exposed. They were just plain low, no underwear in sight.

"Man-ass," Sebastian supplied when he caught me staring.

"Excuse me?"

"It's the latest style from New York. They refer to it as man-ass. Call me old-fashioned, but I prefer to limit my butt-crack viewing to repairmen and dockwork-ers."

I felt immediately better. There wasn't a chance in the world I could compete with the sort of style that would be on display this evening. The pressure was off. My outfit may have lacked panache, but at least no one could accuse me of trying too hard.

"Get whatever you want to drink," Sebastian said, gesturing to the bartender set up in the corner before leaving us to go mingle. "And then why don't you say hello to my publicist, Hillary. You remember her from the reading, don't you?"

But by the time we got our drinks, Hillary was deep in conversation with Man-ass, so I used the opportunity to eat a deviled egg and tell Susan about my first outing as a Big Sister with Deedee earlier that afternoon. I'd picked her up, we'd gone to a movie, and then I'd taken her home.

"That was it," I complained. "Not exactly life-changing stuff."

"What were you expecting? It was a movie."

"And popcorn," I added defensively.

"Did she have fun?"

"It's hard to tell. She's sweet, but not exactly a chatterbox. I find myself doing that thing I know kids hate, where I drill her with stupid questions." I grimaced as I thought back to snatches of our conversation:

How do you like school?

It's okay.

What's your favorite subject?

(Shrug) Language arts, I guess.

That's right. Rose mentioned you want to be a writer.

(No response, as I hadn't officially posed a question.)

What sorts of things do you write?

Fiction, I guess.

Oh? What type of fiction?

Short form.

"She'll open up," Susan assured me. "As to whether or not you can change her life, you'll have to be patient. Sounds to me like she hasn't had much of a chance to let loose and be young. She may not even know how. Maybe taking her out and introducing her to a little fun — even if it's a movie on a Saturday afternoon — maybe that's enough."

"I guess I'm hoping for trumpets and revelations."

"Aren't we all."

It took only an hour or so for the room to fill. Sebastian delivered on those celebrities he promised — that is, provided one used the term *celebrity* loosely. There was a guy I recognized from one of those bachelor shows and a woman who had earned her fifteen minutes of TV fame for drinking a blender full of slugworms and managing to keep it down.

"June! Susan! Come here!" Sebastian waved us over to where he stood with a group of people — one of whom immediately caught my attention, being as she was a magnificent giantess of a woman with pale blond hair, cheekbones you could ski off, and the shoulder span of an Olympic swimmer.

He introduced her as Mjorka, the Latvian model/actress who'd originally been cast to play JJ before I stepped in as understudy to capture the role so brilliantly. Also there was his publicist, Hillary, Man-ass, and Sebastian's boyfriend, Kip, who was adorable in that you-want-to-pinch-his-cheeks kind of way with his goatee and wire-frame glasses.

"I was telling everyone about your list," Sebastian said. "I tried to remember some of the things on it, but all I could come up with was the blind date . . . and running a 5K."

"If I found out I was going to die," Man-ass interjected, "I'd want to skydive."

Susan gave a little hand clap. "Me too!"

I rolled my eyes — enough with the skydiving!

The topic veered to a story Man-ass once read in *Chicken Soup for the Soul* about a man who at age fifteen made a list of 120 things he wanted to accomplish. (I knew the one he was talking about: I'd read it myself at my parents' last Christmas when I ran out of things to do. His list included learning languages, climbing mountains, studying primitive cultures, owning exotic pets, photographing the great sites in nature — things you couldn't imagine any one person achieving in a lifetime. I remember remarking to my mom that it said he'd done most of the things and still managed to get married and have five children. She'd huffed, "Sure he did, but I'll bet he never changed a diaper" — which surprised me, because my mom's rarely cynical.)

"What's so interesting about June's situation," Sebastian said, deftly bringing the topic back around to *moi*, "is that she's completing someone else's list." He turned to me. "What else is on it?"

I named a few off the top of my head. When I got to *Eat ice cream in public,* Mjorka looked puzzled. She asked, her voice thick with accent, "Do you mean while nude?"

"Or while skydiving?" That was from Man-ass.

I shook my head. "You have to understand. The girl who wrote the list used to be very overweight. In fact, she'd lost a hundred pounds. So the simple act of eating in public would be —"

"You Americans eat too much of the potato chips and of the sugars," Mjorka interrupted.

"We do love food," Hillary said agreeably, patting her ample hips.

"You do not love the food. You are afraid of the food. So you eat the garbage. You poison your bodies and become fat and ugly to watch at," Mjorka said. Hillary looked stung.

Kip turned to me. "Sebastian told me she'd recently lost the weight?" I nodded, and he said, "That's so sad. I can't imagine what it must be like to be obese your whole life. People are so mean. I'll bet that list was her first shot at trying to live a normal life. And then" — he snapped his fingers — "gone. She'll never have a chance at happiness."

Um, Kip, I know you meant well, but . . . ouch.

"Why do you all assume that she was miserable?" Hillary challenged. "There are plenty of large people who lead rich and rewarding lives. They have friends and satisfying careers, and yes, they even find love and get married. Not everyone is obsessed with being *model*" — there she cast a disparaging glare toward Mjorka — "thin. I believe you're being incredibly sizeist."

"If she was so happy as you say," Mjorka said, "why would she lose the weight then?"

"Or make a list," Sebastian added.

Hillary snapped, "I have a list, and I'm a happy person!" Apparently not at the moment.

In an attempt to smooth emotions, which

is one of the things Susan does so well, she said, "That's so admirable. What's on your list?"

Hillary reddened, and before she could say anything, Mjorka exclaimed, "Ha! You want to no longer be the fat! That is what is on your list!"

At that, Hillary stormed off, Man-ass followed, and Mjorka, oblivious, went off to say hi to someone she knew across the room.

"Hey . . ." Sebastian turned to me. "So how *are* things going with the list?"

"So far, so good."

"Well, you realize you can't hog it all to yourself. You promised you'd let me participate. All I do these days is write, so I need to live vicariously through you."

"It's true," Kip agreed. "This is the sort of thing he lives for."

"So, June, what have you got for me?" Sebastian pressed.

Thinking of the one task that seemed to be eluding me the most, I said, "I don't suppose you know anyone by the name of Buddy Fitch."

"As a matter of fact, I do!" he cried.

"You do?!" *Ohmygosh,* this was incredible! I started jumping around. The search was over! Boy, what were the odds that Sebastian would know —

I stopped. "You were just fucking with me, weren't you."

"I didn't know you'd get so worked up. Who is he?"

"Beats me. That's the problem. There's an item that says *Make Buddy Fitch pay.* But it's hard to exact revenge on a person when you have no idea who he is."

"Have you done an Internet check?" Kip asked.

I caught them up on what I'd tried so far: scanning the yearbooks, searching on the Internet, talking to Troy, who had called me back to say that the people he'd talked to had come up empty, too.

"Tell you what," Sebastian said. "I've got a couple PIs helping me do investigation work for my new book. I'll have them do some digging into this Buddy Fitch character."

"Oh, I don't want to ask you to do all that."

"No problem. I owe you one."

That was true; he did. Besides, I didn't know where else to turn. It was vital that I find Buddy Fitch. After all, it would be awful to go through all the trouble of racing to finish the list, only to fall one short.

CHAPTER 8

The next few weeks passed quickly. To punish me for being assigned the gas giveaway, Lizbeth refused to ease up on any of my usual deadlines — and, in fact, I suspected she was making up extra work to give me. I stayed late at the office most nights trying to juggle everything. I hadn't noticed how busy I was until my mom called to talk about a finalist being voted off *American Idol* and I realized I'd forgotten to watch. Not the entire season — just a few episodes — but still. (I liken it to those people who get to the end of the day, find they're peckish, and remark, "Gee, I forgot to eat!" That never happens to me, either.)

Even with work heating up, I made time to get together with Deedee every Saturday afternoon — although things with her weren't progressing as quickly as I might have hoped.

I'd been allowing her to choose the activity, and every week she said she wanted to see a movie. Making up for lost time, I'd guess. The only problem, I began to realize, was that it didn't exactly create the sort of bonding experience that would allow me influence over her life. I'd pick her up at her house, we'd drive the ten minutes to the theater, talking mostly about what we happened to observe outside the windows of my car — things like billboards, that lady with the shopping cart, which pizza places offered the thickest layer of cheese. Once at the theater, we'd get snacks, watch the movie, and then head back home. So far, the only life lesson I'd taught her was my trick when buying popcorn: insisting that they fill the bucket half-full of popcorn, squirt on the butter, then fill it the rest of the way up before adding the final buttering. "That way, every bite is greasy," I'd told her wisely. And while she'd seemed genuinely impressed — ordering popcorn like a pro on subsequent visits — I doubted that's the sort of thing Marissa had in mind when she'd written, *Change someone's life.*

In the interest of moving forward on the list, I tried to suggest another activity when I picked Deedee up for our fourth outing. The science center had a special show of actual preserved dead bodies. I thought for sure that'd be a draw — what teenager doesn't enjoy gore?

"But the new Chris Rock movie just came out! I'm dying to see it."

I buckled my seat belt and started the engine. "Wouldn't it be nice to do something new?"

"Pleeeeeeease," she pleaded. "I hear it's really funny. Everybody's seen it. If I don't, I'll be the only person in my entire school who doesn't know what's going on." In her earnestness, she wiggled like an upended Jell-O mold.

How could I say no to that? "Okay. Chris Rock it is."

Everything went as usual until we were at the concession. I heard Deedee whisper to herself, "Shit!" followed by a mumbling in Spanish.

"What?" I asked, but having learned to put a deaf ear to her swearing, I turned my attention back to the guy behind the counter. "No, don't fill it up all the way. Halfway. Then add the butter. . . ." I leaned over to give Deedee a nudge, but she was gone.

I paid for the snacks and attempted to balance them in the paper-thin cardboard carrier — two sodas, a giant bucket of popcorn, a box of Whoppers, and some Twizzlers —

as I scanned the crowded lobby.

No sign of her.

Please tell me I didn't lose her.

I still had the tickets, so she couldn't have gone into the theater. I tried to recall what she'd been wearing. Baggy jeans, I think. A gray hoodie. I shouted into the women's bathroom for her. No answer.

Worry knotted my stomach, but I told myself it was ridiculous. This wasn't a toddler who had wandered into traffic. She was fourteen. The place was silly with teenagers — loud, bright mobs of kids talking loudly and pushing at one another and drawing attention to themselves while pretending that was the last thing they wanted — yet none of them was *my* teenager. This was bad. The Big Sister program surely frowned on losing your charge.

I debated having Deedee paged, even though I knew she would kill me, when I spotted her sitting inside a phone-booth-shaped driving video game in the corner of the lobby. I could see the edge of her arm and pants and part of her ponytail.

"Deedee?" I said, leaning in, trying not to spill the drinks.

"Oh, hey," she said. "Just checking out this game." She hadn't put in any coins. "Game over" remained on the screen from the last player.

"You scared me — I thought I lost you."

"Sorry."

"The movie's about to start."

"Okay." She didn't move, but she craned her neck to look past me, obviously searching for something . . . or someone?

"Is there a problem?"

"Nope. No problem."

After another minute or so, she finally got up, snatching a soda from the tray in my hands, which upset the delicate balance I'd worked so diligently to establish. I fumbled, trying to hold everything together, to no avail. Deedee made a grab for the popcorn, and I managed to save the Twizzlers. The rest crashed in a wet mess to the ground, splashing my pants and earning applause from the people nearby.

As I bent down to clear everything, I heard, "Nice job, Deedee. Real graceful."

I gazed up to see a girl standing there who was probably cute, but all I could see was her smug grin.

"Oh, hey, Theresa," Deedee said nonchalantly. "I didn't know you were here."

Suddenly Deedee's dash to hide in the video game made sense. She appeared to be as glad to see this girl as I was to see Lizbeth every morning.

"Me and Claudia met up with Tony and all them." Then she asked, "Who you here with?"

Deedee, clearly not seeing any way around it, introduced me with a tip of the head. "Her."

I'd been reduced to a pronoun.

Theresa appeared to expect further explanation. Deedee seemed mute, and I couldn't come up with anything that wouldn't shame her further. I understood how embarrassing it must be to get caught at a Saturday afternoon movie with an adult when your peers are there with friends. Was I a family friend? A relative? Would my admitting to being her Big Sister be akin to committing social murder? For lack of anything better, I said, "I'm her parole officer."

To my surprise, Deedee burst out laughing, the purest show of emotion I'd seen from her in the month we'd been getting together. Theresa tittered uncomfortably, not quite getting the joke but obviously wondering if it might be on her.

"Yeah . . . got busted drug running," Deedee said. "Anyway, we better go. Movie's starting."

As we took our seats in the front row — our punishment for seeing a movie on opening weekend — the previews thundered just a few feet from us. I leaned toward Deedee and said, "Was it my imagination, or was your friend Theresa a complete bitch?"

Deedee grunted agreement as she took a handful of popcorn. "She acts like she's everybody's best friend, but the second your back's turned, watch out."

"Big gossip?"

"Yeah, and not too smart, either. She's probably telling everybody I really got a parole officer."

"You don't seem to mind. I guess that's better than her squealing that you were with a Big Sister, huh?"

After taking a slurp of the surviving soda that we were now sharing, she said, "Nah, you're cool. A few girls have Big Sisters. My girlfriend Janelle has burned through three Bigs already." As I said a silent prayer of thanks that I didn't get matched up with Janelle, she added, "It's just that I never get to do nothing with my friends. I'm always baby-sitting my shit of a brother. Every day after school. Most of the weekend. The only time I get out of watching the little *bicho* is when I'm with you. Oh, and once I got to go to a school dance. And even then my mom tried to make me come home right after. I only got to hang out longer because I pretended I got mixed up on the time."

"Clever strategy."

"I thought so."

I shook my head. "It's hard to believe anyone would ask that much of a fourteen-year-old. When do you get to have fun?"

"This is it." Her voice was grim, making it evident how short our outings fell from her definition of fun. "And it's only because that lady Rose from the Big Sister program told my mom that I'd freak out and turn into a ho or something if she didn't give me a break once in a while. Like, go wild with any freedom I might get. I overheard them talking. It was the first time anybody ever made Mami feel bad. About anything." She slurped again. "Rose is pretty funny. She totally gave my mom shit. Said my life needed changing and that she was going to do it."

At hearing that, I nearly dropped my box of Whoppers again. Of all the nerve! Rose Morales wasn't helping me achieve my secret goal of crossing an item off my list after all. The wily minx was competition!

Trying to set the record straight — if any life changing was going to happen here, it'd be me doing it — I said, "I know I'm not as good as having a friend your age, but I'm glad that you and I get to do things. I hope you've been having an okay time."

She shrugged agreeably. "Sure. It's good." She eyed the Whoppers. "You gonna open those?"

After the movie, I suggested we sneak in a little extra time together to hit the M.A.C cosmetics counter, where I bought Deedee a tube of liquid eyeliner. At eighteen dollars, it was cheaper than the movie snacks and — judging by the squeal of delight she gave when I handed over the bag — a much wiser investment toward purchasing her affection.

"So how about next week we skip the movie and go to the beach instead?" I said as we scurried to the car. She was supposed to be back by four, and it was already five minutes after. "I've been wanting to go boogie boarding." (Which of course was ridiculous — anyone who knew me at all would realize I'd never *want* to go boogie boarding. It was just a task from the list. But since Deedee didn't know about the list — and never would, since she was essentially a task on it, too — I was relieved that she seemed to take my comment at face value.)

"All right. I can work on my tan. But ain't no way I'm going in the water. It'll be freezing this time of year."

"I prefer to think of it as refreshing," I countered.

"Yeah, right."

Okay, so I'd brave the waters alone. At least we'd be doing something other than staring at a movie screen. After I got on the road, I asked, "Will you be in trouble for being late?"

"Probably. But maybe not. My mom will be mad at you, not me. I'm supposed to watch Prince Ricky."

"Your brother, I presume?"

"You can't believe what a pain in the ass he is, and my mom thinks he's so perfect. It's always Ricky this and Ricky that. I don't even exist except to watch him. You have no idea."

When we reached a red light, I turned to her and said, "Feel the back of your head." She looked at me as if I'd gone insane. "Go ahead, do it." With a look that said she was simply humoring me, she reached up a hand and ran it over her head. "Notice how it's nice and curved?" I leaned toward her, still keeping my eyes on the stoplight. "Now feel mine. See how it's flat?"

She did and said, "Ew. It is kinda flat." She felt hers again to compare.

"That's because when I was a baby, my parents used to spend their time chasing my brother around. He was hell on wheels. I was an easy baby, so they left me lying in bed all day by myself. Baby's heads are soft, so mine eventually flattened."

Deedee thought about it. "You're lucky you got all that hair. It covers it up. I'd never have known you had a flat head."

"My point is, you're not alone. I understand what it's like to lose out because of a spoiled brother." And I had the deformity to prove it.

The Santa Monica beach near the pier was packed — I remembered too late that there was a big environmental fair and beach cleanup going on. Even though it was off-season, the beach was filled with rows of tents with booths set up on the sand. Music from the sponsoring radio station, K-JAM, blared from speakers — top forty pop and hip-hop music, which I would've enjoyed a lot more if I hadn't had to pay seven bucks to park. Deedee carted a beach bag, and I carried towels and a boogie board borrowed from Susan, which I slung over my shoulder by its leash in the smooth manner of Sinatra holding a raincoat.

The day was clear but windy. Waves broke along the shore as if detonated. Although the air was warm, the water temperature in March would definitely be icy. The surfers wore wet suits (something I should have looked into), but the fact that a few swimmers braved the water in ordinary swimwear gave me hope.

Since we had to pass the fair to get to the water, I figured I could drag Deedee to check and see if there was an L.A. Rideshare booth — while I was at it, say hi to Elaine, the woman who worked weekend events for us. It occurred to me that my sudden interest in my co-worker Elaine might have had something to do with the size of those waves. I knew I'd go through with the task before me, but I sure wasn't in any hurry.

We wandered past a couple of rows of booths until I saw the Los Angeles Rideshare banner. Brie was there alone, and she waved when she saw me trudge up with Deedee. She stood behind a table filled with various brochures as well as key chains, pens, antenna balls, and other cheap, crappy plastic items with our logo on them.

"What are you doing here?" I asked, surprised to see her.

"Elaine got that flu that's going around. I'd told her any time she wanted me to fill in for her I'd be glad to. I get paid time and a half."

Just then, who should walk up to join Brie but Martucci — carting a box, which he set with a thud on the table. "Hey, Parker," he said, looking me up and down. "You here to work?"

"Do I look like I'm here to work?" I wore an oversize shirt as a swimsuit cover-up and was still holding the boogie board.

"How the hell would I know? But if you're here to work, I've got more boxes that need hauling. Brie here's afraid she'll break a nail."

"I just got 'em done," she explained, holding up her nails, which were each painted with tiny flowers.

"Sorry to disappoint you," I said without sincerity to Martucci. "I'm just stopping by."

When I introduced them to Deedee, Brie exclaimed, "So this is your Little Sister! We've heard so much about you. Hold on —" She reached into the box Martucci had brought to hand Deedee a logo pen with a tip like a lava lamp that changed colors as you clicked it. "This is for you. I'm only giving the good stuff to friends."

"Cool," Deedee said, clicking. "Thanks."

Brie turned to Martucci. "How about you go get that box with the T-shirts? I'll bet this girl would like one of those."

"Jesus, you women think I'm a plow horse," he groused. "You know, Elaine pulls her own weight when she's working with me."

"That's because she doesn't have my skills. My job is to attract customers," Brie said. "I can't do that if my nails are all nasty."

He looked wearily at Deedee. "What size you want?"

"Large?" she replied.

He left, muttering something under his breath. When he was out of earshot, I said, "Forget time and a half. If you're forced to work with him, they ought to pay triple your hourly rate."

"What — you don't like Martucci?"

"You *do?*"

"He's all right."

"I just hate the way he sucks up to Lizbeth. And that rattail braid of his is so gross. He's always *feeling* it."

"He's probably scared it might've crawled away," Brie said. "Anyway, I figure I can get him to pick up hoagie sandwiches when he gets back. All this standing here is making me starved. You want a hoagie?"

"I'll pass." Although it occurred to me that if I ate something big, I'd have an excuse to wait thirty minutes before going in the water.

Brie turned her attention to Deedee. "So,

141

hon, you got yourself a boyfriend?"

I couldn't believe she'd ask her such a prying question right off. I expected Deedee to do the clamshell imitation I knew so well, but she made a noise like *pbbbbt* and rolled her eyes as if to say, *Boys.*

"I know that face," Brie said, nodding wisely. "Go on, tell Mama Brie all about it. Who's the bum, and what'd he do?"

"Carlos," she answered, as if saying "dog turd."

"Mm-hmm . . ."

"And he all says he likes me, that I'm hot and all that . . ."

"I know that one."

"And then I find out he's going out with . . ." She paused because it was clearly too awful to say. *"Theresa."*

I cut in. "Theresa from the movies?"

"Yeah. He was there that day, which she conveniently forgot to mention."

Brie shook her head in disgust. "You don't want Carlos anyway. He's a fool, going for a skank like Theresa. You know what I think?" She leaned over and pulled the oversize tank top Deedee wore snug against her. "You got a cute little figure there. You oughta dress real sexy and show that Carlos what he's missing. I got some clothes that I don't wear anymore. They're small on me, but I'll bet they'd fit you real nice. How about if I give them to June to pass on to you? You can keep anything you like and throw away what you don't."

Deedee wearing Brie's castoffs? Her bright and tight Lycra and spandex? That was good for a laugh! That was about as likely as —

"Sure." Deedee beamed. "You got stuff like what you're wearing now?"

"This old thing?" Brie wore a fuchsia tank top over matching short-shorts. "Oh, way better."

Well, isn't that swell? In five minutes she'd managed to do more bonding with Deedee than I had in over a month. Although it was nice to see Deedee open up, even if it wasn't to me. At least it was in my general vicinity.

"Hey, I almost forgot," Brie said to me. "That traffic reporter guy stopped by to see if you were here. Trey . . . ?"

"Troy Jones?"

"Yeah, that's it. He said he's here with K-JAM helping with the beach cleanup. Oh, speaking of that, watch this." She crumpled a brochure and tossed it into the sand. Within seconds, two children holding trash bags ran up and began to fight over who got there first to pick it up. "Works every time! I guess they got more people showing up to pick up trash than they got trash."

Deedee appeared delighted, but I was busy looking for Troy Jones. Hopefully he was gone by now. I didn't need him nosing around while I attempted to check a task off the list — especially one that required so little clothing on my part. "I hope Martucci gets back with that T-shirt soon. We should get going," I said.

Brie eyed the boogie board. "Looks like you've got some fun planned. By the way, we still on for tomorrow night?"

"Yep." Brie was going to accompany me to the Oasis bar so I could cross off another task.

"You still buying?"

"Yep."

We chatted a bit longer until Martucci returned, chucking a box onto the sand this time. Then he rifled through it and tossed a T-shirt at Deedee. "There you go," he said. "Wear it proudly."

"Thanks." She held it up to inspect it. "It's cute."

"You think *that* shirt's cute," Brie said, "you ought to see what I picked out for June to wear for tomorrow. Hoo-ee, it's nice. The top's this silvery blue, real shiny, you know? And it's got these sparkly things right along the —"

"Okay, then!" I interrupted, not wanting Brie to elaborate in front of Martucci as to the location of those sparkly things.

Too late. "Along the *what,* exactly?" he asked a bit too innocently, his gaze dropping to indicate he was making a pretty good guess.

"We'll be leaving now," I said, trying to ignore him, but Brie, clueless, gestured across her chest as an answer.

"Nice," Martucci said. "So what's going on tomorrow?"

"Girls' night out," Brie replied. I began to worry she might start talking about the list, but she simply said, "We're going to this bar called Oasis. That's the name of it, right, June? Oasis?" I nodded, and she continued, "Anyway, the guys there are going to have to pick up their tongues off the floor when June here walks in. She's definitely going to be . . ." She paused to give me an exaggerated wink. "The *hottest girl there.*"

Okay, shoot me now. I wasn't sure who was more amused by Brie's carrying on about me being hot, Martucci or Deedee. Luckily, an actual customer approached, preventing Brie from inflicting any further humiliation. I grabbed our beach stuff and said a quick good-bye, and Deedee and I started the trek to the water before I lost my nerve.

Although I had done a fair amount of body surfing in my day, I'd never surfed on a boogie board. I may be a California girl by birth, but I grew up in the Valley, land of air-conditioning and outdoor pools. Anyone who's ever been in Van Nuys during an August heat wave would understand how Valley girls earned such a reputation for hanging out at the mall. It's shop or melt. And the beach — the beautiful, breezy beach that was over the hill and a forty-five-minute drive away — may as well have been a thousand miles for my parents' willingness to drive us there. (Although I have to admit, now living in Santa Monica, it's embarrassing how few times I've made the short trip to the beach myself.)

Chase had given me pointers when I'd stopped by Susan's to borrow their boogie board. He'd told me to paddle out to where the waves crash. Wait until one is about to break, lie on the board, then paddle like crazy and ride it gloriously into shore. "Wait for your wave," he'd advised, as if I had any idea what that meant.

I set down our towels. I wore a blue flowered two-piece bathing suit from last season — one of the few I could find with a bottom that actually covered a bottom and an underwire on the top. If I'd known at the time how precious and rare this combination would turn out to be — as I bitterly discovered when I tried and failed to buy a new suit in the current season — I'd have bought the shop out of them. Sure, my bare stomach wasn't perfectly flat. But big deal. I've seen women flaunt plenty worse on my bus ride to and from work. Whoever came up with the idea that Los Angeles was filled with tight bodies honed to perfection obviously never rode public transportation.

I grabbed the boogie board. The waves weren't quite the size of billboards, but they appeared ominous enough to a coward like me. Deedee had made good on her promise not to go in the water, settling on her towel.

"You coming to cheer me on?" I asked.

"I'll go up to my ankles," she said, snatching a bag of Doritos to bring with her. "But don't be thinking I'm going any deeper."

Maybe the girl was on to something — the water was so cold that I got brain freeze the second I dipped my feet in. Deedee said, "This isn't so bad." Which, of course, was easy for her to say, not being the one about to go in full-body. It figured: The one time I didn't put something off was the one time it would have been wise to do so. Surely the water would be warmer come summer. Too late now, though: I was committed.

It took me a while to swim out with the board, what with my limbs being numb. Plus every time a wave came, it pushed me back. Eventually — huffing and groaning and cursing the fact that I never finished that junior lifesaving course at the Y back in eighth grade — I made it out past the break, where I gave catching a wave a few tries. The technique I established was to find a wave, fall off the board, and get buried alive in the water, the boogie board attached to my wrist banging into me.

Although growing weary, I dragged my tired body out again and again. I was about to call it a day (after all, the list only said *try* boogie boarding; there was nothing on it about going pro) when I saw what I was sure was my wave swelling gloriously behind me. Right before it hit, I realized I was wrong. Horribly, horribly wrong. This wasn't a wave at all. It was the Chrysler Building. It was Mount Kilimanjaro. It was the Great Wall of China — only standing on its end a thousand miles high and about to come crashing down on me.

Which it did — pummeling me and sending me spinning and tossing so I couldn't tell which was up or down. I hit sand hard a few times but was dragged back up . . . or down . . . or any direction but toward air. Lungs bursting, I made myself follow the instructions the lifeguards used to tell us — not to fight the wave. Just as I did that, it spat me with my board crudely and unceremoniously onto the shore.

There I lay, splayed on the sand, gasping for air, scraped and sputtering.

I heard a man's voice say in disgust, "Watch out for the big lady, Tommy. Don't step on the big lady." A pair of toddler's feet stepped neatly over my head.

Nice. I quit.

I unleashed myself from the board and was about to pull myself up when two more feet appeared. "You okay?"

That voice sounded familiar. I looked up — it was Troy Jones. I yanked myself to my feet, trying to brush the sand off me. It encrusted my face. I was human sandpaper. My swimsuit bottom felt like a full diaper. "I'm fine."

"That was one helluva ride. A bit rough on the dismount."

"I was hoping for style points." Sand fell from my brow into my eye. Trying to restore my dignity, I said as breezily as I could manage, "How's the garbage cleanup going?"

"Good. Not enough garbage to go around, though."

Deedee walked up. "You should go under the pier. That's where the good stuff is. My girlfriend Janelle said she once found a bag of crystal meth under there."

I raised an eyebrow at her. More sand fell.

"Troy," I said, attempting to change the subject and use the moment of distraction to pull the back of my swimsuit to dump some of the sand, "this is Deedee, a friend of mine. Deedee, this is Troy."

Troy put out his hand to shake hers, and Deedee took it, giving him a slow once-over. He wore a K-JAM T-shirt and shorts, and she must have approved of what she saw because she bore the same expression she had at the movie theater — shame at her association with the likes of me. "You know, June don't always look this bad."

"Thanks," I said, sneering.

She attempted to straighten my hair, which was matted on one side and lifting like a bird in flight on the other. "Okay, so it's not so good now. But tomorrow night she's going out, and she's gonna be *bangin'*. Go on, tell him how hot you'll be."

Troy grinned. "Yes . . . do."

"For real!" Deedee continued. "Those guys at this Oasis place aren't going to know what hit 'em."

"I clean up nicely," I said, deadpan.

150

"Did you say Oasis?" Troy asked.

I nodded. "It's a little bar over on —"

"Yeah," he said, "I know it. Used to go there with my sister once in a while. She had a crush on the bartender."

I pulled a soggy candy bar wrapper from my hair and, disgusted, tossed it on the ground. A boy shouted, "I got it!" and ran over to pick it up and put it in his trash bag. Deedee then chucked her empty Doritos bag on the beach and watched in delight as the same thing happened. "I want to see what other garbage we got. This is fun."

After she left, Troy said, "So, you a big fan of boogie boarding?"

"Never did it before."

"Any reason you decided to try it today?"

Sand kept falling in my eyes, and I feared it appeared as if I were winking. "I see we're also going fishing today." When he gave me a curious look, I said, "As in fishing to see if this might be something from the list?"

"Was I that obvious?"

"That's okay. And yes, it is."

He gazed out at the ocean for a moment and then asked, "Did you catch any good waves?"

"I'm not sure. I got going a couple times, but I don't know if that was catching the wave." It occurred to me that catching waves might be like having orgasms — if you're not sure you've ever done it, then you haven't. "Probably not."

"You going back out again?"

Back out? Was he joking? I intended to never go back in the water . . . ever. In fact, in the time since what I considered my near death experience, I was seriously toying with packing up and moving to Montana — or any other state that was dead center and as far away as possible from anything large, wet, and salty.

"Of course I am," I said boldly, my pride winning over anything resembling rational thought.

"I'm going to give you a shove-off." Without saying anything else, he reached up and pulled off his T-shirt, then tossed it on the ground. Well now! He had strong shoulders and arms — working in the fields strong as opposed to standing in front of the mirror at the gym posing strong. And a bit of light brown hair on his chest that led down to firm but not six-pack abs. That was when I noticed the huge scar that ran almost the entire length of one of his legs, crossing from where his shorts ended to his shin at a diagonal.

"What's a shove-off?" I asked, hoping I hadn't been staring too obviously. But he had, after all, removed clothing. It would be rude *not* to look.

"You'll see." He shouted to his fellow garbage collectors that he'd be right back, then grabbed the board. I followed him into the water. It was easier to swim out past the break without the board — and getting back in the water did offer the benefit of allowing me to rinse the sand from my hair and from a few of my more critical orifices.

The water reached him midchest, and I bobbed, hanging on to the board. We were no closer than we'd been when we chatted on the beach, but somehow being in the water made it seem strangely intimate.

Troy proceeded to give me the same instructions Chase had — only he said that when the right wave came, he'd give me a shove.

"So do you surf?" I asked, bobbing.

"Once in a while. Not so much now since I get up at three in the morning for work."

"Gosh, that's the time I'm usually stumbling home drunk."

"Right. You strike me as that type."

"You don't know — I could be," I said, finding myself mildly irritated that it was so obvious I wasn't a party girl, even though he'd clearly meant it as a compliment.

We chatted a bit about his favorite surf

spots, and then he told me to get ready — that the waves were picking up. I clambered onto the board, my arms reaching to grab the top end and my butt and legs dangling in the water. I was pointed toward shore like a rocket ready to launch. Troy was behind and slightly to the left of me — not the proximity to my rear I would have chosen had it come up for a vote.

"When I say go, start paddling," he instructed. I glanced behind me, and a swell began to build. When it reached me, he shouted, "Go!" My hands grabbed at the water, and the wave started to lift the board. Troy put one hand on the back of the board, the other on my lower back, and gave a strong, hard shove.

Suddenly I was soaring. *This* was catching a wave, and — my suspicions had been correct — I'd never done anything like it before. It felt as if the water beneath me had turned into a sea of hands that kept spiriting my board up and forward — gliding and skipping and lifting until I was shrieking with the unexpected thrill of it and wishing that this amazing rush would never, ever have to end.

CHAPTER 9

I'd driven past Oasis probably a hundred times but had never before been inside. I generally try to avoid tropical-themed bars located in minimalls. When Brie, her girl-friend Chanel, and I walked in, however, it was surprisingly large and lively and — for a Sunday evening — crowded.

"Good, there're mostly guys here. Less competition," Brie said, tugging on the snug tank top she wore especially for the occasion because it was the color of baby barf — no worries she might upstage me. Chanel had announced that surely there'd be no brothers at a place called Oasis in a mini-mall so she might as well wear an ugly shirt, too — a gesture I would have appreciated more if I didn't happen to own the same shirt.

No matter. All that was important was that I meet the dictates of #8: *Be the hottest girl at Oasis.*

To that end, I wore the aforementioned silvery blue top with the sequin action going and the low-rider jeans I'd bought for the blind date. I spent forever blow-drying my hair. Truly a child of the eighties, I can't help myself: When it comes to hair, I still equate bigger with better. I did, however, pass on Brie's offer to do my makeup for me. (I'd almost taken her up on it until she'd boasted, "I do one face and it works on *everybody.*")

We took a seat at a high cocktail table in the center of the room. The waitress came by, and Brie and Chanel ordered pink ladies, and I asked for a Chardonnay.

"So now what?" Chanel said when our drinks arrived.

I quickly surveyed the people around us. "I suppose as long as we establish that I'm the hottest woman in the room, then we're free to have our drinks and go."

"I can't see everybody good from here — let's check it out," Brie said. She and Chanel grabbed their drinks and left to case the room. I stayed at the table, trying to be . . . hot? Ugh. Could I please go back to my idea of setting myself on fire? Truth was, I'd never felt so ridiculous in my life. I felt silly because Brie and Chanel were walking around deciding if I was the prettiest girl in the room and even sillier because I kind of hoped I was. I understood what Marissa was after: that thrill of feeling that every eye is on you because you're beautiful, not because you're fat. But most of the eyes here weren't on women, but rather on the TVs in the corners broadcasting a Lakers game.

They returned, their faces a twist of pity. "Over there, by the jukebox, behind that pillar," Brie said. "She's hotter."

Chanel nodded. "The boobs are fake, but she's got kind of a Lindsay Lohan thing going. You know, real fresh but slutty."

I craned my neck. Crap! She *was* hot! "I can't compete with that! Now what am I supposed to do?" I whined. "Keep returning again and again hoping to hit a slow night? There's always going to be somebody more beautiful!"

"You don't need to worry about it," Brie said ominously. "We'll get rid of her."

"What are you planning to do?" I asked, mildly alarmed.

She reached into her purse, and I feared what she might whip out. She merely freshened her lipstick. "We got a few ideas. I figure we'll stand there and talk about a designer shoe sample sale in the parking lot. That ought to get her moving. If that doesn't work, maybe we'll say we saw a rat in the kitchen."

After they took off for their second mission, I was left to sip my drink alone. I was in the midst of checking out the bartenders, wondering which one Marissa had a crush on, when up walked Troy Jones, a beer in his hand and a grin on his face. "You were right, you do clean up nicely," he said.

"Ha, ha."

"I hope you don't mind my stopping by. I was in the neighborhood, mooching dinner off the folks."

"Aren't you fortunate. I have to drive to the Valley to get a decent home-cooked meal."

"You here by yourself?"

"No, my girlfriends are off . . ." *Er, eliminating hot chicks?* "Saying hi to people they know." I glanced over to where Brie and Chanel stood. They were having what appeared to be a loud conversation with much gesturing behind the Lindsay Lohan lookalike's table and being completely ignored.

After I invited Troy to pull up a chair, he gave a nod toward the bar. "That's the guy my sister had the crush on — in the pink polo shirt. She thought he looked like the lead singer from Nine Inch Nails."

It was hard to decide what seemed stranger: that the sweet girl I pictured

Marissa Jones to be would have had a thing for Nine Inch Nails or that she thought anyone in a pink polo shirt could resemble Trent Reznor.

"I see that," I said.

"Thought I'd point it out — in case you needed to know."

It took a second for it to sink in this time. "Fishing again?"

He took a swig of his beer instead of answering.

"It's not about the bartender," I said.

"I didn't think it was. So you don't need to chat him up or anything?"

"Nope."

I knew he was here hoping to see the list, and he had every right to — in fact, I had no claim to it in the first place. Still, I was worried he'd be disappointed. There weren't many crossed off yet, not as many as should have been. To stall, I asked, "So how did you get into traffic reporting?"

"Ah, cleverly changing the subject. I'll tell you, but I'm saving the steamy stuff for my best-selling memoir." He leaned back and gave me an exaggerated dreamy stare. "It started at the age of three when I got my first tricycle. . . ."

"Is this where everything goes murky and we have the flashback?"

"You prefer the short version? Basically, I'm a motorhead through and through. Got my driver's license at sixteen. My motorcycle license the same year. Took me till seventeen to get the pilot's license — and they don't let you fly commercial until twenty."

"So that's what you've always done? Piloted?"

"Actually, I started out racing motorcycles out of high school. Picked up a few sponsors, too. Thought I might go pro. But then I took a spill . . ." He paused to knock on his leg as if it were wooden. "Split my leg open. Messed up my knee. That was the end of my racing career."

I grimaced and said, "That must have been terrifying."

"You know what's weird? My family figured I'd be the one to die young. At the rate I was going, none of us thought I'd live to see thirty." With that reminder of why we were sitting across from each other, I shifted uncomfortably, and mercifully moving on to other topics, he said, "So, what does your boyfriend think of all this?" I tried to remember when I had mentioned Robert when Troy added, "I assume that was your boyfriend who came with you to the funeral."

160

"Oh yeah, we broke up a while back."

"Sorry."

I gave a brief flick of my hand, as if to say, *No big deal, c'est la vie,* because nobody wants to admit they've been dumped and, even worse, that it hurt.

"Hey, what's that you're drinking?" Troy asked. "Let me get you another. . . ."

"Oh, no thanks." I caught a glimpse of Brie and Chanel. They sat at the table with the hotter girl and her friends — whooping over the Lakers game and high-fiving one another.

"Come on," he urged. "That one's almost empty."

"Really, I'm fine. I'm driving."

"Too bad." He gave me what my mom used to call a devil's grin, the corners of his mouth sneaking up. "I was hoping if I got you good and drunk, you might show me that list."

What could I do? It was stolen property as it was. "Fine," I said begrudgingly. "I'll show it to you — but first, I want to make sure you understand that a lot of the things aren't crossed off yet because they're in progress."

"All right."

"I'm working on them."

"Duly noted."

"And it's not fair to cross them off until I've finished them."

He nodded.

"Done them proper justice."

"June . . ."

"Yeah?"

He held out a hand. "The list . . . ?"

I dug it out of where I kept it in my wallet and handed it to him.

He unfolded it and started to read.

20 THINGS TO DO BY MY 25TH BIRTHDAY

1. ~~Lose 100 pounds~~
2. ~~Kiss a stranger~~
3. Change someone's life
4. ~~Wear sexy shoes~~
5. Run a 5K
6. ~~Dare to go braless~~
7. Make Buddy Fitch pay
8. Be the hottest girl at Oasis
9. Get on TV
10. Ride in a helicopter
11. ~~Pitch an idea at work~~
12. ~~Try boogie boarding~~
13. ~~Eat ice cream in public~~
14. ~~Go on a blind date~~
15. Take Mom and Grandma to see Wayne Newton
16. Get a massage

17. ~~Throw away my bathroom scale~~
18. Watch a sunrise
19. Show my brother how grateful I am for him
20. Make a big donation to charity

His expression was serious as his eyes darted over the items. At one point, he blew out a breath and rubbed his forehead. I wasn't sure if I should say anything, so I tossed out a simple, "You okay?"

"Number nineteen's a tough one." I knew the list well by now: #19 was *Show my brother how grateful I am for him.* "It's just that . . . ," he began, and then he stopped. After a moment he said, "Can you excuse me?"

"Of course."

He left the list on the table and made his way to the men's room.

Brie scurried over the moment I was alone. "We haven't been able to get her to leave, but we might be okay anyhow. She's got a bad tooth in the back."

"Lucky me."

"You're lucky all right — I see you got men making the moves on you. That one's a cutie."

"You met him yesterday. He's Troy Jones — Marissa's brother."

"Damn, that's right. I thought he looked familiar."

"I showed him the list," I said, glancing toward the men's room door. "He seemed upset."

"Well, sure. It's hard to accept your sister wanting to go braless."

I winced — I hadn't thought about how personal a few of the items were.

I made Brie leave before Troy returned, apologizing as he sat back down. "Wasn't expecting it to hit me like that."

"I take it you two were tight?"

"She was my baby sister — I was already five years old by the time she was born. I looked out for her, you know?"

A brother looking out for his sister? No, I wouldn't know. I tended to think of myself as an only child — one who happened to have a sibling.

"At any rate," he said, "she expressed her gratitude to me fine in her lifetime. You can cross that one off the list."

Oh, how tempting that was! Reluctantly I said, "Not really." I went on to explain to him the rules Susan and I had set up for the list: that I didn't have to do the tasks in order, that I had to obey the spirit of the law, and that I had to try as best I could to make them my own. "It'd be too hard for me to predict what Marissa might have had in mind for that one, so it seemed more sincere to go after it from my own point of view." Which meant, I added, that I needed to let *my* brother know how grateful I was for him before I could mark it as complete. I didn't mention, however, that it was going to be interesting expressing how I felt about such Hallmark moments as the time he held me at butter-knife point in the kitchen to make me cry.

"Although there is that one here, number fifteen: *Take Mom and Grandma to see Wayne Newton.* That needs to be *your* mom and grandma," I said worriedly. I couldn't imagine they'd want to go with me to see Wayne Newton — which obviously meant a trip to Les Vegas. I had no idea how I was going to pull *that* off.

"They'd love it," he said as if reading my mind. "They call themselves Wayniacs."

I gave a mock sigh. "Every family has its shameful secrets."

He asked to see the list again, and this time when he read it, he seemed to be in lighter spirits. "There are a few things on here a guy doesn't want to think of his sister doing."

"I'll bet."

"But I don't mind picturing *you* doing them."

He gazed up at me, and instinctively I crossed my arms.

"So who'd you kiss?" he asked.

"Some busboy."

"Bet that made his day."

And at that point — damn it — there was no denying it anymore. Something inside me lit up. The groundhog had been awakened in her tunnel and was about to pop her head up to see if the long winter was over. I searched for a mental baseball bat to pound her down. With all the men in the world, couldn't I possibly aim my affections toward a man whose sister I hadn't killed? If we became a couple — and my God, how had my thoughts even progressed so far so fast? — we'd for the rest of our lives have to lie anytime someone asked us, "So . . . how did you two meet?"

"I'll help you with the one about riding in a helicopter," Troy said, and then drained the last of his beer. "Marissa wrote that because I was always bugging her to do a ride-along."

"Ride-along?"

"Coming with me while I do a traffic report."

"I'd love that!" *Stop it!* I scolded myself.

166

Stop with the eyelash fluttering!

Brie and Chanel walked up then, shaking their heads. "They were *robbed.* There was no *way* that was a foul."

After I made introductions, Troy stood to leave. "I'd better get going — I've bothered you long enough." He slid the list toward me. "And for the record, you have that one covered." He pointed to #8: the unbelievably embarrassing reason we were gathered here today.

I shook my head. "Except for Miss Cutie Pie over there."

Brie agreed sadly, "It's true, she's hotter," and tipped her chin toward the competition. Troy's eyes followed our gaze.

He grabbed a pencil from the table display advertising the nachos special. Leaning over the list, he drew a neat line through *Be the hottest girl at Oasis.* Then he returned it me. "Not even close."

CHAPTER 10

The gas giveaway project was stalling since we couldn't find a single gas station that would work with us. Seems there's this little thing called "liability" they were worried about. One gas station manager wanted me to take out a million-dollar insurance policy in case anyone had a heart attack from excitement when we offered to pay for their gas. Even when I tried to explain that the total value of each prize would be fifty dollars tops — and that would only be for those big gas-hog SUVs — he turned me down. "You never know," he said. "My sister-in-law had a spider drop in front of her when she was vacuuming, and it gave her such a bad fright that, boom, that was all she wrote."

I'd been calling gas stations for weeks with zero luck. The date was set for April 16, two weeks away. I was the bride who'd booked the band and ordered the cake but couldn't find a groom that would have her.

At Lizbeth's weekly department meeting, Martucci offered up a lead, a guy he knew by the name of Armando who managed an Umpco station in Burbank. The location had me drooling since it was close to where so many of the major news studios were located.

"What's in it for me?" Armando said when I called him to ask if we could have the gas giveaway at his station. He continued working the register as we talked. I could hear the *ching*ing of the drawer opening and closing.

"It'd be great publicity for your station — plus we'd bring in lots of business."

"How do you figure? Didn't you say you were going to surprise customers? So how would new people be coming to spend their money at my station?"

"Well, yes, but —"

I heard him shout away from the phone, "Not that pump! That one's got a broken handle . . . pump five! Use pump five!" Then he was back. "How much new business you figure we'll get that day?"

"It's more about goodwill. You see —"

"Goodwill! Unless it's green and has a picture of a president on it, I can't use your goodwill. Pump *five*, I said! Jesus, can you count? One, two, three, four, *five!*"

"The idea is that people will see your station on TV or hear about it on the radio and —"

"No shit it's not working, Sherlock! You're at the wrong pump!" he shouted. He came back to the phone. "Not interested."

When I reported to Martucci that I'd struck out when I called, he said, "You *called?* Well, no wonder. You're not going to get anywhere on the phone. You've got to go there in person and talk to him." He pulled a scrap of paper from his desk and wrote down directions to the gas station. "And for Christ's sake, Parker, wear something tight."

"We're on!" I announced jubilantly at the department meeting later that week. Thanks to those five pounds I'd gained — and possibly more, but having dumped my scale, how was I to know? — virtually every item of clothing I owned was tight. I'd gone straight from work to seal the deal. While I'd like to say that Armando was no match for my charms, to be truthful, he'd put up quite a struggle. In the end, however, I prevailed — especially after I assured him that I'd do everything in my power to make sure he got on camera. That, and yes, I'd wear the red top again.

Although I could have gone through with the event with just one gas station committed, Brie had come through with another as well. Some friend of a friend owned a Union 76 near the airport. Everything was shaping up just as I'd hoped.

My confidence was such that I even had T-shirts printed up at Kinko's for the staff to wear. I held up a shirt, which was bright purple with white lettering: *The Great Gas Giveaway* on the front and our logo and phone number on the back.

Lizbeth managed a wan smile. "Cute . . . although I don't know how 'great' it is seeing as we only have the two locations."

I wanted to jab her with a sarcastic, "Oh *yeah?*" but besides the fact that it was hardly the sort of witty retort that she had coming, I absolutely refused to let that woman get to me. This event was going to be a huge success, and that was the best possible revenge for her sour attitude.

After the meeting, Brie pulled me aside and gave me a teasing nudge. "This might be worth a call to your traffic reporter friend. The one who thinks you're *hot?*"

"Shut up," I said, reddening. "I practically begged for that compliment."

But she had a point. I should give Troy a

call to tell him about the gas giveaway so he could mention it on air.

But not yet.

Two weeks' notice to ask for a ten-second plug sounded desperate even to me.

"Look at you! How adora—" I started to exclaim, until Deedee widened her eyes and shook her head vigorously at me to stop me from continuing. "—ble," I finished on a much quieter note.

"Let's go," she said stiffly.

She'd answered the door wearing one of Brie's outfits — jeans jacket over a striped Lycra top and pink pants that rode low on the hips. Sure, the clothes might have been a size too small for her, but it was a refreshing change over the huge shirts and baggy pants. Even though I can't say the outfit was entirely flattering, it begged for comment.

"Buenos días," I called to her mother as I always did as Deedee ran out of the house.

When we got into my car, I said, "What's the deal? Does your mom not want you wearing stuff like that?"

"Are you kidding? She'd love it. She's been on my butt to stop the sagging and dragging for forever."

"I see." I remembered back to Deedee's

mother complaining to Rose Morales on my first visit. Deedee's choice of clothes had obviously turned into a power struggle between the two of them. She wanted Deedee to dress more femininely, and apparently Deedee had wanted the same thing but wouldn't admit it.

"The way I figure it, she only needs to *think* I'm wearing the big clothes." She had a triumphant grin. "I gotta be careful, though, because she's not totally blind. I need to keep it low on the colors if she's around."

"Clever. Too bad you couldn't hide those good grades from her, too."

She caught my sarcasm and returned it in kind. "Rose ratted me out on those."

"You're probably the only teenager in America hiding her good behavior from her mother. Anyway, what I was going to say is that you're adorable."

"Thanks. You're not going to tell her, are you?"

"How?"

"Oh yeah. Heh." Then she added, "She can speak some English, and she understands a lot more than she lets on. They talk English around her at the restaurant where she works."

"She works?"

"Yeah, she works. She's a cook. Real fancy restaurant."

"That's amazing. I'm a terrible cook, and I don't even have a disability. You'd think she'd burn herself, or —"

"She never burns herself. She's too perfect." Deedee picked at a button on her jacket. "I hear every damn day how much she can do even though she can't see. She's always harping on how I need to make something of myself like she has. Not follow so many of the girls who start popping out the kids right away. She wants me to go to college first and make a lot of money."

"Isn't that what you want?"

"Sure, but maybe I want kids first. You know, before I'm all old." She must have realized what she said as soon as she said it, because she added hurriedly, "Not that being old when you have kids is bad." A few seconds passed before she asked, "You ever thought about having kids?"

"Sure. Even though I'm so *aged* that I'm certain my ovaries are shriveled and filled with dust, I may give it a shot."

"Or maybe you can adopt."

"I'm thirty-four. You act as if it's hopeless."

"I didn't mean it that way. It's only that where I'm from, women your age are grandmas."

We met Sebastian and Kip at a laser tag in Pasadena. That hadn't been the original plan. I'd set up lunch so that Sebastian could talk to Deedee about her writing. He asked if Kip could come along, however, and since it'd be the four of us, couldn't we have a little fun? I'd switched plans, and watching them together, I was glad I had. They had a blast. Deedee let loose in a way she rarely did — screaming back and forth in Spanish with Kip, making up Mexican mafioso games, and laughing hysterically.

Unfortunately, the whole concept of laser tag eluded me. The room was so dark that I kept getting lost in the maze. The gun didn't shoot anything I could see, and I never did catch on to how I was supposed to recharge. They made fun of me later because I'd been killed and didn't even know it. Apparently, I walked around for three rounds already dead — nothing but a ghost pulling the trigger over and over with no effect on anyone.

We parted ways at the laser tag, and I took Deedee home. "Good luck sneaking in without being seen," I called as I let her out of the car. "And don't let me catch you doing anything good!"

She rolled her eyes.

The phone was ringing when I walked into my apartment, and when I picked it up it was Kip.

"Calling to gloat about your victory?" I asked. "Because I'm wondering if the term *poor sportsmanship* rings any sort of bell for you."

"I need to talk to you about Deedee," he said, his voice stiff.

"Did something happen?"

"I could be wrong about this . . ."

"Okay . . ."

"But I don't believe I am. I'm speaking as a medical doctor who's worked with a good number of young women recently, almost exclusively Latina, so I know the body type, and I know what their skin tone usually looks like, and —"

"Kip . . . *what?*"

"I think your Little Sister has a bun in the oven."

I spent the rest of the weekend fretting. Could Deedee really be pregnant? She was only fourteen! Of course, Kip could be wrong — but what if he was right? I should say something to Rose Morales. There was probably Big Sister–Little Sister protocol I should be following. Not that a situation such as this would be in the handbook. Not

176

that there was a handbook.

But if I talked to Rose and I was wrong, Deedee would never trust me again.

The devil perched on my shoulder told me to pretend Kip had never called. *Que será, será* and all that. The angel perched on the other shoulder, however — who looked suspiciously like a thin, baby-faced gay man with a goatee and glasses — said I had to do something . . . fast. The things he'd noticed — the protruding belly and the discoloring of the skin — were signs she was getting pretty far along. If that was the case, every day mattered if she wanted to um . . . er . . .

"Wanted to what?" I had asked Kip earlier on the phone.

"*Not* have the baby," he'd replied.

"Oh."

"All I'm saying is that — if that's what she decides — the sooner the better. The worst thing would be if she missed the time when a doctor would be willing to do it. You don't want to know what these girls resort to when they get desperate."

He was right about that.

I didn't want to know.

By the time I met Martucci on Monday for our six-thirty a.m. run, I was no clearer on what to do than I'd been every hour on the hour that I'd woken up the night before.

Yes, it was a crazy time.

Deedee might be pregnant. I was organizing the biggest promotional event of my career. My libido waged its own campaign for me to get in touch with a certain traffic reporter who should hate me but seemed to be indicating otherwise. I had ten items out of twenty left to do on a list that I felt honor-bound to complete in a matter of months.

And I was training for a 5K run three times a week — every Monday, Wednesday, and Friday — with, of all people, Dominic Martucci.

Was it any wonder I was having trouble sleeping?

Originally, I'd hoped I wouldn't need to do anything as drastic as train in order to cross off #5: *Run a 5K.* There was a race coming up in May in Manhattan Beach that I planned to sign up for. I'd recently hopped on the treadmill at the gym, assuming it would be a breeze. After one minute of running — not one mile, one *minute* — I felt as if I were breathing in bricks instead of air. I was gasping and panting and was so exhausted that I nearly let myself get spewed off the end of the treadmill like a doughnut off the assembly line. I clearly wasn't going to make it without putting in effort. Knowing nothing about how to prepare for a run, I asked around the office to see if anyone had any tips. To my dismay, the name Martucci kept coming up. As much as I hated to go crawling to him for advice, I asked him anyway. All he said was, "Sure."

"So are there ways I should go about training . . . or certain shoes that might help?"

"Sure," he repeated. "I'll train you. But I demand one hundred percent commitment. Three days a week. Show up on time and be ready to work. And" — he yanked a box of Hot Tamales candies from my hands — "I suggest you cut down on the crap."

"I don't need you to —"

"How's the running going so far?" he asked, giving me a disparaging once-over.

Not so well. I narrowed my eyes at him suspiciously. "Why would you help me?"

"Let's say it's nice you're doing that list for the girl you ran over."

"You know about the list?"

"Everybody knows about the list."

"Hmph. So much for Brie keeping a secret," I grumbled.

He gave me a friendly swat on the shoulder. "Sorry I missed the day you went bra-less."

So there I was — as I had been the week before — at an outdoor track, doing warm-up exercises. Martucci used the interval training method. I'd walk briskly for five minutes, then run a minute, walk five minutes, run a minute, and so on, until I collapsed in a heap on the dirt, at which point he'd pick me up and make me do it again.

I finished the first set of intervals, and Martucci walked next to me as I wheezed and puffed. He wore snug jogging shorts and a racing-style tank shirt that showed off his wiry muscles. "Hot date last night, Parker? You're more out of it than usual."

"I've got a lot of my mind. A girl I know might be pregnant."

What was I doing confiding in Martucci? Susan had been out of town for the weekend, so I must have been desperate to talk to someone. Either that or I was losing brain cells with every lap.

He blew out a breath. "Tough break. But running is one of the best things you can do. When you get to the third trimester, you'll need to switch to walking. But it's important to stay in shape so you can push when the time —"

"It's not *me*," I snapped. "It really is a girl I know. I met her as part of the Big Sister program a few months ago. Poor kid's only fourteen. What's she going to do . . . I mean, if she *is* pregnant? My friend who's a doctor suspects she might not even know herself — she may be in denial of any symptoms. I can't decide: Should I tell her mom? Or the Big Sister coordinator?"

"Do you like this kid?"

"Yes," I said, surprising myself with the sureness of my answer. "Quite a bit."

"Then get one of those home pregnancy kits. Make sure she's really up the duff before you go telling everybody. If I was this kid, I'd want the chance to tell them myself."

"I hate to say this, but you're right."

"Buy the kind in the blue box — the one with the picture of a rabbit on it. It says pregnant or not pregnant in words instead of having to figure out dots or lines. Makes it less stressful."

"How is it you're such an expert on home pregnancy kits?"

"You're asking that question of an Italian stallion like myself? The women call me 'sperm of thunder.' I don't dare stand too close for fear I may impregnate them with just a whiff of my manhood."

181

■ ■ ■ ■

The next evening, I called Deedee to say I was in the neighborhood and would her mom let her go grab a quick slice of pizza? When I picked her up, no sooner had she shut the car door than I said, "There are two choices for where we can go for pizza. There's Mario's on Culver. Or there's my place, where I have one in the freezer that we can microwave. The advantage of going to my apartment" — I paused — "is that I have a home pregnancy kit there, too. In case you need one for any reason."

She stared at me, saying nothing.

I continued, "Kip had a hunch you might be pregnant."

Still nothing.

"Might you be pregnant?"

She sat back in her seat, closed her eyes, and gave a wet sigh. "I don't know."

Sounded like microwaved pizza to me.

At my apartment, I read the instructions for the pregnancy kit as neutrally as if I were reading off the side of the pizza box instead. "You need help?" I asked as she headed to the bathroom.

"I can pee by myself."

"Sorry. Thought you might want moral

support."

She added apologetically, "You can come in after."

Four minutes later, the microwave dinged. The pizza sat untouched, however, because the stick was ready.

Deedee's hands were in prayer over her face, so I flipped the stick to the side that would show the results.

Pregnant.

Martucci was wrong. I'd have much preferred pink dots over that word staring straight at us.

Deedee closed her eyes and whispered, "I am so fucked."

I grabbed her close in a hug. "Everything's going to work out fine," I assured her. Her body sank against mine. I had to marvel. Just moments ago, I'd been staring at proof that she was surely a woman, yet she'd never before seemed so much like a little girl.

CHAPTER 11

If Maria Garcia Alvarez wondered why a doctor was telling her that her fourteen-year-old daughter was pregnant instead of hearing it from the girl herself, she didn't show it. She seemed as glad to yell at him as at anyone. Kip's face remained placid as they faced each other on the couch, their knees touching, while Maria released a torrent in Spanish. Deedee also sat on the couch, sunk deep in the pillows behind her mother, arms crossed.

Of course, all I could do was watch from where I sat in the armchair. I had no idea what was being said. Kip had taught me the Spanish word for pregnant, *embarazada* (awfully close to "embarrassment," which I found interesting), but the words were coming so fast and furious, I couldn't catch even that.

I had promised Deedee that I'd stand by her whatever decision she wanted to make.

We'd talked for an hour before I drove her home. She'd suspected she was pregnant, she'd told me. Just didn't want to face it. Some simple math — she'd had sex only once with Carlos after the holiday dance she'd been allowed to attend — put her at three and a half months pregnant and due early August. Although what she wanted to do was have the baby and put it up for adoption, she said, she doubted that's what would happen. I was incredulous: It was more than obvious to me that that was the best plan. The girl was fourteen! She was an honors student who wanted to go to college! When I'd told her so, she'd said, her voice flat, "You don't get it. We don't give up our babies. It just doesn't happen."

So Kip was brought in to help break the news and, possibly, smooth the waters for the idea of adoption. "Maybe your mom will be open to it," I'd told Deedee. "Since she wants you to go to college, too." One look at Maria talking to Kip — gesturing wildly with her hands as she continued her rant — made it clear things were going far from smoothly. No wonder Deedee jumped at my offer to help her tell her mom. The woman was terrifying. If my mom acted like that upon finding out I was pregnant, I'd curl into a ball and cry.

I didn't understand a word of what was being said, but I could make a pretty good guess. I had a boyfriend once who watched soap operas on Telemundo — or, more accurately, watched the busty, sexy, scantily clad actresses on the soap operas on Telemundo. He'd supply the dialogue in English over what they were saying in Spanish. Only he'd say things like "My breasts are so very large, they barely fit in this halter top" and "Here is the weapon used to murder Pedro — and while I hand it to you, I will rub my other hand slowly over my body and lick my lips provocatively."

The show unraveling before me was no less dramatic, although lacking in sex appeal. Maria's lines were too numerous to dub, but they clearly centered on insisting that Deedee got herself into this predicament and now it was time to pay the price.

"But Mami!" Deedee cried, although she only whimpered her lines — and let me tell you, she wasn't going to have much of a career in the Spanish soaps if she didn't kick it up a notch. I had to guess the rest of her lines since they were delivered in Spanish, but based on my earlier conversation with her, it would be along the lines of "It was one mistake! I shouldn't have to pay for it forever! The baby shouldn't have to suffer!

186

What kind of mother could I be at fourteen years old? I want to finish high school and go to college and be a writer or a doctor and maybe one day a mom — but someday, not now!"

Maria would then shoot her a stormy look. "You should have thought of that before you slept with the dashing Carlos! Do you think I want to be raising another child at this point? I have a job I love! I am the finest blind cook in all of Los Angeles! And now I'll be responsible for a grand-child!"

"It doesn't have to be that way!" Deedee would plead. "We can find the baby a good home, where she'll be loved and cared for! Isn't that part of being a parent? Making the hard choices?"

"We are a proud people, Deedee, and don't you forget that! Family is everything to us! We cannot turn our backs on family even if it means throwing our own hopes and dreams forever out the window!"

"Oh, Mami! Please, I only want —"

"Ladies, ladies!" Kip would interject, his voice deep and soulful. "Stop fighting. Isn't there enough strife in the world?"

On the drive home, I learned from Kip that even with the language barrier, I wasn't that far off the mark — much to my disappointment.

"Don't be hard on Deedee for not sticking up for herself more," he said. "For her, the idea of giving away her baby probably carries more shame than getting pregnant in the first place. What you and I might call the right choice she sees as selfish — even if she wants it, too. It's just how it is."

"That's so frustrating."

"Anyway, Maria's not ruling out adoption entirely . . . if the parents were relatives or people in the neighborhood that they knew. She agreed to talk to that woman at the Big Sister program to see if she could help her explore options. The burden of raising the child is going to fall largely to her, and she's not excited about it. She'd love to find a loophole. Some way to give the baby a better life without giving away her grandchild."

"But it's Deedee's life. It should be her decision."

"Technically it is," Kip said. "But would you ever want to go up against Maria Garcia Alvarez?"

I shuddered. "Not without boxing gloves and body armor."

"The worst part," I said to my mom, tugging on what I hoped was a weed, "is that she *wants* to do the sensible thing."

188

"Poor girl. I'm sure she's under so much pressure. Is she going to stay in school?"

"She doesn't know what she's going to do. I suspect she's still in shock."

I'd stopped at my parents on Sunday to help my mom with the gardening. They had a big party coming up — also the reason my dad needed that frozen shrimp. When I first arrived, I'd handed him my offering of five bags. He'd accepted them gratefully and then retreated to the living room to fall asleep in front of a golf tournament on TV.

My mom clipped the leaves off the rosebushes as she asked, "Have you ever been pregnant?" She said it so nonchalantly, it took me a second to grasp what she'd said.

"Um . . . don't you think you might have noticed?"

"I'm not so naive. You could have gotten an abortion."

"Oh. Well, no," I answered. "I've never been pregnant."

She nodded. "Just curious."

Now wasn't that a touching mother-daughter moment! I was glad she wasn't curious whether I'd ever *thought* I was pregnant, because then I would have had to say, "Sure, plenty of times."

Not that I made a habit of having unprotected sex or anything. But even with being single 150 percent more often than with a boyfriend, there were still times when the condom broke. Or I forgot the diaphragm on a camping weekend and decided millions of Catholics couldn't be wrong about that rhythm method. Or my period was late for no reason at all, but it was late. The last time I peed on a stick, "yes" or "no" on the strip was the latest in technology. And it had been "no," as always. Yet leading up to the moment when I knew for sure, I had the opportunity to wonder. *What if?* Sure, I've always hoped to go about things in the traditional order, and mostly I felt relief. But there was a small part of me that would have been happy. Things would be uncertain: Would we get married? Would I be a single mom? But either way I'd have a baby . . . somebody to whom I was the most special person in the world. And all I'd had to do to put my life on an entirely new trajectory was lie back, spread my legs, and let it happen.

"Life is ironic, isn't it?" my mom said, handing me a pile of leaves to stuff in a sack. "Your brother and Charlotte have been trying for years to have a baby and can't. This girl has sex once, and poof! She's going to be a mother."

I stopped with my leaf stuffing. That was

it! "I can't believe this didn't occur to me before!" I exclaimed. "*They* can adopt Deedee's baby! Oh, it's perfect. They're not strangers, which I know is impor—"

"Hate to burst your bubble," my mom broke in. "But they're not interested. Believe me, I've talked to them plenty about it. They want to have their own. In fact, Charlotte's doing those hormone shots right now."

"Darn," I said, deflated.

"They're awful, too, those shots. They make you moody and put on weight. She's certainly going about it the hard way."

"Especially that part where she has to have sex with Bob," I said, and gave an exaggerated shudder. And isn't that just like my brother? I thought. Putting his wife through so much misery so he could pass on his lineage.

"Sometimes," my mom said, setting down her clippers and using the back of a gloved hand to wipe her hair off her forehead, "I have to wonder what God's up to."

Wednesday late afternoon I was making a few last ditch calls to drum up interest in the gas giveaway scheduled for the next day. Phyllis called me from Bigwood's office. "What would it mean to you if I said I could guarantee TV coverage for you tomorrow?"

she asked in her fifty-pack-a-day voice.

"I'm not sure I follow," I said. "You have media contacts?"

(*And if so,* I thought bitterly, *could you not have coughed them up during the afternoon staff meeting?* I'd tried my best to beef up the "maybes" I'd gotten from various news crews, but Lizbeth had simply given a tinkly laugh and said, "When they say maybe, it means no. I suppose I'll stop by anyway, just in case.")

Phyllis cleared her throat. "I can make things happen." Suddenly I understood how Woodward and Bernstein must have felt.

I tried not to get too excited, but TV cameras would be quite the coup. It would show Bigwood that I could pull together a successful promotion. And even though it was certain Lizbeth would hog any opportunity to be in front of the camera, I could at least wander by in the background to fulfill #9 on my list: *Get on TV.*

"That would be great," I said, wondering why Phyllis was being so mysterious about the whole thing. "What do you need from me?"

"A favor. You're a writer, and I'm not much with words. I need help with a letter."

"Sure. I'll come up there right now and
—"

"Not here."

Ah. *That* kind of letter. Somebody was searching for a new job. "How soon do you need it?"

"I was hoping you could stop by my house after work tonight. I'm in Culver City — shouldn't be too far out of your way."

"Deal."

"You help me out," she added before hanging up, "and I'll get you all the TV coverage you can stand."

I reached Phyllis's house a few minutes before six o'clock and parked on the street. Her car was already there — pulled into her driveway behind a Harley so massive that it more resembled a motor home than a motorcycle. Maybe those Hell's Angels rumors were true. I stopped to read the stickers on it to see if it'd give me any hints, but they were mostly for seemingly ordinary riding clubs. No skulls and crossbones.

Phyllis came up behind me. "Anything on that list of yours about riding a motorcycle?" she asked.

I turned to give her a wave of greeting and then said, "You know about the list?"

"Everybody knows about the list."

I sighed. "That's not on it."

"You ride?" I shook my head, and she

193

said, *"Never?"* as if I'd admitted I was the world's oldest living virgin. "Wait here." She disappeared into the garage and came back a minute later with two helmets and a leather jacket, which she tossed to me. "So you don't get road rash if we wipe out."

Road rash? Oh no — I agreed to *write*, not *ride*. "Thanks, but we need to get to the letter. I'm in a bit of a hurry."

"Hogwash," she said. "But if you're that worried about time, we'll talk while we ride."

Partly because of my newfound spirit of adventure, but more because I was afraid of Phyllis, I obediently straddled the seat behind her. It was like sitting in a La-Z-Boy; it even had a back bar and cushy armrests. The seat beneath me rumbled, and as Phyllis pulled out of her drive, I thought this was how it would feel to ride a speeding rhino, both thrilling and terrifying. When Phyllis yelled, "How is it?" that's what I told her.

"Most people say it's like an orgasm, but whatever floats your boat."

"So what's the deal?" I hollered over the growl of the engine when we stopped at a red light. "You looking for a new job?"

"It's not about work. I want to write a letter to my daughter."

"Your daughter?"

The light changed, and she roared forward again. We cruised past the movie studios located there and through old residential neighborhoods that were quaint by L.A. standards — brick-and-adobe houses and leafy trees. Over the course of the ride, Phyllis gave me the full story, letting the intimate details of her life scatter along the streets of the city like candy tossed at a parade. The story wasn't anything I hadn't seen a dozen times on the Lifetime Channel: Mom and live-in biker boyfriend have baby. They name baby Sunshine. If that alone isn't enough to piss her off for life, they proceed to drink too much and do far too many drugs and leave her with friends and relatives and foster care from the time she could barely toddle. Eventually Mom goes into rehab, and biker boyfriend goes God knows where, and the daughter, who by that time prefers to go by the name Sally, has put herself through college and has a nice job as an office manager and maybe a husband and kids, but we're not sure, wants to establish a relationship as much as she wants her toenail ripped off at the root, even though Mom has been clean and sober for ten years.

We pulled back into Phyllis's driveway.

Life is funny, I thought as I hoisted my leg high and over the seat. People are living too much or too little, and I wondered if anyone out there is living the right amount.

"You're a good rider," she said.

"All it takes is sitting — I'm good at that."

"Not true. You've got to lean when I lean. There's trust. And anticipation. You'd be surprised how many people flip out when the bike takes a turn and they throw their body weight the other way."

Changing the subject to the reason I'd come over, I asked, "So what do you want to tell Sally in this letter?"

Phyllis pulled off her helmet, and what she said next, she said quietly. "That I know I was a shitty mother."

"Okay."

"And that I'm sorry I hurt her."

"Well then," I said, going to grab a pad of paper and a pen from my car, "let's say it."

CHAPTER 12

The alarm woke me at five o'clock, and as painful as it was, even that was going to be pushing it. I had to be at the gas station in Burbank in an hour. I needed to leap out of bed and jump straight in the shower. Unless I left the conditioner on for only one minute — that'd buy me two more blissful minutes of slumber. . . .

I was out the door a little before six, which was later than I'd hoped. Especially since I still needed to stop at the twenty-four-hour Vons for helium balloons, and — oh, the irony! — I needed gas.

The morning sky was brightening by the time I hit the freeway for Burbank, my Toyota so packed with balloons that if my life were a cartoon, the car would be floating away with me in it.

I scanned radio stations, excited about the day ahead. Martucci and Phyllis were handling the giveaway at the gas station near the airport. Martucci had plenty of experience running promotions, so they'd be fine on their own. I'd join Brie and Greg (who, even though he was the designer and didn't have a clue what he was doing, was the only other staff member I could get) at the Burbank station. If Phyllis hadn't been blowing hot air about her TV media connections, I'd schmooze reporters while Lizbeth took interviews.

The idea was that we'd lie in wait until a car with more than one person pulled up to the pumps. Then — wearing our festive T-shirts and carrying balloons — we'd run up and say, "Thank you for carpooling . . . we're paying for your gas today!" They'd cheer wildly, the TV crews would capture the moment on camera, and it would be splayed over TV sets across Southern California.

Each team had a debit card with a thousand dollars on it, which should last most of the morning. I'd talked with Brie before I left home, and she and Greg were there and ready to go.

I tuned in to K-JAM. Troy had promised to make mention of the promotion several times throughout the morning. True to his word, I heard him report a few traffic snarls, then he added, "And if you're carpooling, today could be your lucky day. The good folks at Los Angeles Rideshare might pay for your gas. They're at secret locations throughout the city . . . so watch out!"

What a guy. I felt the free publicity go *cha-ching!* in my head.

When I picked up my cell phone to let Brie know I was almost there, I noticed I had several messages. Hmm. Must have had it on vibrate.

The first call was from Brie: "We have a problem here. Call me."

The second call was from Brie: "Shoot. We got a lot of people here. You need to call me."

The third call was from Brie: "I told you to hold *on* — June, where the hell are you?"

In fact, every message was from Brie, and her language grew progressively worse with each one. I was still picking up desperate messages from her when my phone vibrated in my hand. "Hello?"

"Where you at?" It was Brie. "I don't know what's going on here, but we got a mess. There's a million people lined up screaming for their free gas."

What was going on? "I got stuck on the 405," I lied, pitiful as it was to do so, "There must be some sort of —"

"Well, get your butt here as fast as you

can. I don't know what to do. It's crazy. Everybody's saying we owe 'em free gas. Traffic's blocked on Ventura Boulevard, and some guy told me it's backed up to the freeway." Away from the phone, she shouted, "Hey, I said hold *on*." Then she was back. "Greg is pumping gas as fast as he can. But people are getting ugly, and we're running out of money, so he's telling them they can have five bucks' worth each and that's it. Your man Armando is *pissed*."

"Any TV crews?" I asked meekly.

"Yeah!" she answered, suddenly excited. "Channel Two is setting up, and the Channel Four truck is trying to get here, but it's tough with all the people . . . Hold on. Lady, I don't pump nobody's gas. . . . *Yeah?* . . . Well, don't make me tell you what you can do with that pump."

"Hold down the fort," I urged. "I'll be right there."

I reached Burbank in minutes, and I parked a few blocks away to avoid the traffic backup. From there, balloons in hand — no telling why I grabbed them, probably clinging to the vestiges of the joyous day it was supposed to be — I started to run to the station at a pretty good clip, thanks to the training I'd been doing with Martucci.

Oh no. Martucci.

He picked up on the second ring. "How's it going?" I huffed, still running, balloons bouncing against one another above me.

"Fuckin' nuts," he said. "But it's handled. Phyllis made a sign that says 'No Free Gas.' We coned off the entrance, and we've got cops here directing traffic."

"Cops? There are cops?"

"They gave us a ticket. The fine's eight hundred bones, but at least the crowd's under control now."

"I don't understand why this is happening. . . ."

"Some guy told me they're broadcasting the locations — all the channels. They're telling people to grab a friend so they have a carpool and head on down to get in line for their free gas. I've got entire fucking families here. A guy drove over from El Monte — that's twenty miles for a damn tank of gas."

"They were supposed to keep it a secret!"

"It ain't a secret no more, babe."

As I neared the gas station, cars were lined up so deep that they were nearly stacked on top of one another, and each had more than one person in it. The honking was deafening. The gas station had two islands with four pumps per island — all were busy. News trucks for Channels 2 and 4 and Fox

News were parked at odd angles at the periphery of the property and were filming the mayhem. Armando furiously directed traffic in and out of the station.

"Hey, lady," a man yelled, leaning out of a pickup, "I been waiting for forty-five minutes. Can't they pump faster? I'm late for work!"

Brie sidled up to me. "We don't need balloons. Looks like everybody knows it's a party."

"This is a disaster," I moaned.

"Not yet, 'cause Lizbeth's not here. *Then* it'll be a disaster. But hey," she said, "plenty of TV coverage!" A TV camera pointed at irate customers while a reporter held a microphone to interview them.

"How much money do we have left?"

"Beats me. Greg took a bunch of candy bars and gum from the snack stand — he's handing them out and begging people to go away. I saw him crying at one point. Them artist types are pretty delicate."

I understood how he felt.

"Thanks for handling this, Brie. These people are insane. It's only free gas! You'd figure we were handing out diamonds!"

"Folks like to get something for nothing. And don't you worry. I've been doing Tae Bo, so nobody better mess with me. But you need to handle it fast. When Greg runs out of candy bars, we could have a riot on our hands."

"Tell you what," I said. "Go find something that you can use to make a sign. Write 'No Free Gas' in big letters and then stick it by that tree. And here —" I handed her the balloons. "Start giving these out to the kids."

"You got it."

I grabbed my cell phone from my pocket and called Susan, who was still at home getting ready for work. "You need to help me," I blurted when she answered. After explaining the situation, I told her to get on the horn — I actually used those words, "get on the horn," that's how crazed I was — and tell the TV stations to stop broadcasting the locations. The gas giveaway was over.

As was my career, probably, but first things first.

Then I marched over to where the news vans were parked. I was in charge here, and I needed to start acting like it. Crystal Davis, a reporter for Channel 5, stood patting her face with powder. She'd been with them for about a thousand years; her face was amazingly preserved, and I don't think that hair would move in a monsoon. I introduced myself, then quickly said, "You need to tell people to stop coming down."

"Are you the one in charge here?" she asked.

It wasn't easy to admit. "Yes."

"Good. We need an interview. Ready?"

"No . . . um . . . yes . . . um . . . Give me a second." Out of the corner of my eye, I spotted Lizbeth surveying the situation and appearing — grrr, not angry or panicked, which would have at least preserved my dignity — but utterly delighted. Her face said, *Gee, all this fun and it's not even my birthday!* I hated her with a white hot heat, but only for a second. Then I remembered that as the senior staffer here, it was her job to do the interview. The thought of her having to clean up my mess cheered me immeasurably.

"Be right back," I told Crystal, and trotted over to my boss. "Lizbeth!" I said breezily. "Channel Five wants to talk to you about —"

"Not a chance."

"But as the —"

"I wouldn't want to deprive you of your big moment. Lou Bigwood showed all that confidence in you — didn't even feel the need to check with me before assigning you the project. Too bad it seems to have gone awry."

If she wasn't going to take the heat for me, I sure wasn't going to put up with her insults. I spun on my heel and headed back to Crystal Davis. As I did, I passed Greg, who was working his way down a line of cars, pleading, "Free gas is over. Here's a Butterfinger. Please go away."

"I'm ready. Hit it," I said to Crystal.

She faced the camera and said, "We're here where a promotion from Los Angeles Rideshare to give away free gas has drawn hundreds of carpoolers eager to get a free tank of gas. With us we have June Parker. June . . . did you expect this sort of response?"

Every fiber in my being wanted to say, *No, you twit . . . and if I ever get my hands on the moron who leaked the station locations . . .*

Glancing over at Armando breaking up a fight between two motorists at the pumps, I said brightly, "We knew people were angry about high gas prices, but no, we had no idea how much."

"Are these people going to get their free gas?"

I answered with an even brighter smile. I'm sure I looked like one of those awful clowns they hire to terrorize children at birthday parties. "We're doing all we can . . . but the good news is that anyone who rideshares saves money on gas!"

Before the interview was over, I managed to squeeze in our 800 number, and I did my best to use my body to shield the view of Greg nearly sobbing against a pickup truck. Then I repeated the exercise with Channels 7 and 4, plus two radio news programs and the *Los Angeles Times* and *Press Enterprise.* As much as I attempted to put a positive spin on things, the fact that each one then went to talk to disgruntled carpoolers was a bad sign.

The police arrived at nine o'clock and shut down the station, slapping me with another fine.

Lizbeth had slithered away at some point. I attempted to make it up to Brie and Greg with promises of all the hotcakes and sausages they could possibly consume . . . my treat, of course.

Armando stepped away from his negotiating with the police long enough to make it clear to me he intended to sue for lost revenue. His crimson bloated face told me that there was no shirt in the world tight enough to placate him this time around.

Everybody knows that the food at Max's Grill is lousy and overpriced, which was the reason I chose to go there for lunch with

Susan. The less chance I had to bump into someone I knew, the better.

"I wish I knew what happened," I said, twirling overcooked spaghetti onto my fork. "I don't think it was Phyllis. She swears she only had time to call one of her contacts before all hell broke loose."

Susan sneered at her meal. "I don't know why you made me eat here. I tried to order the safest thing. Who can mess up a burger and fries?" She lifted the top bun. "Ugh. Is that mayonnaise *and* Thousand Island dressing?"

I continued, "Besides, it wouldn't make sense for her to sabotage the event. She was working at a gas station, too, so she'd be screwing herself. Whereas Lizbeth had nothing to lose and every reason to hope I'd fail. I'll bet she did it."

Susan held her plate toward me. "Take a look at this. I can't tell if that's the pickle or the meat. What do you think?"

"I made every one of those press calls myself. There's no reason it should have gotten so out of hand."

"I mean, it's green like a pickle, but it's awfully big."

"For crying out loud," I snapped, "can we focus here? My job hangs in the balance and you're worried about a pickle."

"Sorry."

"And I believe that's meat."

"Oh, yech, I was afraid so."

I'd spent most of the morning after returning from my apology breakfast with Greg and Brie calling news desks, hoping I'd get a clue as to what went wrong. How did we go from "Maybe we'll send a camera to film you" to "Hey, carpoolers, head on down for your free gas!" And for a bunch of people who ask questions for a living, reporters sure are evasive when the shoe's on the other foot. The best I managed was a guy at Fox News who thought he remembered seeing a fax at one point — but he didn't have it anymore, and he couldn't say who made the decision to air the locations. But hey, there's no such thing as bad publicity, eh?

"At least you handled the interviews well," Susan said.

"Yeah?"

"Definitely. I flipped through the channels, and it was impressive how you managed to put things in a positive light — even if they did make it seem like complete bullshit. I mean, Crystal Davis shows you saying, 'We're excited to see so many people carpooling,' and then she switches to some lady in an SUV about to burst a kidney because she's mad she has to wait for her free gas. As if she couldn't afford to pay for it herself."

I sighed, and as I watched Susan take a cautious bite of burger, I finally asked the question I didn't want to ask. "How bad do you think it is?"

Susan chewed, and I wasn't sure if her grimace was due to the food or my question. Being management, she has the inside scoop, and — even though we've always had a "don't ask, don't tell" policy between us when it comes to work — I can trust her to be honest with me.

"First off, a little perspective: No one died," she said finally. "You're lucky that Bigwood wasn't around — I hear he's at a conference in Fresno. So he's going to find out about it after the fact. It would have been worse if he'd seen it as it was happening. Now what's done is done, and it's a matter of cleaning up the mess. Also, for some reason Phyllis seems to like you." And here she looked genuinely perplexed by that. "I overheard her talking to that new receptionist about what a great job you did. Anyway, Bigwood usually listens to her."

"He does what his secretary tells him to?"

"For as long as I've known him. She must know where the bodies are buried. So that may help you. On the other hand, all those angry commuters — it didn't bode well for the company. And this gas station manager threatening a lawsuit is a problem. I'm sure they can ward him off, but it could get pricey. What I worry about" — she paused to wipe her hands on a napkin — "is that if it starts to get expensive, they'll panic. Then they'll want a scapegoat."

"Baa-aaah," I said.

"I'm not saying they'll come down on you — and you know I'll do what I can to defend you if they do."

"I appreciate that."

"Still, not a bad idea to update your résumé."

CHAPTER 13

When I got to work on Monday, Dr. Death was waiting for me at my cubicle entrance. I shouldn't have been surprised. Martucci had warned me on our morning run that his friend Armando wasn't backing down. He was claiming he'd lost ten thousand dollars and that his gas station's reputation had been irreparably besmirched. "I didn't know he knew words that big," I'd grumbled, to which Martucci had replied, "He's full of shit — if anything, the guy stands to make money. All that publicity. But he'll still try to squeeze what he can out of us." Apparently, he'd been particularly offended that we'd wiped out his snack stand. So I'd spent most of the weekend fretting, although my fingernail biting wasn't limited to the demise of my career. Deedee and I mowed our way through an ice cream the size of an army tank at Coldstones while discussing her options and, to my frustration, getting nowhere. She seemed resigned to giving up her future. By the time Monday rolled around, seeing Dr. Death first thing in the morning was par for the course.

He attempted a smile as I eased past him and asked him in. "I hear you had quite the brouhaha," he said with a chuckle. When I looked at him uneasily in response, he cleared his throat and sat in my guest chair.

Too bad for you, I thought. *If you're going to be the man who fires people, you don't get to make jokes.* Dr. Death was in his late forties with a medium build, round, soulful eyes, and pancake ears. The overall effect was oddly gentle given his reputation; I hadn't been this close to him since the directors' meeting.

Every muscle in my body held its breath. I'd never been fired from a job before, but I'd seen and done enough in my tenure here that I knew it could be brutal. The higher-ups were almost always escorted out immediately — I assume so they couldn't steal files or make disparaging phone calls. I hoped at least I'd be granted a few weeks to get my résumé out there and, more important, continue drawing a paycheck. At my level, what harm could I do? Write a bad brochure? Dangle a participle?

"You're aware we've received a letter from

a lawyer representing a Mr. Armando Bomaritto."

"I heard a rumor to that effect."

"Care to tell me what happened last Thursday?"

Hmm. So he intended to draw blood slowly from the victim. I updated him on everything — from how I'd planned the events, to the phone calls I'd made to reporters, to the events of the day itself. "It doesn't make sense," I admitted. "I made sure everyone I talked to knew not to broadcast the locations."

"No one spoke to reporters but you?"

"Just me."

"Did anyone else have access to the list of reporters?"

"Lizbeth . . . she had me turn over a list of who I called at the end of every day." A thrill shot through me as soon as the words left my mouth. I've watched plenty of detective shows in my day, and you don't have to be Perry Mason to figure out that what I said sounded incriminating. My mind whirled, trying to figure out a way to beef up Lizbeth's role. Oh, to look at Dr. Death, doe-eyed and demure, and say, "I'm sure Lizbeth wouldn't sabotage me, even though she was bitter and envious because Bigwood gave me the assignment, which, gosh, now that I say it out loud, sure sounds like quite the motive. But Dr. Death . . . may I call you Ivan? . . . do you really think she'd do such a thing? Do you *really* believe she'd call my reporter list and tell them to broadcast the secret locations?" Tempting as it was, I simply said, "She's my supervisor."

I was going to be classy and leave it at that, but he pushed. "Can you think of any reason your supervisor might follow up on your calls?"

There was no way to whine, "She'd do anything to screw me," without sounding as if I were the sort of person who'd say such a thing. "She wasn't happy with how things were going, if that's what you mean."

His face told me he meant nothing. Dr. Death was a blank slate. "Was there a contract with Mr. Bomaritto?"

"He and I had a verbal agreement. He'd let us use the site. I'd get him publicity." I left out the part about my promising to wear the red shirt.

"Hmm," he said.

"Is that bad?"

"Is what bad?"

"Not having a contract."

"I'm merely collecting information at this point, and this has been helpful." Dr. Death stood to leave. Relief rolled off me in waves.

He hadn't yet pointed at me à la Donald Trump and barked, "You're fired."

"What happens now?" I asked.

"We're preparing a response to Mr. Bomaritto, and Phyllis is at Costco buying snacks to replenish the gas station's supply."

"Phyllis had to go —"

"We needed coffee," he said, waving me off.

"Plus they have those good sticky buns," I added, which I knew was stupid, but I was nervous. Exactly how close, I wanted to know, was the guillotine blade to my neck?

Although I couldn't bring myself to ask the question, he must have seen it oozing from my pores. He said, not unkindly, "We intend to keep this out of the courts. I don't know yet what that will require. You'll hear from me."

After he left, I checked my messages. There was one from Phyllis letting me know that she was headed to Costco and did I need anything?

Yes, I thought, a giant tray of sticky buns, a fork, and everybody the hell out of my way.

The other message was from Troy Jones. "June," he said, and the rest wasn't easy to make out since he kept erupting into laughter. "I gave your gas giveaway a plug, but I see you didn't need the extra help . . . hahahahaha . . . got the locations from dispatch and I flew overhead and . . . hahahahaha . . . it looked like you were starting a junkyard off the 101 freeway . . . hahahahaha . . . guess I was the only one who kept your location a secret . . . hahahahaha . . ."

Good thing he was enjoying himself, because I sure failed to see the humor.

Troy Jones and I played phone tag all week. It's not easy to get hold of a guy who works in the middle of the sky in the morning and doesn't return calls all afternoon. And I forgave him for mocking me in his phone message because — as it would happen — I needed a favor. A big one. Troy Jones was now officially part of my plan to be the best gosh-darned employee L.A. Rideshare had ever seen. He was, in fact, my entire plan.

After daily messages back and forth, Troy finally reached me Thursday night at home. It was almost nine o'clock when my phone rang.

"Isn't it past your bedtime?" I asked him. After all, I was about to crawl into bed, and I'm not the one who got up at three a.m.

"I catch up on my sleep in the afternoon."

Mmm. I pictured him stretched out on

his couch. Then I pictured him stretched out on his couch with his shirt off. Even better. I was about to insert myself into the scenario — deciding the on/off status of my own clothing — but I swatted down my hormones.

"Anyway," I proceeded, all business, "you mentioned before that you'd be willing to take me along on a traffic report."

"Any time. You name it."

"Well, yes, thanks. But I'm wondering if I can ask a huge favor. You know how the gas giveaway kind of got out of hand —"

"There's an understatement," he interjected. "They're still talking about it at work. A buddy of mine, Ryan, drove down . . . brought his daughter with him so he'd be a carpool. He said it took him three hours to get out of the traffic mess, and nobody was getting any gas. I heard there were fistfights."

"Only the one!" I protested. "The gas station manager broke it up. And speaking of the manager, he's suing."

"You're kidding, for what?"

"Loss of income, pain and suffering. The usual. Since I was more or less in charge, I might get fired. So if you could take my boss up on the ride-along as well, she might cut me slack. Especially if she'd have a chance to give a pitch for ridesharing on air. I don't know if you can do that, or —"

"You might get fired over this?"

"Quite possibly."

"I had no idea." He groaned, "I left you a message *laughing*."

"Don't worry about it."

"You must think I'm such an ass."

For a minute there, yes. "Nah."

"Well, the ride-along's no problem. There's plenty of room for two. I can't guarantee you'll get on air, though. I'll have to run it by the producer. Depends on how bad traffic is, whether or not there'll be time. I'm usually more open on Fridays, so if that works for you . . ."

"Sure, Friday's perfect."

We set up a ride-along for the following week. The helicopter he piloted was based at the Van Nuys Airport, a few miles from my parents' house. "I go up at five," he said, "so if the two of you can be there at four-thirty, we'll have time to get you situated."

"Four-thirty? As in the morning?" I gulped. "Hoo boy. Mind if I wear my jammies?"

"Wear whatever you want. It's radio." He paused and then said, "What kind of pajamas?"

My mind flashed to my favorite pajamas.

Flannel shorts and a T-shirt with little Snoopys on it. Sexy lady! "I'll surprise you," I said.

"Sounds promising."

He gave me directions to his hangar in the airport, and when I thanked him again, he said, "Looking forward to it. By the way, you have any problem with heights?"

"Nope."

"Speed?"

"Fine with it."

"Flips, turns, nosedives, midair stunts?"

"How 'bout you drop me off before you get to that part? But don't rule it out entirely. I'm sure my boss would *love* it."

The next morning, I marched boldly into the office — head held high for the first time since the fiasco. As soon as I could tell Lizbeth about how Troy Jones would be working with us, she'd sing a different tune about me. She'd throw her body in front of Dr. Death to preserve my job. Granted, it was only the one ride-along, but there was no need to get into picky details.

Lizbeth was in a closed-door meeting all morning. I was editing my newsletter when I noticed Dr. Death hovering near my cubicle. My heart froze. No . . . not before I had a chance to spring my surprise on Lizbeth . . . he couldn't. That was the problem with these cubicles. No place to hide. If only I could . . . Oh, wait . . . he passed me by. I exhaled a breath. Close call.

When I felt the chill from the air recede, I peeked around the corner. I saw him stop to talk to Brie and then go into Lizbeth's office.

I escaped to the deli downstairs to get doughnuts and Diet Coke. There was no way I was going to risk an encounter with Dr. Death before I had a chance to talk to Lizbeth. By the time I checked back to see if he'd left and if she was available, it was almost noon. Brie sat at her station, thumbing through an *Ebony* magazine.

"Can I see Lizbeth now?"

"She's gone."

"Damn! I was hoping to catch her so I could —"

She lifted her head. "You didn't hear? She's *gone.* Dr. Death fired her an hour ago. Escorted her out the door. He gave her enough time to pack up a couple boxes, and that was it."

"Lizbeth was *fired? Lizbeth* was fired?"

"Tossed out on her skinny behind."

"Why?"

"Beats me. Nobody knows. She didn't see it coming, I'll tell you that. I know she's white, but I never seen anybody that white. She looked like a ghost seeing a ghost."

"That's unbelievable."

Lizbeth . . . fired! I couldn't get my mind around it. *Ding-dong, the witch is dead.* I should have been elated, should have been dancing with the Munchkins in the streets. But I stood there, numb with confusion. How could Lizbeth possibly have gotten fired? "It's so strange," I muttered.

"Yeah, and you want to know the saddest part? She took her TV. Now how am I going to watch *The Guiding Light?* Shoot — and Buzz was about to find out whether Olivia's been cheating on him with his evil twin."

Rumors flew the rest of the day. They ranged from Lizbeth getting fired for sabotaging my gas giveaway (my personal favorite and one I did nothing to squelch) to a lovers' quarrel between her and Bigwood.

Finally, I couldn't stand it any longer and went to find Phyllis. She was close to Bigwood. Maybe she'd know. Mostly likely she knew. The question was: Would she tell?

"Hey, Phyllis," I said, peering into her space. It was a windowless room that sat off of Bigwood's office. Papers were stacked against every wall and littered her desk. She had a door, though — the only secretary to have one, underscoring her clout. "Got a minute?"

"Sure. What's up?"

I pointed toward where her office led into Bigwood's and mouthed, "Is he in there?"

She shook her head. I shut the door behind me and helped myself to a mini Snickers from a dish on her desk, then took a seat.

"First off, I'm not in here to gossip," I said. "I am hoping to get information."

"About . . . ?"

"Why Lizbeth was fired."

"Last I heard, she was embezzling. Or was it that she was discovered trying to use one of those blowup dolls to ride in the carpool lane?"

"I'm serious," although I'd heard that last one myself from Brie minutes earlier. "You may think that this is none of my business, but I am involved. I was in charge of a gas giveaway that went badly. The next thing I know, my boss is being escorted out."

Phyllis tipped back in her chair, her hands forming a steeple in front of her face. "So are you here to take the blame or the credit?"

"It's not like that. I'm not going to fake any love for Lizbeth. She was the worst boss I've ever had. I'm thrilled that she's gone.

But Dr. Death . . . um, I mean Ivan . . . did a lot of poking into what happened. If Lizbeth messed up my project, I deserve to be told."

"What makes you think I'd know?"

"You know everything."

"Point taken." After regarding me a moment longer, she said, "You're not hearing this from me. I'm telling you because I owe you one. Lizbeth was squeaky clean, and so, for the record, were you. As best we can determine, a guy at Fox News took it upon himself to stir things up. The other TV stations followed suit."

"If that's the case, why don't we say something? We look like fools, and it wasn't even our fault!"

"Lou's chummy with people high up at Fox. They all belong to the same country club. Anyway, the gas station owner wanted blood. We gave him blood. Lizbeth's. It was the easiest way to stay out of court."

"That's so awful. It wasn't even her fault."

"You'd rather you got canned?"

"Of course not." I took another Snickers, a question forming. "But why *wasn't* it me? I was in charge of the project. Plus, I'm the one the gas station manager was so angry with."

"That I don't have the answer to. I suspect

it may be that Lou sees potential in you . . . thought you might deserve another shot. And you know, with Lizbeth gone that means there's a vacant position now."

Or in other words, just because I was in the house that landed on Lizbeth didn't mean I couldn't yank off her ruby slippers.

"When are they going to post the position?" I asked.

"Didn't you learn anything from the last time you got passed over for the job? That's not what Lou's about. He doesn't put people in management unless he sees that spark in them. Then rules and protocol be damned. They're hired on the spot."

"Spark? Come on, Phyllis, who are you kidding? He hires eye candy."

"Is your friend Susan only eye candy? Am I? If you want the job, prove yourself. The braless stunt you pulled was brilliant." I felt myself go hot with embarrassment as she continued, oblivious that it hadn't been an intentional career move. "That's enough to get noticed, but it won't close the deal. You've got to deliver the goods."

"Deliver the goods! I am not sleeping with Lou Bigwood!"

She tipped her chair forward so that she landed with a thud and gave me a hard stare. In that moment, I could picture her around the pool hall with the other Hell's Angels, talking trash and chugging cigarettes. I wondered if that was why Bigwood kept her around — because he was afraid of her. "Do I strike you as a pimp? I thought you were bright, but you're not getting it. *Do* something. Make it big so it wows the pants off him. And do it soon before he finds a honey who's willing to wow him first."

CHAPTER 14

My dad was sitting on the front porch drinking a glass of wine and listening to Roy Orbison on a boom box when Deedee and I walked up carrying our overnight bags.

"Lawn's looking good, Dad," I said, and then I introduced him to Deedee.

He shook her hand hello. "We're barbecuing steak for dinner — you like steak?"

"Sure. Love it."

"I was afraid you might be one of those vegetarians." Then he turned to me, apparently out of small talk. "Your mother's inside."

It was Thursday evening, and the ride-along with Troy was the next morning. I was spending the night at my parents' house since they lived only a few miles from the Van Nuys Airport. If I had to report in at four-thirty a.m., I was cutting the drive as short as I could. I'd invited Deedee to join me — it wasn't as if Lizbeth needed the seat anymore, and I thought the girl could use a special treat. Even if I had a chance to talk on air, I knew it wouldn't be enough to wow Bigwood. But it might, I hoped, get his attention — not to mention cross two items off my list while I was at it.

"Honey, I'm home!" I shouted as Deedee and I made our way into the kitchen. My mom stood at the counter, chopping vegetables for a salad. Something spicy was cooking, and it smelled divine.

"Jeez, you look so much like your mom," Deedee said quietly, and I guess on first glance we did — same wild hair, only she wore hers short. And Doris is where I inherited all those curves. I got her chin, too, which is slightly pointed, but thank the Lord I didn't get the Delaney nose, which suits my mom but if you ask me is beaky on the rest of her family.

"So this is Deedee!" Mom exclaimed. She set down her knife and marched past me to give Deedee a quick hug. "I've been looking forward to meeting you. June tells me she's been having so much fun with you."

As we set our bags on the floor, my mom asked me, "How was the drive out?"

"I took the 405," I said. "It was how it always is — a mess."

She shook her head and then said in a joking voice, "I always say that traffic is like the weather. Everybody talks about it, but nobody *does* anything."

"I try!" I protested.

Ignoring me, Mom said to Deedee, "Are you excited about your helicopter ride?"

They started to talk about the morning to come — a safe topic. I'd primed my parents ahead of time. No talking about the baby. In fact, no talking about *any* babies or baby-related topics. As far as they were concerned, there was no baby. Deedee was six months along, and her belly was starting to pop. She was back in the oversize clothes, however, so you couldn't tell. She said she hadn't told anyone at school and, so far, nobody'd guessed.

Deedee, my dad, and I helped carry the food out to the dining room table and took our seats. Dinner was soup, salad, "Oprah" oven fries, and steak from my dad's grill. My mom had set the table with tiki-themed place mats and dishes. The cutlery had palm tree designs, and the water glasses were painted with hula girls.

Dinners at my parents' house had gotten progressively more elaborate since my father retired. He'd always been relegated to the grill, over which he is lord and master. But in the past couple of years, he's tried his hand at a bit of experimenting in the kitchen — a salad here, a pasta dish there. Mom must've felt threatened, because suddenly she was adding sauces and trotting out new recipes the likes of which we'd never seen before and saying things like "Martin, this salad you made is delicious. Hey, did you guys know that a baboon can make a salad? They can! I saw it on the Discovery Channel!" Dad was edging into what had always been my mother's domain, and enjoying a good meal as I do, I wasn't above fueling the competition.

"Dad, those steaks sure smell good!" I effused as my mom carried in bowls of soup and set them in front of us. "Mmm, and Mom, is this soup homemade?"

My dad poked at his bowl. "What is this?"

"In honor of Deedee's Mexican heritage, I made taco soup." My mom gave Deedee a smile and said, "Now I know it's not a traditional recipe, but I thought it would be silly of me to try to make a dish that you probably get at home every day, only better and more authentic. A friend of mine got the recipe at her Weight Watchers meeting, and . . ."

I have no idea what she said after that because my brain was buzzing as if bees had set up shop in there. Did she say taco soup?

The taco soup?

I was about to ask what was in it when I tuned back in to hear my mom say, "And truthfully, it's nothing but opening a bunch of cans."

Deedee dug in. "If weawwy goog," she said, her mouth full of hot soup.

"Gracias, señorita," my mom said, showing off that she had about as vast a command of the Spanish language as I do.

I regarded the soup as if it were a murder weapon, which it sort of was. Then I thought, *What the hell, I'm starving, and it smells delicious.* I took a spoonful and blew on it before tasting it. Okay, it was pretty good. *Weawwy goog,* in fact, I thought, scooping up more. Why not? It wasn't as if the soup had been driving the car.

"Do you enjoy school?" my mom asked Deedee.

"It's okay."

"June tells me you're an honors student. Good for you! So, do you have a boyfriend at school?"

Deedee poured ketchup over her oven fries, looking as if she'd like to crawl under the table. "Not really."

I shot my mom a look. What was she doing? Had I not made it clear there would be no talk of babies, and didn't the fact that

Deedee was pregnant imply that there was, in fact, a boy in the picture, at least at one point?

My mom barreled ahead, pretending not to notice the daggers I was shooting at her. "You will. You'll have lots of them, that's for certain. You're such a pretty girl."

Deedee seemed increasingly uncomfortable, so in an effort to get my mom off whatever oddball track she was on, I said to Deedee, "She's right, you are . . . but don't put too much stake on anything my mom says. She used to think that I was cute when I was your age, too."

"You *were* cute!" my mom insisted.

Dad gave a chortle. "Didn't she have those braces? And the eye patch?"

"It's not my fault I had a lazy eye! And it was only for a few months!"

Deedee cheered instantly. "An eye patch? Serious?!" And she made an *arrrgh* noise like a pirate — as if I hadn't heard that every second of every day that I wore it. "Got any pictures?"

"Sorry. There are no pictures of me because I was so ugly . . . *and* the second child. If you want to see my brother, however, we have about a million photos of him." Then I patted the back of my head to remind her of the neglect I'd suffered.

"Don't you listen to her, Deedee," my mom said. "She may have had an . . . *awkward* phase for a while there, but that's exactly my point. By the time she reached high school, she'd blossomed. Truly, it's the best time of your life. I can't wait for you to get out there and experience it all. With your brains and beauty, I'll bet you have big things ahead of you."

Ah. So that's what she was doing. I'd been baffled at first, until I realized that this was Doris Parker's one-woman public service announcement to try to convince Deedee to give the baby up for adoption. Not so subtle, but an A for effort.

Deedee responded by putting her attention to sawing at her steak, to the point where my dad said, obviously annoyed, "Hey now, you ought to be able to cut that with a fork."

Dessert was rhubarb pie and ice cream served on the back patio to the sounds of the bug zapper killing flies and my father's complaints that the Bloomingdales next door recently landscaped with low-water plants — cactus and rock gardens — instead of grass. "Can you believe it? What do they think this is, Death Valley? They ever hear of a water hose? Next thing you know, they're going to be installing one of those

232

solar panels."

"Your parents are a riot," Deedee said as I showed her to my brother's old room, where she'd be sleeping. It was only nine o'clock, but since the alarm would go off at three a.m. we were both eager for an early turn-in.

"They sure liked you," I said. "I wouldn't be surprised if they're downstairs right now adding you to the will." Then I left to shower, not daring to leave it for the morning in case I overslept. It was quarter to ten by the time I'd blown-dry my hair, and I'd already done the finger-counting thing and realized the most sleep I could hope for was five hours. Ugh — how did Troy Jones do this every night? Before going to bed, I noticed a light on in Deedee's room. I gave a knock and went in. She was under the covers, still in her big shirt, reading one of my brother's old comic books. "I can't fall asleep this early," she said.

"I can. I have a remarkable gift for slumber. It's waking up on time that I'm worried about."

"Me too. I set the alarm."

"Good — between the both of us, one should manage to roll out of bed." I sat on the edge of her bed. "You need a lullaby?" I started to sing, "Gitchy gitchy ya ya da da . . ."

She set down the comic. "You told your mom that I'm pregnant." I attempted to put on an innocent face, but she said, "I'm not stupid."

"Sorry. She's my mom. I couldn't *not* tell her."

"At least she was nice about it. My mom screams at me all the time. I'll bet yours never yells at you."

"In defense of your mom, I'm a bit old for that."

"But when you were a kid, I'll bet your parents didn't yell."

I thought about it. "Probably not much. We Parkers aren't big yellers, but that doesn't mean they didn't come down on me if I deserved it."

She snorted. "Yeah, right. What'd you ever do wrong?"

"Plenty."

"Forget it. You're too goody-goody. I bet you never did anything bad your whole life."

"Sure I have!"

"Like what? What's the worst thing you ever did?"

Maybe it was the taco soup or the thought that I'd be seeing Troy Jones in mere hours, but Marissa was on my mind, and before I

even thought about it, I said, "I killed someone."

"I mean *serious.*"

I'd regretted it as soon as I said it, so I
tried instead to come up with some other
crime I'd committed to appease her. Unfortunately, sneaking into the spiked punch
and puking at Kathy Berz's graduation
party was the best I could do, and it seemed
downright charming compared with killing
someone. I sputtered and stammered until
Deedee said, "Shit, you *did* kill somebody!"

"Nah, I was —"

"Bullcrap — don't take it back now. You
did."

I sighed. "You're right, I did. It was an accident." I turned my attention to picking a
loose thread from the comforter. "Only it
was my fault, so I don't know if 'accident' is
the right word." I told her about giving
Marissa a ride and the car crash. At
Deedee's urging, I went into the details:
from the dresser toppling off the truck, to
how I'd veered, to my first ride in an
ambulance. Of course, I didn't mention that
Marissa was Troy's sister or anything about
the list. The last thing I wanted was for
Deedee to suspect she was part of it.

"So how did she die?" Deedee asked when
I'd finished. I gave her a blank stare, and

she said, "I know it was a car crash, and the dresser falling, but what *exactly* killed her?" She said it without a shred of pity or empathy. She wasn't being ghoulish, either. It was simply information she wanted that I hadn't adequately provided.

"She wasn't wearing a seat belt, so when the car rolled, she got tossed."

"Like through the window?"

And here was the strange thing: I felt as if I could finally say it. The details of that night that I'd kept from Susan, my boyfriend Robert, my parents . . . everyone. It had always been my fear of their kindness. That their sympathy would have been more than I could bear. All I'd admitted to them was that Marissa died when the car rolled — as far as they knew, that was it. "The windshield," I told Deedee matter-of-factly. "She crashed through the windshield."

"She got cut to death?"

"No. As I understand it, she died because my car . . ." I took a breath before continuing, "It landed on her."

"On what part of her?"

"I don't know — all of her, I suppose."

"Gross. What'd you do?"

"Nothing," I answered, yanking the last of the stray thread from the comforter. "I did nothing."

Granted, I'd been pinned by the air bag with a banged head and no clue about where Marissa was. But really, all I'd done was hang there. Twiddling my thumbs. Singing la-de-da. Waiting to be rescued while the entire time I crushed Marissa Jones to death. The worst part: At no point did the police or hospital staff comfort me with "She died quickly." They always say that, and in its absence, I was left to assume that the opposite must be true.

I stood to leave. "Well, it's late, I'm going to sleep," I said as I clicked off the light, and out of habit I repeated what my mom said to me every night even when I'd been too old for her to tuck me in. "Sweet dreams."

The alarm sounded, and I smacked it off. Ugh. I felt nauseated from sleepiness. Three a.m. Why didn't I pull an all-nighter? At least I'd already *be* up instead of having to wake up.

After dragging myself out of bed, I dressed in the jeans and long-sleeved T-shirt that I'd left out. I yanked my hair into a ponytail, then went to check on Deedee, who sat on the edge of her bed looking as if she'd been pulled from the dustbin and set there. "It's the middle of the friggin' night," she groaned. She wore the same clothes she'd slept in and — after throwing on her tennis shoes — pronounced herself ready. Then she crawled under the covers and told me to wake her up again when it was time to go.

Pride forced me to make at least a cursory attempt at makeup. My eyes were slits, so I tried as best I could with mascara and eye shadow. Later, when the puffiness receded, I'd get to see if my aim was on the mark or if I wound up resembling Bette Davis in *All About Eve.* Whatever. If Troy was hoping for foxy ride-along companions, he needed to switch to the afternoon drive-time shift.

The Van Nuys Airport was small and catered to commuter planes and helicopters. Deedee and I made it there a few minutes early and easily found Troy's hangar. He was there already, dressed in jeans and a hooded sweatshirt, drinking coffee and looking over some papers. Outside the hangar we passed a bright yellow helicopter with *"K-JAM — Getting L.A. Jammin' "* emblazoned on its side.

"Morning, ladies!" Troy called when we approached.

"Morning implies sunlight," I replied grouchily. "This is not morning."

"So," he said, clapping his hands together,

"let me show you around. How about I start with the coffeepot?"

He showed us the operation there. His circumstance was unusual, he explained, because most traffic reporters worked for a traffic reporting service — he was an independent who worked directly for the radio station. K-JAM was the top-rated morning show. That's why Lizbeth had been drooling to get on air.

"You ever meet Fat Boy?" Deedee asked Troy, referring to K-JAM's morning DJ, who — at least based on the billboards I'd seen around town — had earned his nickname legitimately. He was about four hundred pounds of pure wacky Latino, and in the billboards he wore thick glasses, a hat, and nothing else but a Speedo.

"Sure. I'll be on air with him this morning, but we won't see him. He's at the radio station."

"Fat Boy's so funny," Deedee said. "I like it when he calls people pretending to be a old lady."

"You listen to K-JAM?" he asked her.

"Yeah, while I get ready for school."

"So what's your opinion of my traffic reports?" he asked her, leading us toward the helicopter.

She gave it some thought, then said, "You

could be funnier. Crack jokes. You do a good job talking about the traffic, I guess. I can't be sure since I don't drive yet." She grinned at him. "For all I know, you make it up — there's not any traffic at all."

"So you're on to me already."

A stocky man sporting a baseball cap and a beard came over holding a doughnut bag. Troy introduced him as his co-pilot, Dickie Ruiz. "Dickie and I need to go over a few things. You might want to hit the ladies' room," Troy suggested. "You won't have another chance for a couple of hours." Deedee and I must have looked panicked, because he said, "I can make an emergency stop if you need it."

"I gotta pee every ten seconds these days," Deedee whispered as we made our way to the bathroom.

"How are you feeling?" I asked. "You going to be up for this?"

"Oh yeah. This is the coolest thing I've ever done."

We met back up at the helicopter a few minutes later. Troy said, "Good news, June. We're down a sponsor, so I'll have a chance to throw you a couple questions in the seven o'clock hour. Anything you want me to focus on?"

While I was trying to decide, Deedee said,

"Ask her what's her favorite song."

"Thanks," I said, "but it needs to be more about ridesharing. Maybe you could ask about the new rail line to downtown?"

"Boooooring," Deedee said.

Troy said he'd see what he could do to keep things lively and then opened a door to the helicopter. "Ready?" he asked. He and Dickie helped us climb in back, where there was just enough room for Deedee and me to sit comfortably.

"Where are the parachutes?" I asked as I buckled in. "Does my tray table serve as a flotation device?" I was babbling because my belly was starting to do nervous flips. I'd never been in a helicopter, and even though I'm not afraid of flying, I wasn't sure what to expect. Plus I'd be talking live on the radio, so it was a double whammy of nerves. I felt I had a lot riding on this, knowing Lizbeth's position was open.

Troy fiddled with some controls, and Dickie handed Deedee and me headsets — the huge kind that fit like earmuffs. Each one had a thin microphone that pulled forward. "Once he starts those chopper blades, it's going to get loud in here. You'll need these to hear what's happening on the radio station. Use the mikes to talk to us here in the chopper — it's easier than shouting. June, we've powered the mike on yours so you can talk on air, too." He smiled. "Do I need to remind you of the words you can't say on the radio?"

"No, that's okay."

"I wanna hear them!" Deedee said.

"*Fuck*'s a no-no," Dickie replied. "You can't say *fuck*."

"What about *shit?*" Deedee asked. "Because I swear that sometimes they bleep it out, but there are other times —"

"*Shit*'s not allowed," Troy cut in. "But you're right, it sneaks through once in a while. And June, feel free to talk all you want about how incredibly good-looking I am. There's no ban on words like *stud . . . sexy . . . godlike . . .*"

"*Egomaniac,*" Dickie added, passing his bag of doughnuts back to us. "It kills him that he's stuck in radio and the ladies don't get to see that pretty face of his."

We dove into the doughnuts until Troy gave us a one-minute warning; then we got ourselves ready. When he kicked the helicopter into gear, the sound of whirling blades was deafening, even to us inside with the doors closed. "I always thought that was fake!" I shouted. "That you sat in a studio and played a tape!"

Dickie answered by pointing to his ears

and mouthing, "Headphones."

"Oh, right." Deedee and I scrambled to pull on our headphones, and I adjusted my microphone.

Troy asked, "Can you hear me?"

Deedee nodded. I gave a thumbs-up.

"Here we go," he said, and the helicopter lifted. It hovered for a moment and then flew up and forward. My insides did a dip, and Deedee gave an excited whoop.

"Everybody okay back there?" Troy asked.

Deedee nodded again. I gave another thumbs-up.

I could hear Troy chuckle in my headphones. "You guys can talk," he said. "I'll give you plenty of warning when we switch over to on air. And Deedee, you don't need to worry. Only June's mike goes live."

Did he have to say the word *live? Arrrgh,* as I'd have said in my eye patch days. The doughnut danced in my stomach.

There's nothing to be scared about, I told myself. It wasn't as if Troy would ask me tough, probing questions. I could handle this, especially after living through the gas giveaway debacle. My brain seemed to be buying the pep talk. My digestive system remained doubtful.

I forced myself to concentrate on the view while I listened to the radio station, which was playing that Black Eyed Peas song that, now that I'd heard it, would be stuck in my head all day. The night sky was taking on a grayer hue, and it looked as if the sun were considering making an appearance. (And I didn't for a second forget this was a twofer for the list: both #10, *Ride in a helicopter,* and #18, *Watch a sunrise.*)

Our flight had started in the Valley, and within minutes we were making our way over the hill. I'd flown in planes over Los Angeles plenty of times, but this was close enough that I could make out the sights. Dodger Stadium . . . the Getty Museum . . . the mansions along Mullholland Drive. Even the 405 Freeway seemed lovely, winding as it did up the hill, dotted with the headlights of early morning commuters.

Troy turned to us. "What do you think?"

"Who'd have thought traffic could be so pretty?" I said.

"Well, if you find this traffic pretty," Dickie remarked, "wait until rush hour hits. It's a freakin' work of art."

Deedee pressed her face against the window. "This is so awesome. Nobody's gonna believe me when I tell them."

Troy did the first few traffic reports, and as he'd warned me, the radio feed shut off in my headphones. I could hear Troy's voice, but Fat Boy's responses were dead air. Troy put on his "radio guy" voice — huskier and more enthusiastic than how he usually sounded. So far, traffic was moving smoothly, and it sounded odd to hear only one side of their banter. At one point, Troy said, "I don't know, Fat Boy, it's been a while since I've looked that closely at a monkey," leaving me to wonder what could have prompted that sort of response.

We buzzed past the Hollywood sign as the sky changed from gray to orange. The letters looked every bit their forty-feet height from this vantage point. "Thought this might be a nice view for the sunrise," Troy said to me, the only acknowledgment he'd made of the list.

Then the helicopter veered left, and Troy said, "I'm heading to check on the 101 — I'm getting word of a crash there. June, I'll probably bring you in on the next go-round."

"Sounds good!" I chirped.

Barf.

I tried to quell my nerves, restricting myself to happy, ridesharing thoughts. *Plug the 800 number . . . plug the 800 number . . .*

Whatever you do, don't swear . . . and definitely don't say fuck. Fuck, now I have it in my head . . . it's like that Black Eyed Peas song, and I won't be able to get it out! Oh, shit . . . I mean, fuck . . . Oh no, I'll be spewing cusswords as if I have Tourette's and —

"All right, we're good to go," Troy said. "I'll start with the traffic news. From there, June, I'll intro you and then toss you a question or two."

"Make them easy," I said queasily.

He turned his head briefly. "Nothing but softballs, baby." Looking back at his control panel, he said, "Now, it'll be the same as before. You'll hear my voice in your headset. You'll hear yourself, too. And I'll be able to hear Fat Boy, but you won't. Don't worry — he knows to only let me cue you. Got it?"

"Got it."

The radio sounds disappeared, and I again heard Troy's voice describing a traffic tie-up on the 101, the 405 at the Sepulveda Pass, and the sluggish 90 past Riverside. Then he continued, "If you're getting tired of traffic, I've got with me here in the K-JAM JetCopter a lady who can tell us about how to avoid the mess . . . June Parker with Los Angeles Rideshare."

Here it came. My heart thumped. My stomach growled from nerves so loudly that I was afraid it could be heard over the helicopter blades.

He continued, "So, June, what would you say to somebody who's sitting alone in their car right now, wishing they were anywhere but on the freeway?"

"Well, Troy," I said, and as soon as I said it, Dickie whipped around to face me, his expression a complete panic.

"We've got dead air!" he hissed. "I can't hear you!"

Not knowing what to do, I continued, "I'd tell them —"

But Troy's voice cut me off. "I mean, besides get out and walk. Heh, heh. Right, Fat Boy?"

"What the f—" Deedee began, but stopped short. I could hear her voice in my headset. She figured it out at the same time the rest of us did. Her mike was on, and mine wasn't.

Dickie picked up the wires leading from the controls to us. We must have switched the headsets when we took them off to eat the doughnuts. I froze with panic: *What should I do?* Troy put a finger in the air to say, *Wait . . .* and then he said, "That's a good point you're making there, Fat Boy."

With that, Deedee sat up straight and bleated into her microphone, "June here! You know what, Troy? I always say that traffic is a lot like the weather. Everybody *talks*

247

about it, but nobody *does* anything."

Troy didn't miss a beat. "So true. And what *should* they do?"

"For starters," she said, her eyes wide with excitement as she continued, "they should carpool. I mean, if they're lucky enough to have a car. Especially since gas is, like, a million dollars a gallon."

"Remind me not to go to the same gas station you do," Troy joked. I was a wreck, but he seemed to be taking it in stride. Dickie reached back and gave Deedee's arm an encouraging squeeze.

"Bus," I mouthed to her.

"And if they don't got a car," she continued, "then they can take the bus. Shoot, my mom is blind, so she's *gotta* ride the bus everywhere, and she does fine."

"Good for her," Troy said.

I'd reached into my purse and grabbed a pen, and I quickly wrote the company's 800 number on the back of the doughnut bag and held it in front of Deedee.

"Yeah, so I don't want to hear nobody complaining that they can't do it. If she can ride the bus and she can't even see, then somebody who's got everything going on ought to be able to do it, too."

"I can't tell you how glad I am that you came to share that with us today, June,"

Troy said. He could hardly hold back his grin. He was *enjoying* this!

"You're welcome," Deedee said proudly. "Oh, and if they got any questions, they need to call 1-800-RIDESHARE. Which is more than seven numbers, but I guess it works okay anyway."

Troy wound up the report, thanked the sponsors, and then the radio came back in my headset again.

"Deedee, that was great!" Troy exclaimed. "You're a natural."

Dickie slapped her leg in congratulation.

I tried to sound enthusiastic when I said, "You did better than I would have."

"Can I do another one?" she asked eagerly.

Dickie shook his head. "Let's not press our luck."

"Shoot. I wanted to give a shout-out to my girlfriend Rebecca."

To round out the tour, Troy whipped along the beach, deserted save for a few surfers at this early hour, and over the giant Ferris wheel at the Santa Monica pier.

After we landed and climbed out of the helicopter, it was all I could do not to kneel and kiss the ground. Good old terra firma! Fun as it had started out, I'd never been so glad to have something over with. The people of Los Angeles now thought my mother was blind and that I'd use double negatives, but that wasn't even the problem. I'd blown it. Again.

In the moment that we realized my microphone wasn't working, it was Deedee who'd stepped up with a plan. Left to me, it would have been the longest silence in radio history. Only after the fact did I realize I could have simply leaned over and talked into her microphone until we had a second to switch headsets.

I moped and tried to appear as if I weren't, as the others seemed amped from the ride.

"Besides being on the radio, the best part was seeing that car accident," Deedee chattered on. "They looked like toy cars. And that one was totally upside down. It was so awesome."

"You know what's interesting," Dickie told her, "is that most traffic reporters don't use the term *accident.* You'll notice they call it a 'crash' or a 'smash-up.' Saying 'accident' makes it sound as if it can't be helped."

"I never thought of it that way," Deedee remarked.

As he spoke, I'd exhaled a breath but seemed to have forgotten how to draw it back in. Then everything started to collide inside me. The taco soup . . . my talk with Deedee the night before . . . seeing Troy

Jones and not having enough sleep and eating only sugar for breakfast and blowing the interview and Deedee was pregnant and why didn't I just talk into her microphone and all that coffee and there's no such thing as an accident because they're crashes and smash-ups but not accidents because somebody must be at fault and the worst, worst, worst part of all . . . Troy's glance sliding over to me because he'd heard what Dickie said, too. And in his eyes I saw the one thing I couldn't take — the thing that was as good as pouring lighter fluid on the smoldering fire of my emotions. I saw pity.

"Pardon me, I need to . . ." I gestured toward outside, as if there were important errands I'd remembered I needed to handle. I hurried out, and as soon as I was beyond where they could see me, I ran the rest of the way to the side of the building.

Then I threw my back up against the wall, and the waterworks began.

My chest heaved to gasp air. Tears hurled themselves from my eyes as I let loose racking, heaving sob after sob. I knew the noise I was making — I'd heard it before when I'd visited San Francisco's Pier 39, where dozens of sea lions played on the docks. In my case, it was a bark of awful, confused misery. It was Laura Petrie on *The Dick Van*

251

Dyke Show when she used to cry in her falsetto, "Oh, Rob!" It was the girl screaming in a slasher film. It was a Mack truck's brakes squealing on the freeway. It was ugly and undignified, and I couldn't make myself stop.

I felt hands on my shoulders. Troy scooted me down so I was sitting — flat against the wall, hugging my knees. Then he moved my arms and spread my legs apart. He pushed gently on my back so my head dropped down between my knees. "Breathe," he directed. "Take a slow breath in, then let it out."

"I . . . I . . . I . . . caaaaan't . . . huh a huh . . ."

"Shhh. Deep breath in." And he breathed in deeply and then exhaled to demonstrate. "Come on, do it with me."

And in between snorting out sobs, I managed to get in a few breaths, then a few more; then after a while I was breathing in synch with Troy and, frankly, feeling foolish there with my head between my knees.

His hand rubbing my back was nice, though. I was also A-okay with the way he sat next to me, his body grazing mine.

As I lifted my head, and before he could get full view of the damage, I used the underside of my shirt to wipe my face. It emerged soaked with mascara, tears, snot, and heaven knew what else.

Troy had stopped rubbing my back and shifted so he could see me better. (And what a view I'm sure it was!) "Dickie didn't mean anything by it. It wasn't about you."

I shrugged my answer.

"He doesn't know about the accident. And hey, see that? I said 'accident.' Because that's what it was."

At this point, because my eyes were puffy and I'm sure my nose was red, so basically I had nothing to lose, I said simply, "Why are you so nice to me?" It was both a question and an accusation.

"Why wouldn't I be?"

"Do I need to state the obvious? Because if I do, then this —" I made a gesture toward my eyes — "could start up again."

"Please don't do that."

"The fact is, I was driving. You have every right to blame me for" — and there was no way to say it without saying it — "your sister's death. You should hate me. I find it hard to understand why you don't seem to. You're either a saint or . . . well, saint's pretty much my only idea."

"Excuse me while I go call the news desk, because that's the first time anyone's ever called me that."

"I'm serious."

"I know. All I can tell you is that I get plenty angry about what happened. But not at you. Trust me, if I ever get my hands on the bastard who couldn't tie a dresser down to a truck . . . and then didn't *stop* . . ." He shook his head. "You don't want to be there. As far as I'm concerned, you didn't do anything wrong. You survived, and I wish my sister had, too. That's it."

I nodded, missing the warmth of his hand on my back. As much as I'd enjoyed the comfort, however, I knew there was something that I needed even more: the truth. I'd been running from it for a long time, and now it was time to face it. "Troy, I want you to answer a question for me, and I want you to answer it honestly."

"Okay."

"Promise?"

"Sure." His brows pulled together in curiosity. "I promise."

"When your sister died, was it . . . right away? Like instantly? Or . . ." I let my question trail off.

I saw his Adam's apple jump. His mouth opened and then shut again. What seemed to be a lifetime passed, and at last he said, "Yeah. They said it was instant."

He was truly the worst liar I'd ever seen.

I had my answer. Only it wasn't the one I'd wanted. The weight I'd hoped to have lifted gave an evil chuckle from its perch on my shoulders.

Troy got himself up from the ground and then extended an arm to help me up.

"That was quite a radio interview Deedee did, huh? She's a pistol." He was obviously trying to change the subject, interject levity into the moment. What the heck, I'd play along. I clasped his hand and let myself be pulled to my feet.

"Yeah, and I can't believe you," I said, forcing mirth into my voice. "Egging her on like you did."

"Gotta go with the flow. And hey," Troy said, giving a playful tug at my pants, "what's up with the jeans?"

"There's nothing wrong with jeans. You're wearing them. Remember . . . radio and all that?"

"I'm disappointed, that's all. I was specifically promised pajamas."

"You're not missing much," I assured him, brushing at my bottom. "My pajamas are no big thrill. Half the time I wind up just wearing underwear to bed."

As soon as the words escaped my mouth, I winced with embarrassment.

Troy gave a low chuckle. "I was disappointed before. Now I'm devastated."

CHAPTER 15

My parents didn't argue often. But when they did, my brother and I had an uncanny ability to choose these times while their equilibrium was off to ask for things. A later bedtime. Pizza delivery. The combination to the liquor cabinet. It was risky. You could get your head snapped off. Yet there was also the chance that you'd get a "yes" that you'd never, ever get otherwise. We didn't even have to hear the fight or know for a fact it had happened — it was as if we could *smell* the vulnerability. I can't even say it was deliberate, at least on my part. It was pure childhood instinct that drove us to pounce when the prey was weakened.

It was the same sort of instinct, I'll assume, behind Deedee saying to me now — as I was still reeling from the news that Marissa's accident had in fact been the worst-case scenario — "I've been thinking."

"That explains that smoke coming from

your brain," I quipped.

I was driving her to school after the ride-along with Troy, and we'd gotten mired in the rush-hour traffic that had looked so lovely from the sky. It was butt-ugly down here. I was stuck behind a huge truck with a naked woman silhouette on the mud flaps and a "My Kid Can Beat Up Your Honor Student" bumper sticker. Somebody nearby hadn't passed smog inspection because I was choking on fumes. My car had moved about a foot and a half in the past hour.

"I'm pretty sure I got somebody who can adopt the baby."

"Deedee, that's wonderful!" I exclaimed, and the words kept gushing out. "I can't believe you didn't tell me before this! Is your mom okay with it? Oh my gosh, I'm so excited for you! Who is it? Did you find relatives?"

"Sort of related," she said.

"Yeah?"

"A sister."

I looked over at her in utter confusion. "A sister? You never told me you had a sister."

"A big sister."

"Wha— ? Huh — ? You have a big sister? How is that — ?" And then it struck me.

Ho no. Was she out of her mind?

"Tell me you're not referring to me."

"Why not?!" she challenged. "It'd be perfect! You could be the mom — and we'd all hang out together and do stuff."

"But Deedee —"

"You want a baby. You said so yourself."

"I meant more *someday.*"

"I'm not due till August."

I gave a sigh.

"You don't exactly have all the time in the world," she said ominously.

"Do you know something I don't know? Because I was planning on sticking around for a while."

"You know what I mean."

"I can see why the idea would appeal to you. And I'm flattered, I am. But if you haven't noticed, I'm *single.* Wouldn't you rather the baby go to a married couple?"

"I don't know any married couples. I know you."

"There are agencies where they'd introduce you to people who —"

"That's not gonna work. You know that. My mom is never gonna let the baby go to just anybody. And I don't want that for her anyway. How do I know how some stranger's gonna treat her? That she's not gonna get smacked around or put down all the time? Or *worse?*"

"Her?" I asked. "Did you —"

"It's a girl."

"Congratulations," I said; then I added gently, "Believe me, the idea of adopting the baby is very tempting. But sweetie, your mom's never going to go for this."

"Yeah, she is. We already talked about it."

"You did?"

"I mean, it was my idea. Even way back when I only thought I might be pregnant. After you and Kip came over, me and my mom talked about it. And then last night, spending that time with your family, I knew for sure."

I blew out a breath.

"I don't have much family," she said. "Mami's is mostly in Mexico. I don't even know my dad. And you'd be an *awesome* mom. Plus you got that big place with a pool. The baby would have grandparents living close by. And I'd be, like, her big sister."

Traffic started to clear — there'd been backup due to a crash . . . a smash-up . . . whatever you want to call it. As I got close to where the accident happened, I slowed to rubberneck. I waited all this time, I might as well get my show. Not much to see. Fender bender; no injuries as far as I could tell. All this to watch two people exchange insurance information.

We picked up speed, and I fiddled with the air vents, trying to get a breeze going. "It doesn't bother you that I'm not married?"

"Might be even better. You'll give the baby more love that way. You don't have anybody else. All you got is each other."

"What if I get married?"

Deedee made a sound like "Heh."

"It could happen!"

"Ah, that'd be okay. You wouldn't marry a guy who didn't want a baby, too. You know, I think Dickie liked you."

"Dickie?"

"He was totally flirting with you."

"You don't mean Troy?"

The girl must be brighter than I gave her credit for. "Why, do *you* like Troy?" she asked sweetly.

"No! I thought you might have the names mixed up. I assumed Troy because you met him before . . . at the beach."

She started to singsong, "You really liiiiike him . . ."

"Shut up."

"You think he's seeeeexy . . ."

"This car is still going slow enough. I can shove you out and probably not even get a ticket for it."

"You want to kiiiiiiss him . . ."

I snipped, "Can we change the subject?"

"Fine. You gonna adopt my kid or not?"

Out of the frying pan and into the fire.

"I need time to mull it over. This is a lot."

Deedee nodded, whereas I was utterly shocked by what I'd just said. I'd mull it? Surely the answer needed to be a swift and simple no. Yet, as soon as Deedee proposed the idea of me being a mom, all I could think about were those few minutes of waiting for a pregnancy test result. The same mix of yes and no stirred inside me. I wasn't yet willing to open my eyes and look at the results — especially since this time it was up to me what answer appeared. Instead, against all logic, I'd just given Deedee a maybe.

"Just don't take too long deciding," she said. "If you don't do it, I gotta start buying baby stuff. And sign myself up for independent study. And those guys said they were going to get me a student internship at the radio station in the fall. I can't do it if I got to worry about a kid, so I'll need to call them and tell them no."

Sensing my chance to divert Deedee from the topic of adopting her baby, I said, "Oh, an internship? That's great! You must have really impressed them. What sorts of things would you be doing?"

"Nothing if I got me a baby to take care of," she said dully.

So much for diverting her attention.

After I dropped Deedee off at school, that Mariah Carey song "Hero" came on the radio. When it got to the part about how I'll finally see the truth — that a hero lies in me — I felt a catch in my throat. It wasn't a full-on sob. I prefer to save that sort of thing for where people can see me, apparently. This was more a quick bubble of emotion. A hint at the roller coaster to come.

When I finally got to work, Susan was the only one who noticed it wasn't me on K-JAM. Everyone else told me, Good job! Way to go! Phyllis popped her head into my cubicle to say, "It's a start."

My mom had left a message. "Why are you going on the radio saying I'm blind? I understand if you want to give carpooling a heartwarming angle. But couldn't you have made your father blind? He doesn't have to go to work and face people." Then she sighed. "Ah well, maybe I'll get one of those handicapped spots now."

For the next week, the only thing I could think about was adopting Deedee's baby.

It wasn't as if I didn't have other things to occupy my mind. Work was a madhouse. I had to pick up the slack for Lizbeth's being gone, even though there was no talk yet of (me) replacing her. Plus, it was near the end of the fiscal year, so those projects I'd procrastinated on had come back to haunt me.

But my world went on autopilot, and I had one thing on my mind. For the first time, I could relate to that annoying way that women get so consumed about pregnancy and babies. In fact, I now offer my profound and immediate apologies to every woman behind whose back I made gagging motions when our conversation managed to again focus only on baby clothes, bassinettes, and spit-up.

Out of nowhere, I'd become obsessed with babies. Even when I was running errands one day, my car steered itself to a Babies R Us — or, as I've called it any other time I've had to go there to buy a shower present, Downtown Hell. But this time I meandered the aisles, gushing over the tiny outfits. Mentally picturing how I'd turn my spare room into a nursery.

That was, I scolded myself, *if* I adopted the baby.

But that was crazy. Of course it was crazy! Wasn't it?

Suddenly I was noticing babies everywhere. I couldn't get enough of them. I found myself cooing at them. Asking their mothers how old they were. Did they sleep through the night? Were they on solids yet? "Mind if I give 'em a hold?"

I'd gone to a park a few days before and had a conversation with a mom with two toddlers. I told her about the baby I was going to adopt as if it were fact and not speculation. And I liked the way it sounded coming out of my mouth. *My baby* will be here in August. I'm making all sorts of plans for *my baby.* Of course, then the woman went and wrecked it all by saying, "Your husband must be thrilled." To save face, I had to say, "Yes, my *partner* is beside herself." She piped down pretty quickly after that.

A chance like this would never come along again, that was for sure. It felt as if I'd won millions of dollars in the lottery and I was studying the ticket, deciding whether or not to cash it in. On the plus side, I'd be rich. On the down side, I'd never know if a potential suitor loved me for me or for my money.

Hell, who was I kidding? I'd take the cash.

The idea of a baby, however, was much trickier.

One thing was certain: I needed to think

things through on my own before I opened debate to the floor. Sure, getting input from friends and family would help me sort things out. That was, if I had a different group of friends and family. In my case, it was guaranteed I'd be bombarded with opinions. Better to know where I stood and then see if the winds of public opinion could topple me.

Having recently discovered that lists can be quite helpful in setting one's life on a new course, I pulled out a pencil and piece of paper and made a list of my own.

REASONS TO ADOPT THE BABY

1. *There is a baby who needs a mother*
2. *I would be awesome mom — would never yell at child and would feed her organic vegetables and hardly ever doughnuts*
3. *Am 34*
4. *Almost 35*
5. *May be only chance to be a mom*
6. *Could cross off #3:* Change someone's life *in bold strokes*
7. *Taking action = getting what you want from life, i.e., Alison Freeman**

Reasons Not to Adopt the Baby

1. *Being a single mom perhaps not all it's cracked up to be*
2. *I want a baby, but do I want a baby now?*
3. *Could I love baby that wasn't "mine"?*
4. *Possibility of suddenly meeting man of dreams, having fairy-tale wedding, and starting own family with own biological children sooner than expected, i.e., Alison Freeman**

*Alison Freeman: former co-worker, single, living in a crappy apartment, with no romantic prospects on the horizon. Then she hit age thirty-five and said to hell with waiting for Prince Charming. She bankrolled her life savings into a tiny but cute two-bedroom house and signed up at the local sperm bank. While having her new kitchen remodeled, she and her cabinet guy fell in love. Bucking conventional wisdom to play it cool lest you scare a man off, she notified him, "I intend to get pregnant within six months. It can be yours. Or it can be Anonymous Donor #433's. You choose." They married within three months and now have two adorable girls.

As soon as I wrote the pros and cons, I dismissed #3 under Reasons Not to Adopt the Baby. Of course I'd love the baby. Look at Angelina Jolie. Would anyone ever believe that a woman who wore a vial of blood around her neck could form a maternal bond so deeply and so quickly? Yet she can't seem to collect enough of the little tykes. Love wasn't the issue.

There were decidedly more yeas than nays on the list. But that alone wasn't enough to tip the scales. What was the weight of each argument? Was there any one that trumped them all? Was there a deal breaker in there? I couldn't be sure. Perhaps I could call my old friend Linda who'd done the boyfriend spreadsheet for me to see if she could whip up a logical calculation determining what I should do now.

I sighed and tossed aside the list. This was not a decision I'd make logically.

It would be an act of the heart.

Whatever I chose to do — to adopt or not to adopt — my life would be forever altered. This could be my chance to make up for everything I'd ever let slide.

Then again, it could be the biggest mistake I'd ever make.

"So am I crazy for considering it?" I asked

Martucci on our Monday morning run. I was running a nine-minute mile at this point. More important, what I was doing resembled running, versus the walking with spurts of gasping and collapsing I'd started out doing. Without a bathroom scale I didn't know if I'd dropped any weight, but my skinny clothes were fitting better. That was a hopeful sign.

"Sounds as if you've more than considered it. Sounds like you've made up your mind. And it's great you're going to adopt this kid. Being a parent is the best thing that can happen to a person."

I'd learned enough about Martucci from running with him to know that he didn't have children himself. Or a wife, for that matter. Not sure about the girlfriend — I preferred to remain ignorant. "What do you know about kids?"

"With these Italian genes? I've got thirteen nieces and nephews. Two more in the oven as we speak. My brother in Pittsburgh's got a wife that pops them out like toaster pastries." He glanced at his watch. "Okay, let's move it. Sixty seconds of sprinting . . . go!"

I hurled myself around the track. The 5K race was in two weeks. I wasn't going to win it, but thanks to my training, I wouldn't make a fool of myself, either. After the minute, which felt like an hour, I slowed to a jog again. "You plan to have any of your own?" I asked, huffing. "Kids?"

"Someday. I'm in no hurry. God favors us men. We can spread our seed even when we need a gallon of Viagra to get it up. A woman in her thirties, though . . . I'll bet your clock's ticking like a bomb."

"It wasn't before. I mean, I knew I wanted kids. But I was never panicked about it. Now all of a sudden I am."

He mulled it over and then said, "Makes perfect sense. It's like how sometimes you don't feel hungry. But you go by a fast-food place and smell the food. Next thing you know, you're starved. It's not that you didn't need food before. You just didn't know how hungry you were until food came along."

"Exactly!" Who knew Martucci was so wise? "But why is it," I asked him, "you think I've made up my mind?"

"You told me point-blank when you got here that you were going to adopt a kid in a couple months."

I stopped in my tracks. "I did?"

Martucci circled back around and stood jogging in place in front of me. "Yeah."

"Just like that? I said it?"

He reminded me of the conversation, and

he was right. I'd said it. Popped out of my mouth. *I'm going to adopt a kid in a few months.* It hadn't been "I might" or "Maybe I will." I'd said, "I'm going to." That was when I realized. It wasn't a decision of the mind. Or even of the heart.

It was pure gut.

And my gut said yes.

Yes, yes, yes!

"Oh, my God!" I said. "I'm going to be a mother!"

"Congratulations."

"Thanks." My mind swirled with endorphins and excitement. Even my elbows felt buzzy. Oh, I knew there was still much to do before anything was 100 percent certain. I'd need to get a lawyer that specialized in this sort of thing, or at the very least download legal forms off the Internet. I'd have to sit down with Deedee and her mom to work out the kinks. But there was no doubt in my mind, or in my belly, anyway: I'd do what it took to make it happen.

"So what's your family say about this?" Martucci asked.

"I haven't told them. I haven't told anybody."

"I'm the first to know?"

"Guess so."

"Parker, I'm honored." He grabbed me

271

and engulfed me in a hug. I cringed as sweat poured off him, running down my neck and soaking through my clothes. Although, I reminded myself, I was about to be a mom (!), so I'd need to get used to dealing with bodily fluids as bad as or worse than this. "I had no idea you thought so much of me," Martucci said, releasing me from the hug.

I used my shirt to wipe up his sweat. "Are you kidding? You're my jogging buddy."

No need to hurt his feelings. Martucci had been easy to tell. He was the flagpole I'd run it up, confident that he'd salute. I suspected the other people in my life might not be quite so easy to win over.

CHAPTER 16

#3 Change someone's life
#5 Run a 5K
#7 Make Buddy Fitch pay
#15 Take Mom and Grandma to see Wayne Newton
#16 Get a massage
#19 Show my brother how grateful I am for him
#20 Make a big donation to charity

With seven weeks left until Marissa's birthday, I called an emergency meeting at the Brass Monkey. A bar near work famous for its happy hour, it was also the scene of the crime, where I'd kissed the busboy months prior. Although today must've been his day off. Or he'd quit, tired of sexual harassment from the customers. Maybe he'd spotted me and was hiding in the back. At any rate, I didn't see him.

I'd gathered the troops — Susan, Brie,

and Martucci — promising I'd buy all the two-dollar margaritas they could suck down. Because I needed help. Desperately.

The cold, hard truth: I was getting scared. Marissa had started the list with two items crossed off. I'd completed eleven. Seven remained. Although I'm no math genius, even I could see that I had to pick up the pace if I was to succeed. And, true to form, I'd left the hardest for last. Sure, I could rally. But with so much of my focus now on adopting the baby, I feared I might not.

It was karaoke night, so once again the place was hopping. And for the record, there wasn't enough tequila in my drink, and perhaps in the world, to make me sing karaoke. I gave a prayer of thanks to Marissa on a daily basis that she hadn't put that on her list. Nonetheless, the singing served as a lively backdrop, and who doesn't enjoy hearing "I Will Survive" being bludgeoned by two drunk Japanese ladies?

The four of us sat at a corner table, shoveling chips into our mouths and poring over the list. I clarify: not the list itself. To avoid the risk that drinks might get spilled on the original list, I'd written the remaining tasks on a separate piece of paper. Marissa's list had become like the Declaration of Independence — a priceless document to be protected in a glass box (or in this case, my wallet) until such time as it was ready to be presented and toured about to the masses.

"We know what you're going to do to change someone's life." Martucci beamed, riding high on the fact that he was the first to know about the adoption.

"I can't believe you're gonna have a kid," Brie added.

Susan's fingers tapped on the list. "Although a backup plan might be a good idea . . . in case the adoption doesn't go through."

"It'll go through," I said with more confidence than I felt.

Two weeks ago, after my revelation to Martucci, I'd hired a lawyer. There were so many factors to work out that I hadn't thought about, such as paying for hospital extras, the birth father's rights, and so on. But so far, so good. Deedee started crying when I told her I was going to adopt the baby — that was, after having Kip call her mother to make sure Maria was okay with the plan. On the couple of visits I'd had with Deedee since then, she'd chattered endlessly about how it was going to be so cool when she and I were *both* big sisters.

Although the adoption smacked strangely of a business deal at this point, I knew it would feel real the moment I held the baby in my arms. Still, I was trying to stay on the down low in case everything fell through. I hadn't even mentioned it to my parents. It was hard enough to keep my own emotions from spiraling out of control — it'd be cruel to tell them they were going to be grandparents only to snatch it away.

Of the handful of people I'd told so far, the only negative reaction was from Susan, which didn't surprise me. She kept asking, "But why?" so many times that I started to wonder if I were actually talking to her five-year-old sons. About the hundredth time she'd said, "I never got the feeling that a baby was that important to you," I'd turned to her and snapped, "That's because it never felt *possible* before. I also don't walk around talking about how I want to sleep with Orlando Bloom, but believe me: The day he shows up wearing nothing but a towel and asking me if I'll rub lotion on his back, the answer, for the record, is, Hell, yes."

"A backup plan's not a bad idea," Martucci said, shaking me from my thoughts. "In case you fail at changing this girl's life. What else could you do?"

We sat silent. A beefy guy in a cowboy hat sang that country song about living like you

276

were dying. A good choice since he was in fact dying onstage.

"Money," Brie said. "I always say, 'Money changes everything.'"

"Cyndi Lauper said it first," I joked, only to meet a table of blank stares. "It was a song! Don't make me go get that karaoke list and prove it!"

Martucci smacked the table excitedly. "Lottery tickets! You buy a hundred lottery tickets and hand them out to people you know. One of them hits, and boom, you've changed that person's life."

"Ooh, that's a good one," Brie said, and then turned to me. "I got Lotto numbers I play, so ask me before you buy mine. I always play my age, my birthday, the number of guys I've had sex with —"

"Lotto numbers only go up to forty-six," Martucci said, and chortled.

"I know. That's why I got to split it up."

"It's settled, then. Even though I'm certain that the adoption will work out" — here I narrowed my eyes at Susan as if daring her to challenge me — "the Lotto is the backup plan. So that's one down, six to go. Moving things along . . ."

"What's your rush? You may as well enjoy your nights out while you can," Susan purred. "It's the last you'll have of them for a long while. That's how it is when you have kids."

I scowled at her. "You're out. You have kids."

"They're home with my *husband.* Do you have one of those?"

Ouch.

My expression must have shown the sting because she said, "I'm sorry. That was out of line. I'm worried about you, that's all. Being a single mother isn't easy — believe me, I know plenty of them. But I'll play nice. I promise."

"All's forgiven," I replied, and I meant it. For every bit of haranguing Susan was giving me, I knew she'd also be the first to help me when the time came. Lord knew I'd need plenty of baby-sitting.

"Next: *Run a 5K,*" Martucci read from the list. "That will be handled this weekend, you stud muffin."

"Martucci's running with me," I told Brie and Susan. "Anyone is welcome to join us. Brie . . . you run?"

"Depends." She shoved a chip in her mouth. "Somebody chasing me?"

"I'll take that as a no."

Susan promised to bring Chase and the boys to cheer for me, and then it was on to one of the more troublesome on the list:

#7, *Make Buddy Fitch pay.*

I reported to them how Sebastian had recently called me with an update. His private investigator had searched the United States and found three guys named Buddy Fitch. There was a sixty-eight-year-old retiree in Florida, a thirty-seven-year-old autoworker in Michigan, and a forty-four-year-old in Texas, currently unemployed. That was it. Sebastian explained that it had been particularly challenging, with Buddy being a common nickname. For all we know, he'd said, Buddy could've been a special name between him and Marissa. It might be a dead end. Crossing my fingers for luck, I'd called the Buddys. I'd told each one that I believed he knew a Marissa Jones and that he might want to know she'd passed away recently. And I'd turned up nothing.

"They claimed they'd never heard of her," I moped.

"You should've said she left them something in her will," Brie said. "I bet that'd jog their memories."

My heart sank. "That would have been perfect! Like those police stings where they bring in a bunch of criminals and tell them they've won a prize. I blew it! Now I'm no further than when I started."

"Not necessarily," Martucci said. "The list says, *Make Buddy Fitch pay.* It doesn't say *which* Buddy Fitch. So choose one of them and do something vengeful. I vote for the autoworker. Can't pick on a retiree or some guy out of a job. That'd be low."

Susan was appalled. "And arbitrarily playing a trick on someone because he happens to have the right name *isn't?*"

"Susan's right," I said reluctantly.

"It doesn't have to be real mean," Brie suggested. "You could do something a little mean. Like short-sheet his bed."

"Right. I'm going to fly to Michigan to short-sheet a guy's bed."

She shrugged. "All I know is that *I'd* hate it. Gotta stretch my legs at night. Otherwise they cramp up."

"We'll back-burner this one, I guess." I sighed. "Sebastian told me his PIs would keep working on it. Plus I contacted Troy Jones to see if he'd ask around one more time. *Somebody* Marissa knew must be able to tell us who this guy is. Which now brings us to number fifteen on the list. I have to take Mom and Grandma to see Wayne Newton in Las Vegas."

"Your mom and grandma or hers?" Brie asked.

"Hers."

Susan's brows furrowed. "Are you sure Wayne Newton is in Vegas?"

"He has a regular gig there," Martucci answered, and then opened his eyes wide in protest. "Don't all of you smirk at me. It's common knowledge."

"It is," I agreed. "There are tickets still available for his weekend shows during the next few months."

Brie guffawed. "That's a shocker."

"And," I continued, "at my request, Troy checked with his mom and grandma. They're going to make themselves available for whatever date works for me. He says they're quite excited."

"Really?" Susan asked. "I realize they're grateful you're doing the list. But I can't imagine how they must feel . . . losing a child. Nothing could be worse. Aren't you worried that it's going to be . . ." Her voice trailed off, searching for the right word.

"Weird?" I supplied. "Uncomfortable? Potentially the worst, most miserable trip to Vegas in the history of my trips to Vegas, and that includes the time somebody stole my purse and I got a sunburn so bad my eyelids swelled shut? Yes. I am worried about that. Thank you for reminding me."

I had no clue how I'd pull it off. I'd met them only once, at the funeral, and I'd spoken as few words as possible. According to Troy, this list was such a bright light for them. How could any trip to Las Vegas possibly measure up to their expectations? Especially a trip on my budget.

I started to outline my idea — that I'd drive the Joneses to Vegas, we'd see the show, stay the night, and come back the next morning — when Martucci cut me off. "You can't do it half-assed. From what you're talking about, they probably had more fun at the funeral. This needs to be a party. Keep 'em busy and keep 'em drunk."

"A party? I don't know if I have what it takes to pull off something so —"

"Of course you don't," he agreed. "I've got it covered. I know a fellow at the Flamingo."

"Is this like your friend who runs the gas station?" I asked. "The one who's suing us?"

Susan shook her head. "He dropped the lawsuit. Bigwood wouldn't go into details. I don't know if the guy realized he didn't have a case. Or maybe he was satisfied that an employee was let go. Either way, it's a done deal. No lawsuit."

I hadn't realized how the lawsuit had still been nagging at me until I felt my body release the worry. It was over. Nobody else much seemed to care. It was as if the threat had never even happened, save for the fact that Lizbeth got fired.

"So as I was saying," Martucci continued, "I'll tell my buddy we might give away free trips to Las Vegas as part of a rideshare contest, and we're on a reconnaissance mission to check it out. He'll comp us rooms. Shit, Vegas this time of year? It's so damn hot they're giving away hotel stays in cereal boxes to get people out there."

"We?" I asked. "*We* are on recon mission?"

"I'll drive the Rideshare Mobile. There's plenty of room for the mom and grandma, too." He sat back triumphantly. "And there you have it, Parker. A party."

"I'm in," Brie said. "I'm good with moms and grandmas."

Susan gave me a pleading look. It said, *Don't make me go, please don't make me go.* Susan hates everything about Vegas — the noise, the buffets, the smoking. She doesn't understand why people would pump a hundred dollars in a slot machine and get nothing when they could use that money to buy nicer shoes. The shows are tacky. Everyone wanders around drunk. In other words, everything I love about the town. But is she a friend or what? Because even though she'd rather eat the margarita glass she was holding, she'd go if I wanted her to. I did want her help, but nobody likes a wet blanket in Vegas.

"Martucci," I said, "that sounds fantastic. And Susan, you're excused — you don't have to go."

Her exhale of relief nearly blew me from the table. I picked up the list again. "Las Vegas also takes care of a couple of these others. Number sixteen: *Get a massage.* Easy enough. And number twenty: *Make a big donation to charity.* I'll simply win a fortune at roulette and then give it away."

Martucci and Brie nodded in agreement, but Susan cried, "You can't count on that! Do you have any idea the odds of winning?"

"Thirty-five to one on a straight-up bet," Martucci answered.

She threw up her hands. "Whatever."

"I guess that's it," I announced. "I want to thank you guys for coming and for your —"

Brie grabbed the paper from me. "What about this one? Number nineteen. Says, *Show my brother how grateful I am for him.*"

"Huh?" I tried to make my face go blank.

"Your brother or her brother?" Martucci asked.

I slumped down in my seat. "My brother."

"I keep forgetting you have a brother,"

Susan said. "Isn't that terrible?"

"What — is he an asshole or something?" Brie asked.

"He's fine. It's only that 'grateful' is such a strong word."

"So what are you going to do?" Susan asked.

"I've got that fund-raiser party at my parents' house in a couple weeks." I paused to look at Susan. "You and Chase are coming, right?"

"I wouldn't miss your dad's shrimp cocktail for the world."

"My brother and his wife, Charlotte, will be there, too. So my idea was . . ." I hesitated because it was so weak. "That I'd write a letter and tell him what a good brother he was. Give it to him there. Even if I have to make stuff up." I braced myself, waiting for the mockery.

"That's nice."

"Yeah."

"I'd love to get a letter like that."

"You really think so?" I asked.

"You know what'd be good," Brie added. "Put a picture of the two of you together in it. Maybe from when you were kids. You got a nice picture?"

My mind flashed to a photo my mom kept framed on the mantel. In it, Bob and I are babies — I'm lying on my side on the floor, and he's making an expression of surprise. My mom said he used to do that to me when I'd first learned how to sit. He'd tip me over and then pretend it was an accident.

"I'm not sure about the picture," I said.

As I tucked the wet, salsa-stained list in my purse — good thing I hadn't brought out the original — a baritone voice so deep that it nearly vibrated my chair said behind me, "Pardon me . . ."

I turned around to see a man the size of a tank and the color of hot coffee who was flashing a smile so striking that it was making other parts of me vibrate . . . until I realized that the killer grin was aimed at Brie. "There's been a terrible mistake," he said smoothly. "I'll have to talk to the bar owner. Because how could they be so foolish as to hide such a lovely lady away in a corner?"

"Crying shame, ain't it?" Brie agreed.

He held up a karaoke list book. "Perhaps . . . a duet?"

She grabbed her purse and slid off her chair. Then she took his hand and walked away without so much as a glance good-bye.

"I'd better get going, too," Susan said. "You want a ride?"

We left Martucci to cheer Brie on, both of us blinking from the sunlight when we walked outside. It'd been so dark in the bar, it was easy to forget it was only six o'clock.

As we walked to the car, Susan said, "I can't believe you're going to Las Vegas with Martucci. He's so" — she wrinkled her nose — "smarmy. And what's with that little ponytail?"

"Rattail."

"It looks like a caterpillar crawling up his neck."

"Aw, Martucci's not so bad once you get to know him," I said. "He's just rough around the edges."

CHAPTER 17

Martucci twisted, hands on his waist, warming up for the run. The morning of the 5K race was cool, with a gray, heavy sky that we at the beach call haze but anywhere else they'd call drizzle. "Here we are. Together again. Can't get enough of me, can you, Parker."

"You consume my every waking thought," I replied, pulling my leg behind me to stretch my thigh muscle.

"Damn. Not in the dreams yet. It'll happen . . . only a matter of time."

I'd worn a tank top, stretchy shorts, and a sports bra so industrial that it could hold the lid on a boiling pot. Martucci was in a similar outfit — only minus the bra and with a terrycloth band around his head. Later, when the sun peeked through the gloom I'd be glad not to be overdressed, but for now I had shivers and goose bumps all over. Or maybe that was the thought of

Martucci showing up in my dreams.

Hundreds of people stretched and jogged in place around us. The race was due to start in fifteen minutes. It would begin at the pier in Manhattan Beach and then proceed through town — a town, I noticed on the drive over, that was much hillier than I'd remembered. I hadn't encountered anyone from my cheering section yet, but they'd promised to be there, standing near the finish line so we could go to breakfast after the race. Not only was Susan bringing her family, but Kip and Sebastian were coming, stopping to pick up Deedee on the way.

"By the way, we're set for Vegas," Martucci said. "I scored rooms at the Flamingo."

"Oh, good!"

"Last weekend in June. Friday and Saturday night. My contact there coughed up three rooms. I figure that's a room for me, one for you and Brie to share, and one for Mom and Grandma."

"Perfect."

"Damn shame I couldn't swing getting you your own room — you about to be a mother and all. You need to find a stud and have a last fling."

"Forget it. There will be no flinging."

"I don't know . . . from what I hear, babies

suck up a lot of your energy. It could be a long time before you get any action. Maybe months."

Months? Ha! "I once went three years without sex," I said.

I might as well have slapped him. His eyes welled up. "My *God.* How did you stand it?" His hand grasped my shoulder as he said earnestly, "We're friends, and I want you to understand that I'm here for you. And that I'm not above a mercy fuck."

"Thanks. I can't tell you how much I appreciate the offer. But I'm going to Vegas for one reason and one reason only: to get things done on the list. Anything else is —"

Before I could finish, a kid bumped into Martucci and sent him stumbling into me. "Watch it, buddy!" he snapped.

"Dude, it was an accident." The kid appeared to be about ten years old, with red hair, wiry limbs, and wall-to-wall freckles on his face. "You okay?"

"He's fine," I said. "He didn't mean to yell."

"Yes, I did," Martucci snarled. "Crap. My ankle's twisted." He sat on the ground to examine his ankle, and the boy bent over him. Above the race number he wore on his back he'd written in thick marker "Flash."

"Flash?" I asked. "What's with that?"

He turned to me with a smile. "That's what my dad calls me. 'Cause I'm so fast."

Martucci motioned to the boy to help him up. "I saw a guy selling sodas by the pier. I'm going to see if he has ice."

"I'll go," the boy said, and he was off, as they say, in a flash. Minutes later, he returned with cupfuls of ice and paper towels. We wrapped Martucci's ankle.

"Is it a sprain?" I asked. "Should we hop you to a medic?"

"It'll be fine, but I'll need to keep off it," he said to me. "Afraid you're on your own for the race."

"On my own?" Hands on hips, I gazed bleakly up at the hills. "Boy, I wished we'd trained on hills."

"You never ran hills?" Flash asked.

"Not a one. Not so much as an incline. Plus, I'm used to this guy barking orders at me," I said, tipping my head toward Martucci.

"What's your time?" the boy asked.

"I'm running a nine-minute mile."

He nodded, considering it. "Be right back."

The race organizers started lining people up to start, so I did my final stretches. Martucci coached me from the curb. "Keep your pace. When you get to a hill, you're naturally going to slow down. Don't let it intimidate you. And nothing flashy, Parker. You just want to make it to the finish line."

"Got it."

He held out a fist to me. When I stared at him, perplexed, he said, "You're supposed to tap my hand with yours. Like 'rock' in rock-paper-scissors. It's a jock thing."

Jeez, what happened to plain, old-fashioned high-fives? I did it, then left to line up in my spot. People jockeyed for position around me, even though this was a community event and not a hard-core race. Trying to ignore everyone, I jogged in place, waiting for the pop gun to signal "go," when the boy came up next to me.

"Hey, Flash," I greeted him. "What's up?"

"Don't jog so hard right now. Move back and forth a little bit or you'll wear yourself out." I did what he suggested, and he said, "My dad said it's all right if I run with you."

"Thanks, but you don't have to do that. I don't want to slow you down or —"

"I injured your trainer. It's only fair."

With that, the gun sounded and we were off. Instantly, it was as if everyone were running through a sieve. The fast ones slipped through to the front, and the rest of us found our places slogging along at our own paces.

We started along the Strand, the board-
walk that runs adjacent to the sand, with
the ocean to our left and multimillion-dollar
homes to our right. A light breeze blew off
the water, and my body kicked effortlessly
into gear. My training was paying off. I tried
to make conversation with Flash, but he put
a stop to that, saying, "Lady, if you can talk,
you're not running hard enough."

I'll be darned — he was a mini Martucci.

A mile later, we turned up a street to run
past shops and restaurants and — yum! I
smelled pancakes! One more turn and, "Oh
no, look at that hill — it's a wall!"

"You can do it," Flash assured me. "Go
like this —" He showed me how to lean
forward a bit. "And then follow my pace."

"Isn't there supposed to be special equip-
ment for mountain climbing?" I huffed ir-
ritably. Ow. Ugh. Arrrrgh. Errrrgh. "Don't
you get —"

"Don't talk," he admonished. "Run."

Muscles arguing and protesting all the
way, I made it to the top. Flash high-fived
me without breaking stride. "I knew you
had it in you!"

That was the steepest hill, and after that
the run was cake. The route wound us
around so we ended not far from where we
began. Yards from the finish line, I heard

my name being screamed, along with cat-calls and various inspirations such as "Work it, honey!" and "You go, girl!" I gave a victory wave to my pep squad and then, heart pumping, crossed the finish line. Twenty-nine minutes. Not bad, considering the hills.

There were plenty of runners doing their postrun stretch — for all I knew, a few were already home eating bon-bons. But I'd made it, and not even in last place. Not even close to last. It was especially sweet since I'd never successfully done anything athletic before in my life. My sports history was tragic. Like in fourth grade when my brother talked me into signing up for softball, where it turned out that the only skill I learned was the art of the deal. I'd negotiate with the pitcher, the shortstop, and the third baseman as I ran out to left field, briefing them on the ways they were to cover for me should the ball come my way. But nobody had to cover for me today. I was officially a jock.

My cheering squad came over as I ruffled Flash's hair. "Thanks for the help, Coach. I couldn't have done it without you."

"Yes, you could," he said, his freckled face serious. "You can do anything. I believe in you. Remember that."

"Okay, then," I said, not knowing quite

what to make of him. I had to marvel as I watched him jog back to his dad. How did these children come into my life all of a sudden? Where had they been? Were they always there and just hiding?

A towel hit me in the head. "Nice job, champ," Martucci said.

"Why, thank you."

After that, Susan, Chase, and the twins, Martucci, Kip, Sebastian, Deedee, and I all went to breakfast at Uncle Bill's, the pancake house I'd passed during the race. Sitting at the table, I couldn't help but smile at the ragtag crew I'd assembled over the past few months. C.J. spilled the syrup onto Joey's lap. Kip kept eating off Sebastian's plate. Susan started absently cutting her husband's pancakes before Martucci pointed out what she was doing, and we spent the next ten minutes making fun of her.

But it was Deedee who brought down the house when she blurted, "Shhh, hold on," and then grabbed my hand to place it on her belly.

And there it was. The baby kicking.

It was as if the room and its noises and people disappeared and the only thing that I could see or hear or smell or taste buzzed up through my fingertips.

This wasn't a business deal anymore.

This was a child.

And I'd never before been so close to holding her.

CHAPTER 18

"You sound like a jealous wife," Phyllis teased. "Are you going to start checking his collars for lipstick?"

I'd spotted Lou Bigwood getting into the elevator with a woman. A beautiful woman. She was the third I'd seen him with that week. Naturally, I sprinted to Phyllis's office to get the story. Why I bothered I didn't know. All she'd tell me was the woman's name and company. I could've gotten that reading the sign-in sheet at the reception desk — which I'd already done.

"Is he interviewing people for Lizbeth's job?" I asked.

"No."

I narrowed my eyes at her suspiciously. That had been too easy. "Now let me put it another way: Could one of these women possibly be given Lizbeth's job?"

"Yes."

I flailed my arms. "So he *is* interviewing, then!"

"No. Lou doesn't interview."

Talking to Phyllis was like going down the rabbit hole. Nothing quite made sense, yet everything was clear. I needed to make my move soon.

Whatever it might be. I still hadn't a clue what might impress the boss into giving me the promotion I so richly deserved. "How long do you figure I have?" I asked, bracing myself for another of Phyllis's noncommittal answers.

"Hard to say."

"Suppose there's a gun to your head. Then what would you guess?"

"Three weeks."

"Really? That fast?"

"No, but there's a gun to my head. I'll say anything."

I had Phyllis schedule me for a meeting with Bigwood a few weeks away — a Friday afternoon before he was due to go out of town for a conference. It was vital that I get to him before he left. He'd met Lizbeth at a conference. I couldn't risk a repeat performance. Even though I had plenty on my plate already, I'd never forgive myself if I let him hire another little lovely — someone with that mix of aggression and beauty that seemed to draw him — while I sat by and did nothing.

My phone was ringing when I got back to my cubicle. I picked it up, and it was Troy. As soon as I heard him say hello, I felt my lips turn up and my IQ involuntarily drop. Yes, the crush was in full effect. Getting worse, in fact. Troy had been acting as go-between to help me work out a plan for Vegas with his mom and grandma. We'd exchanged brief, polite phone messages rather than actual calls so far, but they were enough to send my blood pulsing.

The trip to Las Vegas was set for the last weekend in June, and he'd said his mom and grandma were looking forward to it. In fact, everything seemed so tied together, I was surprised to hear from him now.

Unless something was wrong. Maybe they'd changed their minds.

I gnawed on a fingernail. "What's up?"

"Oh, it's you," he said, sounding surprised. "I expected your voice mail."

"I can take a message for me if you'd prefer."

"The real thing's much better." We exchanged the usual *how are yous;* then he said, "I'm calling to offer my services if you think you might need me in Vegas."

Services? "What — escort?"

"Actually, yes. If you need help with Mom and Gran, I'd be glad to do what I can." Then he added hurriedly, "Of course, I'd get myself up there . . . book my own room."

I found myself saying, Of course, come on up. The more the merrier. But concerned by what might be underlying his offer, I added, "Are you sure your mom and grandma are comfortable with this trip? Because it's not worth doing it for the list if it's going to make them —"

"They're excited, I promise, although I'd be lying if I said there won't be sad moments for them. That's why I thought it might be good if I was there. Just in case."

In case what? Susan's comment about how losing a child was the worst possible thing she could imagine floated back to me. Was this too much to ask of a grieving mom? I had no way of knowing if he was being honest about their being up for the trip, but I decided to trust him. "Okay," I said. "But you don't have to go up on your own. You can ride with us. We're leaving Friday at three."

"I appreciate the offer, but I've got a meeting that afternoon," he said. "I'll ride the bike up, so I'll probably get there before you anyway."

"Yeah? You believe that your motorcycle

can take our Rideshare Mobile?"

"You don't really call it that, do you?"

"Sure do. It's a thirty-foot motor home with the words painted on the side in giant letters. I hope your mom and grandma have a high tolerance for embarrassment."

"They're Wayne Newton fans — of course they do. And yes, I can beat you there. I'll get to ride around traffic. You'll be stuck in it."

"Ah, but you're forgetting that we can use the carpool lane."

As soon as I said it, it struck me. I must have gasped because he said, "Everything okay?"

"You're a genius."

"Thank you for noticing. Any reason in particular you're telling me now?"

"You gave me a great idea for work."

"Just now?"

"Yeah, and it might get good media. There's even a chance this one won't cause rioting in the streets."

"That's too bad," he said. "I've come to expect exciting things to happen when you're around."

Friday night, I sat in my apartment, reeling with frustration. I'd spent hours rummaging through photo albums and yearbooks, only to come up empty-handed. The next day was my parents' party, where I'd give my brother the letter showing him how grateful I was for him. I ought to be able to come up with one tender moment to reminisce about, but I couldn't.

Dear Bob:

I'm writing to express my gratitude for the time that you and your friends decided it would be "funny" to pin my junior year homecoming date against the wall and ask him what his intentions were with me. Hilarious!

Love,
June

P.S. It was especially amusing because, although he and I only went to the dance as friends, I believe he may have wet himself.

Dear Bob:

I can't thank you enough for keeping a photo of me wearing my eye patch in your wallet and showing it around as often as possible. How many girls have a brother who carries a photo of them? I'm flattered and, it goes without saying, grateful.

Shiver me timbers,

June

Dear Bob:

Please accept my most humble gratitude for the people you brought into my life — especially all the girls who pretended to be my friends, only to spend the entire time fawning over you once they got to the house. Your popularity and magnetism remain an inspiration.

Yours in family and friendship,

June

Dear Bob:

Words cannot express my appreciation for my recent weekend visit to your home, during which you took off for a golf outing the second I arrived. It was a great chance for Charlotte and me to bond. She cooked delicious meals, and we went shopping and watched movies together and did girl stuff, even though, at least according to birth records, *you* are my actual relative.

Warmest regards from your sister,

June

Dear Bob:

How on earth did you ever get Charlotte to marry you? She's so genuine and warm, and I like her a lot. Did you blackmail her?

June

"Hello?" My mom sounded wary when she answered the phone.

"What's wrong?" I asked. "Did I catch you at a bad time?"

"Oh, it's you, honey. No, it's fine. I thought you were somebody calling to cancel. This is always the point when guests start pooping out. The Kolesars just called to say they're going up north. Your father and I have been holding this party the exact same weekend for ten years, and they RSVPed a month ago."

"I'll be there," I assured her.

"Well, then that's one for certain. Hope you're hungry."

The party was the annual fund-raiser for a scholarship my dad helped start in memory of his best friend, George Ku, a teacher who died of cancer. It's fifty bucks a head and all the food and drinks you can stuff down. It usually draws a crowd of a hundred or so. I was feeling guilty because normally I'd help out with the chopping and dicing and whatnot — I'm not much of a cook, but I make a fine scullery maid. But I'd been avoiding my parents as of late, tempted to blurt that I was going to adopt Deedee's baby but not wanting to say anything until it was certain.

"I know you're busy," I said, "but can I run something by you?"

"Sure. I'm spinning the lettuce. I can do that and talk at the same time."

"I'm working on the letter for Bob that I told you about. And I'm having trouble coming up with memories to share."

"Tell me what you have so far."

" 'Dear Bob.' "

Silence.

"That's it?"

"I was hoping you could fill in the blanks."

She sighed. "Was I such a horrible mother? How could you not have a single happy memory from your childhood?"

"I have plenty of happy memories. Remember that time we went to New York and realized that we'd accidentally left Bob home alone? And then we . . . Oh, wait . . . that was a movie."

"You love your brother!" she insisted.

"Sure I love him. He's my brother. Only there are times I don't particularly like him."

"Bob was a wonderful brother to you."

My hands were poised at my computer keyboard. "In what way," I asked cagily, "would you say he was a wonderful brother? And try to speak in complete sentences."

"Oh, for Pete's sake. Okay. How about when he signed you up for softball?"

"That was one of the worst experiences in my life!"

"I thought it was sweet how he went to all your games."

"He went to my games?"

"Didn't miss a one. It wasn't his fault you were terrible. No offense. I'm only going by what you told me."

My fingers typed away: *Bob, I'll never forget seeing your face there in the stands, cheering me on. . . .* "What else you got?"

"Oh, hold on." She shouted away from the phone. "Martin! The water's boiling!" Then back: "Let's see . . . there were so many things. You always put on those cute plays for us . . . charged a dollar admission. And how about that time we saw the movie *The Birds*? He walked you home from school every day for a week because you had this crazy idea that you were going to get attacked."

"That movie was terrifying!" As I typed, *Bob, you've always been my protector,* I made a mental note to never let *my* child watch such a scary film. What were my parents thinking?

"Goodness . . . Oh, hang on again, the pan's boiling over." The phone was set down, and I heard clattering and shouting to my dad about whether or not he wanted the stove turned off.

When she finally came back, I said, "Sounds like you have things to handle there. I'll let you go."

"I do need to run to the store again." There was a pause, and then she said, "But sweetie? Give your brother a chance. I know he wasn't always overly affectionate when you were growing up. He could be a bit of a pill. But the two of you had your moments. You were always watching TV or playing games or listening to those albums. You know, he's changed over the years. You should see him with Charlotte. He dotes on her, treats her like a queen. I don't know, maybe he needed to grow up. And — now, don't be mad at me for saying this — but maybe you don't always give him a fair shake."

After hanging up, I went back to typing the letter, wishing I'd set out to show my gratitude to my brother in an easier way — like baking him a pan of brownies or offering to wash his car. Still, I managed to scrape together a few reasons I was grateful to have him as a brother. Turned out Sebastian Forbes wasn't the only one around here who could write fiction.

Mrs. Mankowski waved a shrimp in the air. "If I were going to die tomorrow, I'd go skydiving."

"Good heavens!" my dad replied, clearly horrified. "I'd much rather die in my sleep."

My mom had to explain, "Martin, I believe she meant *before* she died."

The list was the talk of the annual Ku party. I'd been there since two o'clock, and in that time I'd learned more than I ever wanted to know about my parents' friends' unfulfilled dreams. Lots of skydiving, traveling, scuba diving, ballroom dancing, and novel writing has gone undone, I'll tell you that. Poor old Mrs. Gorman said she wanted to learn a foreign language, and her husband — who'd taken to finishing her sentences because she kept forgetting what she was going to say — snorted, "Why don't you start with English?"

As soon as I saw my brother's wife, Charlotte, I was glad I hadn't brought up the adoption yet. She was easily thirty pounds heavier than I'd seen her last. More than that, she looked dour and bloated. Her normally heart-shaped face seemed to have tipped upside down, and her blond hair hung limp and dull. I've heard those hormone shots are miserable. If you're going through that and are, to date, still childless, I'm assuming babies in general are a sore subject. I'd called Susan before the party and told her to remind Chase that the subject was off-limits. I knew he got the message, because as soon as he walked in, he caught my eye and pantomimed turning a key at his lips.

After a few hours, the party had dwindled to immediate family, Susan and Chase, and a few assorted neighbors. The sun was going down, and the blazing Valley heat was finally ebbing. My parents had fans and misters going all day — it'd been a scorcher. We sat on lawn chairs in a circle on the patio, that lazy party-almost-over feeling setting in.

I took a swig of my light beer, my beverage of choice for the day. My dad makes a killer mai tai, but I don't go near them. Those babies sneak up on you. "I don't get the attraction to skydiving," I said. "Knowing me, I'd leap into midair and then realize I forgot to wear my parachute. Or I'd be wearing my parachute, but I wouldn't even have fun because I'd be so worried about pulling my cord on time."

Susan — who apparently didn't get the memo about the mai tais — slurred, "As shoon ash the boysh are grown, I'm gonna shkydive. Ish my life'sh dream." Chase caught my eye and winked. The wink said, *Bet I'm going to get booty tonight — and it's not even a holiday.*

"How about you, Bob?" my mom asked. "What would be on your list?"

"Hard to say. At this point in my life, I don't worry about those sorts of things. I've got Charlotte, a great house, a solid job . . . I don't need to 'do' things to feel fulfilled."

Hello — was that my brother who said that? It *looked* like my brother. Same brown, short-cropped hair, same Delaney nose, same teen idol dimples. It was starting to make sense why Charlotte couldn't get pregnant — aliens had obviously kidnapped my brother and were wearing his body as a disguise.

My mom shot me a look. *See?*

Charlotte beamed. "Can you believe this guy?"

Susan lifted her mai tai to take a sip but missed her mouth. "That'sh beautiful, Bob. Jush beautiful."

"That's what I'm always trying to tell my brother," my dad chimed in. "He's always boasting about how his kids did this and that . . . one's a doctor . . . one's a big la-de-da producer. And I think, *What a blowhard. My* kids won't wind up doing a damn important thing in their lives! They won't save anybody's life! Won't write a novel! Hell, my daughter's pushing forty and she's not even married!"

"I'm thirty-four!" I sputtered.

"And you know what?" he continued. "That's because we Parkers know what life's about. It's about being with your friends, drinking and having a good meal, listening to Roy Orbison on the stereo. It's not about your silly doctorates and your 4.0 grade-point averages."

He lifted his glass in a toast in the fading light, and we all did the same, with me wishing my father could learn a new form of bragging.

"Well, I'm glad there are only six things left to do," I said, bringing the discussion back to the list. "Then I can go back to being the same lovable loser I used to be."

Mrs. Mankowski preened at me. "So is there anything on the list about finding a husband?"

"Tick tock!" Mr. Mankowski felt compelled to add.

And to think I used to go over every summer and help those people make jelly.

"June will get married when she meets the right guy," my brother (or so he appeared to be) said.

"Thirty-four is nothing," Charlotte agreed. "And these things can happen so quickly. I'll bet one day she'll call out of the blue and surprise us. Tell us she's in love and getting married."

Just as I was wondering if I could sneak into the house and add an addendum to the gratitude letter I planned to give my brother before he left, Susan waved her mai tai around drunkenly and said, "Acshtually, June *doesh* have a big shurprishe!"

A chorus of "What!?" "Tell us!" "Surprise!?" rang up from the group.

I was going to kill her. "I don't know what she's talking about," I said, trying to make a face that said, *Who you going to believe: me or the drunk?*

"I'll bet you met a fellow!" Mrs. Mankowski cried. There was my answer.

"Ish a biiiiiiig shurprise."

"You'll have to excuse my wife," Chase said. "She tends to hallucinate when she drinks."

Mrs. Mankowski improved her guess. "She met a fellow and *she's engaged!*"

"The shuprishe ishn't a guy. Iish a gii-
iiiiirl."

Chase shushed Susan. My father paled.
"Oh dear." There was much clearing of
throats.

"Ish time you told everbody. The happy
day is almosht here!"

"Is that legal now?" Mr. Mankowski asked.

Susan was *so* going to pay for this. I was
going to reserve a spot in hell for her where
it's Las Vegas 24/7.

"I'm not a lesbian, okay?" I snapped. "The
surprise is not that I'm gay."

"Oh, thank goodness," my dad whimpered. "How would I ever face my brother?"

My mom elbowed him. "We would have
loved you anyway, honey."

"So, what *is* the surprise?" Bob asked.

Out of fear that Susan would blurt it out
anyway, I said, "It's not final, so that's why
I didn't want to say anything. But when
Deedee has her baby in August —"

"Deedee's her Little Shishter," Susan
provided helpfully.

"As I was saying, when she has the baby,
I'm going to adopt it."

If silence has a sound, then it became very,
very loud at that moment.

Susan broke the quiet. "June'sh gonna be
a mommy!"

"By yourself?" Mrs. Mankowski asked.

"Yeah. The girl's only fourteen, and she was going to raise the baby herself otherwise. And I've always wanted children, so it seemed . . ." I let my voice trail off. I don't know what reaction I was expecting, but this wasn't it.

My mom rubbed her forehead. "I don't even know what to say."

"Congrashulations! Thash what you shay!"

"We've caused enough damage. We'll be going now," Chase said, hefting Susan up. He nodded to my parents. "Thanks for the party."

"Yesh. Shank you very mush."

Charlotte jumped to her feet. "Congratulations," she managed to whisper through the tears that were starting. "That's wonderful news." She turned and ran into the house. Bob followed her.

It got quiet again, and then my dad said, "You're not adopting this baby with another woman, are you?"

I didn't dignify his question with an answer and instead went to check on Bob and Charlotte. When I got inside the house, Bob was wheeling a bag from his old bedroom.

"You're leaving?" I asked.

"Yeah. Charlotte's in the car."

"Bob, I'm sorry. I didn't want to say anything today."

"Don't worry about it. We're going to hit the road. I was about to come say goodbye."

"Mom told me everything you've been going through, and —"

"I've got to run . . . don't want to leave Charlotte sitting there."

"Can I go talk to her?"

He shook his head. "It's nothing personal, June. It's going to take her a while to wrap her head around your news. We've been wanting a baby for so long."

"But Mom told me you didn't want to adopt."

"It still hurts. That's all I can say." He reached an arm around me to give me a quick hug. "Congratulations."

"Thanks," I said softly. Then I handed him the letter in an envelope. "It's no rush reading it. Just stuff I wanted you to know."

From there, the Mankowskis couldn't scoot out fast enough. My parents and I cleaned up the party without a word about the baby. We were tipsy and tired, and the Parkers never talk about anything if it can possibly be avoided, and thank goodness, at that point it could.

■ ■ ■ ■

It wasn't until the next morning, over a breakfast of leftover tiny sandwiches, that I had a chance to discuss the baby with my mom. I let her tell me every parental horror story to try to dissuade me from making a rash decision. I nodded patiently and smiled as she outlined the sleepless nights and hurt knees and sassing back I could expect.

"Don't get me wrong," she said, sipping her coffee, elbows on the table, "I'm delighted I'm going to be a grandma. And you might have to get a bigger apartment to handle the stuff I plan to buy that kid. I just wonder if you've thought this through."

"Sometimes it's all I think about."

She set down her cup. "I'm going to play 'what if.' *What if* the perfect man comes around tomorrow and says, 'I want to marry you, but you have a child'?"

"Then he's hardly the perfect man, is he?"

"No," she replied. "I suppose not."

"Now let me play 'what if.' *What if* the perfect man never comes around?"

"Oh, sweetie," she said, clasping my hand across the table. "He will."

CHAPTER 19

At the last minute, Marissa's mom and grandma begged out of the ride I'd offered to Las Vegas. Instead, they said they'd fly up and meet us at the hotel. I suspected they weren't eager to spend five hours on the road trying to make conversation — which might have offended me had I not been dreading the very same thing. I'd need every minute of the drive to psych up for the weekend to come, which was why I was about to bitch-slap Brie if she didn't stop talking about what a long-ass drive this was, and why didn't we bring DVDs for the player?

It was eight o'clock by the time Martucci pulled the Rideshare Mobile into the Flamingo parking lot. We checked in and headed up to our rooms. Marissa's mom and grandma had already arrived, but Troy hadn't. (And, ha! I'd *told* him those carpool lanes would save us time. Plus, Martucci had driven straight through. Brie and I were able to use the bathroom in the motor home, and apparently Martucci had a bladder the size of an oil tanker.)

After calling Kitty Jones, Marissa's mom, to arrange for all of us to meet in the lobby in an hour, I collapsed on the bed.

"What is it about sitting that makes me so tired?" I whined. "It makes no sense."

Our room was your standard two beds, dresser, and TV. From the window we could see across to the Bellagio. The fountains in its man-made lake were in the middle of doing their laser water show. It was both beautiful and grotesque, considering how much water was being wasted in the middle of the desert.

Brie disappeared into the bathroom, and I closed my eyes to relax. The next thing I knew, she was saying, "C'mon, wake up! We got partying to do." When I opened my eyes, Brie stood over me, squeezed into a white halter top and white leather pants. Her hair — these days a shoulder-length weave streaked with hot pink — was pulled high in a ponytail.

"Darn," I said. "That's what I was going to wear."

"It's almost nine. I sure hope you plan to spiff up."

Begrudgingly, I dragged myself off the bed. This was nothing I was looking forward to — why had I let Martucci talk me into a party? I should have simply flown them up for the Wayne Newton concert and flown them home.

Too late for that now, I thought, dressing in a short skirt with no stockings, heels, and a fitted jacket over a tank top. I brushed my teeth, slapped on a bit of makeup, and fluffed my hair. A good long look in the mirror — followed by more makeup and fluffing — and I was ready to go.

"Okay, we've got to work out a code," Brie said. "If there's a sock on the door handle, it means don't come in."

"Oh hell, no. I'm getting a good night's sleep. Don't even think about bringing a man here."

"It's not like I'd let him spend the night."

"No! No men! Are we clear?"

"Every party needs a pooper, that's why we invited Ju—"

"Excuse me?"

"Fine. No need to get your panties in a bunch. I got it."

I'd arranged to meet Kitty and Grandma next to the giant six-foot slot machine in the lobby, and it was a good thing I'd been so specific. I'd have never recognized them otherwise. The grandma eluded my memory entirely, and Kitty Jones had seemed small and faded when I met her at the funeral — as if she'd been washed and run through the dryer at too high a heat. That was to say, nothing like the woman standing before me, who had a healthy at-the-beach glow. Mid-fifties, robust, and with a layered blond bob, she appeared so much the part of a California girl grown up that it seemed odd when I'd heard the twang of a midwest accent when she spoke.

"June, it's so nice to see you. I'm Kitty. You remember my mother, Mrs. Jameson?"

"Call me Gran. Everybody does," said the tiny woman next to her. She wore a velour tracksuit, and her curly hood of brunette hair was clearly a wig, which she adjusted without a hint of self-consciousness.

I introduced Brie and then asked, "How was your flight?"

"Went without a hitch," Kitty replied.

"Although you got to pay for a bag of peanuts," Gran barked. "Can you believe it? A dollar fifty for a lousy bag of peanuts that used to be free! And you can forget about getting a real meal."

"Oh, are you hungry?" I asked. "Because we could get dinner."

"Thank you, but we grabbed sandwiches

at the hotel deli," Kitty said.

"Eight-dollar sandwiches," Gran added. "You'd figure at that price it'd at least have had that fancy mustard, but nope. Plain old French's yellow."

"Whatever you do, don't drink the bottle of water in the room," Brie said, her voice a warning. "You assume it's free, but there's a small note on it that says it's three bucks. They're counting on you being too drunk to notice or too thirsty to care."

"I'd never be that thirsty," Gran said. I noted she didn't mention she'd never be that drunk.

"Hey, where's Martucci?" I asked, partly out of curiosity and partly because I was running out of small talk.

"He's our friend who drove," Brie explained before turning to me. "While you were doing your Sleeping Beauty thing, he texted me to say he was playing five-card stud. Unless we needed him, he'd see us in the morning."

Kitty glanced at her watch. "Troy should be down any minute, but I don't want to keep you waiting."

"No rush," I said. "The only thing I need to do is book a massage for tomorrow."

"That sounds divine," Kitty gushed. "Oh, would you mind terribly if we tagged along?

A girls' day at the spa might be fun. And then Wayne Newton in the evening. What a delightful trip this is going to be!"

I debated whether to mention that the massage was one of the items on the list but decided not to bring it up. It was so much easier to pretend that this was a typical Vegas getaway and not the strange odyssey that it was. The list at this point was the elephant in the living room — it was gigantic, and it smelled something awful, but damn it, we were all going to carry on a conversation around it as if it weren't there.

Kitty was ringing Troy to see where he was when he showed up — and talk about your cool drinks of water in the desert. Black slacks, a casual silky shirt, the beginnings of stubble along the jawline. Mmm.

"Look at you," Kitty said, giving him a hug hello. "You must be beat. Have you been up since three?"

"Yeah," he said good-naturedly, and then hugged his grandma as well.

I was hoping I might get in on that hugging, but he gave a nod to Brie and me. "Girls. How's it going?"

"Never better," I said as we all walked the few steps to the hotel's casino area.

Brie rubbed her palms together. "I want to find me a drink and then a craps table —

in that order. Should the craps table have a fine gentleman or two at it, all the better."

"I'm with you on the drink," Troy said. "You're on your own on the men." He nodded toward a bar. "What's everybody having?"

He took our orders and left to get our drinks. Kitty said, "Anyone up for blackjack?"

"Too much sitting around for me," Brie replied. "Craps you get to scream a lot and jump up and down."

As if on cue, a cheer went up from one of the craps tables. It was a group of guys, most in cowboy hats, whooping it up. Even though the table was already mobbed, Brie said, "That's my table. Bring me my piña colada when Troy gets back, will you?"

Kitty, Gran, and I stood for a while, watching the scene. "You gamble?" Kitty asked me.

"A bit. Roulette's my game. I plan to win big tonight."

"You sound confident. You must be feeling lucky," Gran said.

And there it was again: the elephant. Yes, I planned to win money . . . to donate to charity. Another item from the list. The list I was busy pretending didn't exist, even though it was the sole reason we were here.

After Troy returned with the drinks, Kitty and Gran went to find nickel slots. I figured those weren't exactly going to win me the big bucks, so I was glad when Troy turned to me and said, "You up for hitting the tables?"

"Love to."

It was prime time in the casino. We could find only one seat open at any of the roulette tables, and that was at a twenty-five-dollar minimum bet table. Although I'm usually more of a five-dollar-bet kind of gal, I grabbed the one available stool. "You have to bet big to win big," I said with bravado.

Troy rifled through his wallet and held out a hundred-dollar bill. "Here, you bet for me."

I waved it away. I have a few basic rules for Vegas that I live by, which are as follows: Dress slutty, accept any free drink that comes your way, and always, *always* bet your own cash.

"Watch . . . ," I boasted, turning to the table and setting down five twenty-dollar bills, "and learn."

Also at the table were an elderly couple, a drunk guy who at first glance I thought was asleep, and four girls who were clearly at a bachelorette party since one of them wore a bridal veil.

The dealer — an Asian man whose name tag said José — gave me twenty-five green chips. "To match your eyes," he said, smiling.

Troy leaned close. "I never noticed that you had fluorescent green eyes."

"I was hoping he'd give me purple," I whispered, "to go with my skin."

Five spins of the roulette wheel later, I was broke.

"Hard to believe you didn't even get a corner of a number," Troy remarked, quite unnecessarily. The drunk guy had a wall of chips in front of him. My only consolation was that the bridal party hadn't fared much better than I had.

I set down another hundred dollars and said to José, "Hit me again."

This time I got an edge of number 27, which gave me a six-to-one payout. That was enough to keep me alive for another five minutes before I busted again.

"There's no love at this table," I said with a frown, getting up. "Maybe the slot machines will be luckier." I scanned the casino, which was really bustling now with gamblers and crowds of people passing through to head to dinner or shows.

"Quarter or dollar machines?" Troy asked.

"Quarters. You witnessed both the beginning and the end of my high-roller days."

"If you're not feeling up to it, we don't have to gamble."

"Yes, we do," I said grimly. "I intend to win a big pot of cash so I can donate it to charity. Cross one off the list."

"Ah, I remember that one. Well, I'll pitch in anything I win tonight — and no matter how late it gets, we won't give up until we're flush." We walked up to two unattended machines sitting side by side. "How about these?" he asked.

"They're great . . . especially since I'll get to sit directly under that sign that says, 'Loose Slots.' What woman wouldn't love that?"

"Oh, how you tease."

Lord knows I would have liked to, if I hadn't been so worried about everything going right.

"So, Troy," I said, aiming for nonchalance as I perched on the edge of the stool and fed a twenty into the machine, "how's your mom doing, anyway? She certainly seems okay, but I don't know her so I can't tell."

"She's doing fine."

"Should I give her a copy of the list? Or talk about it more? I mean, I haven't been —"

"June, don't worry. It's going perfectly.

She and Gran are touched that you're doing this."

"Because I could make a photocopy of it. I'm sure the hotel has a copier."

He grabbed the scruff of my neck in a massage. Warmth shot through me. "I swear you can relax."

As if with his hand on me like that!

A waitress came up then to take our drinks order. Troy ordered a beer. Sensing a long night ahead, I asked for a coffee with whipped cream. "Lots of whipped cream," I said.

"Do you want a parasol with that?" she asked sarcastically.

"Ooh, yes! Please!"

After she left, I hoped that Troy would resume massaging my neck, but instead he said, "So how's work? Avert any crises lately?"

"Yes, as a matter of fact. I have a big presentation with the boss next week. If I do well, I could get promoted to management," I said. "That's why I was so happy on the phone the other day when you helped me come up with an idea."

"A promotion? I must've missed something. Last time we spoke, you were about to get fired."

I pulled the handle on the slot machine

and won twelve quarters. "That's the sort of roller coaster my life's been on."

"No kidding. So what's this big idea?"

I suddenly became self-conscious as I was about to say it out loud. What if it was stupid? Better to find out now than with Lou Bigwood, I supposed, but I didn't want to appear foolish in front of Troy, either. Hesitantly I said, "A street race. Well, a highway race, to be accurate. What I'd do is set up two cars to race in rush-hour traffic. One would be a guy driving alone, and the other would be carpoolers."

"I'm not sure I follow. It wouldn't be much of a race at rush hour. What would they be able to do — twenty miles per hour?"

"That's the point. The guy driving by himself would have to deal with traffic. The carpoolers could use the carpool lane. They're almost guaranteed to win. It'll be a live demonstration of how the carpool lanes are faster."

"I came up with that idea? I *am* a genius."

"Do you really think it's good?"

"You'll have media all over that. Believe me, you've got nothing to worry about. That manager position is yours."

"Well, I have to be realistic. You're into racing. I'm not so sure our CEO is. He may not get it."

"If he's a man, he'll get it. We can't help ourselves — we have some sort of imperative to drive vehicles fast. Drink beer. Wage wars. But if you're concerned, how about I come to your presentation and help you out? We could give your boss a live demonstration."

"Are you serious?"

"Sure, why not? I'll drive my car in a regular lane, and you and your boss can take the carpool lane. I'll even wear racing gear so it's obvious you're not going up against a little old lady. I'll look pro."

This felt too good to be true. I waited for the other shoe to drop. "It's next Friday at three o'clock," I said cautiously, expecting him to tell me it wouldn't work.

"I'll be there. Count on it."

Giddy, I gave the slot machine's arm another pull. *I'll be there. Count on it.* Aside from, "No, no, I insist, *you* take the last piece of chocolate," are there any words that tug more at a woman's heart?

I was pondering this happy thought when Kitty and Gran walked up.

"There you two are!" Gran said. "We've been over at the nickel slots. I'm up fifteen big ones. You should've seen it."

"Way to go, Gran," Troy said. "Although

you might want to donate that to the fund we're starting. June is trying to win money for charity. In fact," he said, easy as pie, "it's one of the items for the list. Marissa wanted to make a big donation."

I glowered at Troy — did no one explain to him that mentioning the elephant was forbidden?

"Oh, how wonderful!" Kitty exclaimed. "Ma, we'll have to pitch in our winnings!"

Considering her outrage over the eight-dollar sandwich, I expected Gran to balk, but she said, "Shoot, I'd have played the quarters if I'd known."

Kitty turned to me. "What charity?"

"She didn't specify. A lot of groups collect out here in the streets. Was there one Marissa was particularly fond of?"

"Drinks!"

The waitress returned and hefted Troy's beer and my coffee with whipped cream and — yes! — a parasol.

As I grabbed my drink and tossed tip money on the waitress's tray, I heard Kitty squeak, "A parasol."

"Hmmph?"

Kitty suddenly had that grayish, washed-out look I remembered from the funeral. "A parasol," she mumbled. "Marissa . . . she always loved parasols in her drinks. Even as a little girl, if we were at a restaurant, she'd insist they put one in her milk. Who gets a parasol in her coffee? I'd expect it in a fancy drink, you know . . . but coffee?"

Tears slid down her face, which seemed to have crumpled and turned into a wadded tissue before me.

Troy jumped to his feet and put his arm around her. "It's okay, Mom. Everything is okay."

"I'm sorry," I sputtered. "I didn't . . . I mean, that is, I —"

Troy pulled Kitty aside to comfort her while I stood there, dumb and confused.

Gran clucked. "Here we go again."

"I feel terrible," I moaned. "I shouldn't have . . ." What? Ordered a drink with a tiny umbrella? How could I have possibly known?

"Don't you fret," she assured me. "You're doing the best you can. We know that. It's just, the little things sneak up on you. Kitty can brace herself for a weekend where we're going to see Wayne Newton to help complete a list . . . and by the way, I'm quite excited about that. I'm his biggest fan. But sometimes you get blindsided. She didn't see the parasol coming. No one could have."

Gran went over to take Kitty's elbow and lead her away. Troy came over to me. "My mom could stand to call it a night."

"Of course."

"See you tomorrow?"

"Sure."

A lesser woman might have noted that surely Gran could have handled Kitty — that if they took Troy, too, I'd be alone.

All alone.

In Vegas, surrounded by clanging machines and groups of people drinking and cheering.

Yes, a lesser woman might have felt sorry for losing a wild night of gambling and flirting — and a promise from Troy that he'd stay and help win the pot of money.

She might have even mildly resented the sight of three bodies retreating toward the elevators while she stood there alone, cashing out the money left in her slot machine.

Two quarters made a tinny *chink, chink* noise as they hit the tray.

The stress of the day caught up with me then, pulling on my body. Sleep. I needed sleep. There was no reason I couldn't put off gambling until the morning.

But before I went back to my room, I wandered by the poker area. I needed to connect with someone. *Anyone.* I was starting to realize how hard this weekend was going to be, and I didn't want to face it by myself. And there was Martucci, still sitting at the five-card-stud table. I'd never been so happy to see him.

"Martucci!"

He grunted a greeting toward me, not taking his eyes off his cards.

I stood behind him. "Have you been here all night? How's the game going? Are you winning? Is that a good hand you have there?"

One of the other players tittered.

Martucci took a twenty-five-dollar chip from a pile in front of him and handed it to me.

"What's this?" I asked.

"Go play something."

"Wha— ?"

He frowned at me. "Parker, I've got a game going here."

"Fine."

I stomped away, and upon not seeing Brie (*please, let there not be a sock on the door when I get upstairs*), I gave up. It was time to close my eyes and put an end to this day. Cut my losses.

On my way to find the elevators, I passed the roulette table where I'd lost my money earlier. There was a new dealer, and the bachelorette party was long gone. The only person at the table was the drunk guy, whose wall of chips had dwindled to an anthill.

What the heck. The dealer spun the wheel, and before the ball settled, I set down Martucci's chip. Number 11. Marissa's birthday. As the ball clattered to find a spot and the dealer waved his hand to indicate no more bets, I remembered, *Shit! Her birthday was the twelfth! I've bet the wrong number!*

"Lucky number eleven!" the dealer announced.

I'd won.

Nobody was there to cheer. The drunk guy didn't even notice. I'd never won that kind of money before, yet strangely, I felt nothing. I'd gotten more excited the time I won a carpool mug in the company raffle.

The dealer slid me 875 dollars in chips without comment.

I'd been to Vegas often enough to know it wouldn't be hard to spend my winnings. I stepped outside the casino, where crowds still bustled even at this late hour. The warm night air cuddled me like a blanket. I'd barely cleared the casino entrance when I saw a nun in full habit holding a collection can that read, "Fund for Abused Children."

"You a real nun?" I asked her. There were plenty of scams around here, but then again, there were plenty of genuine charitable organizations glad to take advantage of people who'd lost all sense of the value of a dollar.

"Yes. I'm with the St. Thomas parish here in town."

A cop stood a few feet away, which seemed a good sign. Besides, the sooner I unloaded this cash to charity, the sooner I could cross the task off my list and be done with this day. That seemed as good a reason as any to trust her.

I held up my chips. "You take these?"

"Absolutely."

I slid the chips one by one into the collection can.

"God blesses you, my child."

"Great. I'll take any help I can get."

CHAPTER 20

With sleeping in and then taking our sweet time having breakfast the next morning, it was one o'clock before we hit the pool.

"Goodness, it's a zoo!" Kitty exclaimed, assessing the scene. To my relief, she was back to her old self — or at least the self who was trying to buck up as best she could.

Calypso music floated through air so thickly hot that you could almost see the waves of sound. We wove through a sea of bodies to a group of lounge chairs next to the pool. Brie had reserved them before she'd stumbled in our room at eight a.m., waking me long enough to tell me that I'd missed quite the party at the Hard Rock.

After a general jockeying for chairs, I wound up between Martucci and Kitty. Troy was on the other side of his mom, with Brie at the very end of our row. Gran had opted to take a nap in the hotel room rather than lie outside getting sunspots and risking heart failure in the heat — a choice we heartily supported.

Brie immediately collapsed facedown. "Wake me in an hour. I'll need to turn over."

I stripped to my swimsuit and was bending over to rifle through my bag for my book when Martucci gave me a hard slap on the butt.

"Hey!" I protested.

"*This,* people, is the result of expert coaching!" he boasted loudly. "This body is entirely my creation."

Before I could clock Martucci one, Kitty remarked, "God may have had a little to do with it."

"Well then, praise the Lord," Troy said.

His mother swatted the back of his head. "Show some respect, young man."

"I thought I was!" He laughed.

With that, I started to wonder if I'd somehow conjured my own form of hell: a place where a smart, cute, funny guy kept flirting with me but nothing could come of it, especially with his mother literally between us.

Plus, as part of this hell, Martucci was asking me to rub sunscreen on his back.

"Normally I say sunscreen is for pansies," Martucci explained, holding out the bottle, "but I don't trust this desert sun. It does wicked things to the skin."

He turned so his back was to me. Across the width of his shoulders was a tattoo of an eagle, which seemed to flap its wings as he flexed to lie down. Didn't it figure? Mere feet away was a back I'd enjoy giving a good rubdown, and here I was, smearing lotion on Martucci, trying not to wince when I had to lift the rattail out of the way.

"There, done," I proclaimed moments later, even though he was still white with the lotion I'd barely grazed over him. I grabbed my book — a trashy paperback I'd bought at the hotel gift shop — and settled into my chair.

"Aren't you going to put on sunscreen?" Troy asked.

"Yeah," Martucci piped up, "I was looking forward to watching you rub it all over yourself."

Ugh! "Martucci, you are such a pig. And I already put some on in the room. You're supposed to apply sunscreen half an hour before sun exposure. Therefore, *you* are currently frying, whilst I, in my wisdom, am only allowing enough rays through to give me a golden hue." Then I buried my nose in my book, signaling the end of conversation.

Martucci passed out almost as fast as Brie

had. I attempted to read but was distracted by Troy shifting from his front side to his back, adjusting the lounge chair, sighing, coughing, and then flipping back over to his stomach. Finally he sat up and said, "How long are we going to lie here?"

"It's been fifteen minutes," I said.

"It's so hot. I thought it'd been a couple hours."

"It's not the heat," Kitty said to me, glancing up from her magazine. "He's always this way. The boy can't sit still."

"Yes, I can," he said, and then he stood. "Think I'll swim a few laps."

"See?" Kitty said smugly.

I peeked over the top of my book as he walked to the end of the pool and dove in neatly. Then he attempted to swim laps, which was probably like trying to jog through a minefield with so many kids playing and people floating around on air mattresses.

"It's so good to see him swim," Kitty said. "We wondered if he'd ever be able to. He told you about his motorcycle crash, didn't he?"

I set down my book. "Called it a spill."

"Heh. *Spill.* That scar's just a small reminder of what he went through. He didn't walk for a year, and then he had a terrible limp for several more. Did he mention that?"

I shook my head.

"He put me through the paces, I'll tell you that. I wondered if either one of us was going to survive his teenage years."

"Yeah, he said that he always thought —" And then I stopped.

My unsaid words hung in the air, and I hoped Kitty wouldn't catch on, but she said, "That he'd go before Marissa."

"I'm sorry. I didn't mean to bring her up. Here you are trying to relax and have a good time."

"Don't worry. I'm glad to talk about Marissa. It's funny how people are afraid to mention her name — as if by saying it, they'll remind me that she's gone. As if I don't already know that every second of every day."

"That's got to be tough."

"Some days are better than others." She gave me a reassuring smile. "This day is a good one."

I took a moment to let her words sink in. "Do you mind," I ventured, choosing my words as carefully as I could, "if I asked what Marissa was like? All I know about her is what she wrote on the list. And a few things from yearbooks Troy let me borrow.

I'd love to know more about her."

"Oh, I'd love to tell you. She was such a cheerful girl, you know. Never let things get her down. Funny. Bright. And she always had a hobby going — I remember for a while there she was into sewing. She made all of the draperies in our house. Then it was model airplane building of all things. And that girl loved children. She always said she was going to adopt a houseful of kids when she grew up — you know, poor kids who had nowhere else to go. I guess she had a thing for the underdog. Perhaps it was those years of being overweight that made her more sensitive to others. Mostly, though, I'd have to say she was a sweetie. I suppose every mother says that about her daughter, but with Marissa it was true. She was always thinking about other people. Wanting to make a difference in their lives."

Well, that last part sounded familiar.

"Were you aware that one of the things Marissa wrote on her list was to change someone's life?"

Kitty seemed pleased. "Troy didn't tell me that one, although it sounds like her. He mentioned that there was one about riding in a helicopter . . . and getting a massage . . . and, of course, losing the weight. A few others. I understand that there are twenty things . . . ?"

I nodded. "I don't have the list with me here, but it's right up in the room. I could run up and get it if you want to see it."

"That's okay. Truthfully, before I see it, I'd rather the whole thing be finished."

"From your mouth to God's ears," I said, holding up crossed fingers.

"What do you mean — is it difficult?"

"Nah. Although it's not an easy list, that's for sure. Some of the tasks are definitely challenging."

"Like having to take her crazy family to Las Vegas?" Kitty said, her voice teasing.

"Not at all! This has been wonderful. And to be honest, I needed it."

"Oh? How so?"

"Well, I guess I'd let myself get totally caught up in getting everything completed on time. So much of my focus has been on hurrying to check things off. I want so desperately to succeed. But being here with you gives me a new perspective. It reminds me of why I'm doing the list in the first place."

She shifted to face me. "Why are you doing it?"

Ah, the million-dollar question.

I decided to be honest, since we were having this heart-to-heart. "I suppose it started out mostly as guilt. I felt so awful about everything."

"The accident wasn't your fault, June."

I shrugged. How could I say it? It wasn't about regretting how I'd veered out of the way and rolled the car. Or that I'd asked for that damn recipe, making her unbuckle her seat belt. Or, for that matter, how I'd offered Marissa a ride in the first place. Granted, I'd spent plenty of time lamenting those things, but the idea of fault wasn't what propelled me forward. It was more the fact that two people were involved in an accident, and I couldn't help but suspect that the wrong one walked away. "I want to make it better. That's all. I know what I'm doing isn't much, and it doesn't change anything. But —"

"It's a lot. I can't tell you how grateful we are that you're doing this. All of us. Troy can't stop talking about how impressed he is you've taken this upon yourself."

"Oh, good."

"Not to put any pressure on you, but once we found out that Marissa was making such a big deal out of her twenty-fifth birthday, we decided to throw her a little party. We're having it at that Oasis bar that she was so fond of. Nothing fancy. We'd love it if you could come. Invite anyone you'd like. And, of course, bring the list."

"I'd be honored. And it should be finished by then. *Will* be finished. That's the deadline."

"So I'm told." She paused. "You know, I didn't even know she'd made a list. Usually she was so open about that sort of thing."

Not liking the hurt look that crossed Kitty's face, I said hurriedly, "Maybe she was embarrassed by the things on it. There was one about going braless. No offense, but it's not exactly the type of thing you want your family to know about. And another one about wearing sexy shoes."

"That explains it!" Kitty exclaimed. "For the life of us, we couldn't figure out why she'd been wearing those silver shoes. They were so not her style. Then again," she added, sighing, "who's to say? She'd lost all that weight. There were probably a lot of things she was ready to try."

My stomach twisted, but there was nothing accusatory in Kitty's voice as she continued, "Okay, June, I know I said I didn't want to see the list, but tell me: Was there anything on it about finding love?"

I mentally reviewed the list. "Not really. Although one of the items was to go on a blind date."

"Really. Did you do that one?"

"Yeah. The guy turned out to be gay."

"How funny! Oh, it makes me wonder how it would have been if Marissa had had a chance to do the list herself. Would she have met someone special on that date? The love of her life, even?"

"Oh, Kitty . . ."

She waved away my concern. "It's a nice thought. It doesn't make me happy exactly, but I feel as if she's here with us."

"If it's any consolation, I can assure you Marissa would have had better luck than me on the blind date."

At that, Kitty tipped her head toward Martucci, who was snoring so loudly that it sounded as if trucks were downshifting on the nearby highway. "So what's the deal with you two? You have a little thing going on?"

"Martucci and me? Definitely not. We're friends."

"I think he's handsome," Kitty said. "You don't find him handsome?"

"We're work buddies. That's it."

My gaze moved to Troy. He sat on the edge of the pool, tossing a ball to a group of little kids. I tried not to drool. He looked darned yummy, and it had been so long since I'd had so much as a bite.

"That's a shame," Kitty said, picking up

her magazine. "Call it a mother's intuition, but I swear there's romance in the air."

After checking into the spa and changing into the white terry robes they'd provided, Brie, Kitty, Gran, and I sat in the lounge area waiting to be called for our treatments. The room was decorated in soothing greens, and there was the scent of eucalyptus wafting through the air. It was hard to believe this was in the same building as the casino and its bright lights and chaos.

I was bathed in peace . . . until a man stepped into the room. I said a silent prayer that he wasn't assigned to me. I'd never had a masseur before, and this one looked as if he could snap me like a twig. He had a redwood build — broad-shouldered, with his body forming a slick V at his waist. His waist-length black hair was pulled into a ponytail, and his features, while striking, seemed chiseled from granite. If I saw this guy in a dark alley, I'd faint.

Please don't call my name. . . .

"June Parker?" His voice was an engine rumbling.

Figured. "That's me," I said, standing and pulling my robe tight around me.

The ladies were atwitter, mumbling their approval.

"She hit the jackpot on this one — what a gorgeous face. Like a Greek god!"

"Look at those *hands*."

"Like catcher's mitts."

"I've never seen such big hands!"

"And you know what they say . . ."

"That's feet they say that about."

"Who cares? Anyway, with such an impressive front, I can only imagine what —"

Brie gave me a shove. "Get going. We want to see him walk away."

I waved good-bye to them. They cooed like proud mothers sending their baby girl off to lie naked on a table while a total stranger rubbed his hands over her.

He introduced himself as Runner and escorted me into a dimly lit room barely big enough for the massage table. The drill was the same as usual: He left while I stripped and lay facedown on the table underneath a blanket. When he returned after I'd called out that I was ready, he was all business.

I wished I could have said the same for myself. Something about being naked and so near such a bastion of masculinity had me . . . well . . . *thinking*.

"Do you prefer hard or soft?" he asked innocently enough.

"Hard," I gulped, not so innocently.

"Okay. Let me know if it's too much."

347

He began massaging my back and shoulders in deep, firm strokes. I could hear him breathing as he worked. He was careful to keep me covered. I felt his hip graze against me, but it was all very clean and on the up-and-up and wholesome and, cripes, I was so horny. There was no getting around it. The candles . . . the soft music . . . a man's strong hands gripping me and rubbing me . . . his raspy grunts as he threw his weight into it. How could I not have filthy thoughts? Even though I would have been horrified if his hands actually wandered, that didn't mean I couldn't entertain the fantasy that they might.

He moved my towels around and then dug his fingers into the flesh of my thighs. It was all I could do to suppress a moan. I wondered how many women threw money at him and asked for the "full service" massage.

I wondered if he said yes.

And how much money would it take?

Not that I was interested, mind you.

Simply curious.

Runner told me to turn over onto my back, and then he covered my eyes with a cool cloth. My mind wandered, first to thoughts of work . . . and the list . . . and then to thoughts of Troy Jones swimming, the muscles on his back rippling as he dug through the water. The way he'd smoothed the water from his hair when he'd stepped out, completely wet, his swim trunks clinging to him.

I must have sighed at the memory, because Runner murmured, "This feels good?" His hands gripped my hips, pushing firmly up and down, which brought me back to the moment.

"Mmm-hmm."

"Good."

He continued, making a noise from deep in his chest from all that pushing and thrusting and grabbing. I was trying to do that thing men do to stave off arousal, think of something neutral like baseball — only I was imagining buying that new set of plates I wanted at Pottery Barn — when I sensed Runner shift so that he stood behind my head. "We're almost finished," he said.

I felt his hand rest to put pressure on my right temple. Then his other hand pushed on my left temple. Then his other hand pushed firmly into the crown of my head.

His other hand?

I distinctly recalled him having only two hands when we started, so what was that pressing into my head?

Oh no — it was his penis. He was jamming his erection into me. I felt it rubbing against my hair, making firm, hard circles. I must have been sending out signals. He probably thought I was enjoying it!

I had no idea what to do. It was one thing if I'd asked — *Hey, would you mind sliding your throbbing manhood against me?* — but I'd done no such thing! Boy, if he thought he was getting the full 15 percent tip after this . . .

I needed to say something. Make it clear that he was out of line. Because although I was still covered by the towel, I felt naked. Exposed. *How could he?*

He made a noise . . . *mmmm* . . . yet I lay there with the cloth over my eyes, doing nothing. At the very least, I needed to slap him. Or report him!

Mustering my courage, I pulled off the cloth and opened my eyes. When I did, I realized that he wasn't digging his penis into me. He wasn't even standing behind me. He was to my side. One of his huge hands stretched across my face so he touched both temples at once.

Which left his other hand free to touch the top of my head.

"How was it?" he asked warmly.

"Great," I said, trying not to blush.

Was it my fault the man had freakishly

large hands? Anyone could have made the same mistake.

As I threw on my robe to join the other women before going upstairs to get ready for dinner, it occurred to me that that pent-up sexual energy had to go somewhere. And I knew exactly where.

It almost seemed unfair not to call Troy Jones and give the poor boy a running start.

CHAPTER 21

"This is your motorcycle?"

"Something wrong?" Troy asked, handing me a helmet.

"Where do *I* sit?"

"Ah, I see you've been spoiled." Then he patted the back half of what didn't seem to be a particularly large seat. "Right here. Plenty of room."

When Troy had offered to give me a ride on his motorcycle, I'd told him I had riding experience. It was only a few miles to the hotel where Wayne Newton was performing. Although we could have taken a cab with Kitty and Gran, they wanted to go early for the buffet, which I chose to skip in favor of a nap and a vending machine dinner. Besides, Troy had said he was itching for a ride. As I had an itch of my own to scratch, it seemed reasonable to take him up on his offer.

That was, until now. This bike was nothing like Phyllis's Harley. Where was my motor home on two wheels? Where was my bucket seat? There wasn't even a sissy bar. One bump in the road and I'd go flying off the back.

Troy helped me buckle my helmet, and then he climbed on the bike. I straddled behind him, leaving a reasonable distance between us. When I tried to feel the seat behind me, there wasn't one. My butt was hanging off the end.

Why did I have to wear these stupid shiny pants? Sure, they were cute, sort of a bronze color . . . and I'd paired them with a black stretchy tank top and high heels. I was very Las Vegas — a little trashy, a little shimmery.

But I should have worn clothes with traction. Rubber. Surely I had something rubber in my closet I could have brought. I'd bet anything that Brie did.

Troy started the engine, which sent up a panic flare to my brain. This was crazy — I was taking a cab.

I was about to jump off — tell Troy that his bike wasn't big enough for the both of us — when he reached back. With one arm, he gave me a firm tug so I was snug against him. Then he pulled on my arms to place them around his waist.

"Don't want to lose anybody," he said.

Oh.

Well, this was cozy.

We pulled out of the parking garage and onto a side road, and I thought about Phyllis's comment about me being a good ride. Troy leaned forward, and I leaned with him. It felt perfectly natural. There was anticipation. There was trust. There were my boobs and crotch smashed up against him and his firm muscles beneath my grasp. I couldn't help myself — I let my hands wander to his chest. Nothing too randy. Just enough so it could be mistaken for me getting myself adjusted.

Traffic on Las Vegas Boulevard was stop and go, but we wove through the sea of cars at traffic lights — one of the advantages of being on a motorcycle. A good thing since we'd let ourselves get a late start.

The sun was low in the sky, and the air seemed to glow as much as the lights of the casinos we passed. My hormones buzzed. It was having Troy so close . . . and being kind of scared on the bike . . . and breathing in his scent of soap and heat . . . and the dense evening air . . . and the rumble of the bike beneath me . . .

Just then, a light stopped us. Troy held the weight of the bike with one leg, shifted around to face me, and started to speak: "So how is the —"

But conversation wasn't what I had in mind. I'd had enough of being coy. It was time to make my move.

I flipped up the bug guard on my helmet and then lifted his. Then, my hand on the back of his neck, I pulled him close in a lip-lock — or at least I tried to. Before my mouth got anywhere near his, our helmets collided.

I scowled, trying to see if I tipped my head a bit . . .

"It can't be done," he said, and he reached to unbuckle his helmet. "But I have to say, I like the way you think."

Traffic started moving around us. The SUV behind us gave a quick tap on its horn.

"Light's green," I said, my disappointment obvious.

"Mmm-hmm." His gaze never left me as he continued to lift off his helmet.

"People are honking."

"Let 'em."

He reached toward me, obviously intent on unbuckling my helmet.

"No!" I protested, laughing. "Are you crazy? The light's green! We're in the middle of the street — blocking traffic!"

Troy gave a good-natured sigh, but still he

didn't turn around. His hand slid over my back, resting on the skin between my shirt and pants. Unable to reach my face through my helmet, he settled for gently kissing my bare shoulder. Let the kiss slide up to my neck. I felt his breath hot against me as he murmured, "June . . . you have no idea . . ."

Oh, I had an idea all right.

If my habit was to burrow like a groundhog, at this point I'd popped up from the hole I'd dug. In fact, I was practically running around wild, tearing up the fields and humping people's legs.

But there was also the SUV inching closer behind me. And the fact that the concert was going to start soon.

"Seriously, we need to go."

"Fine. But I feel I should warn you, I'm a man who finishes what he starts. So that means that those gorgeous lips" — he traced my mouth lightly with a fingertip — "are mine."

It was fifteen minutes to showtime when we pulled into a parking area in front of the hotel reserved for motorcycles. Troy locked the helmets to the bike, and we hurried into the casino. Although Kitty and Gran would have already picked up their tickets at the box office, I didn't want them to miss any of the show waiting for us.

"I can't believe I'm rushing to see Wayne Newton," Troy groaned.

Kitty waved to us from near the entrance to the showroom. "There you kids are! We were starting to worry. Ma's already inside." She handed us each a ticket and bustled us through a curtained doorway. As we walked, she chattered on about the buffet and the people they'd met in line and the "Waynabelia" — that was, the Wayne Newton memorabilia — that they'd bought at the souvenir stand.

Our table was dead center and jutted up against a divider. It wasn't close to the stage, but I was pleased to see that it had an unimpeded view. Kitty and Gran sat on one side of the table, and Troy and I slid in across from them. The table was covered in drinks. "Thirsty, Gran?" Troy joked.

"Ha, ha. We took the liberty of ordering for you," she said. "You get two free drinks with your ticket. I got the feeling if we didn't order them now, we may never see a waitress again. So drink up."

Kitty lifted a fruity drink — sans parasol, I couldn't help but notice — and said, "A toast." We each grabbed a drink. I had two huge tumblers of white wine in front of me, one of which I raised as she said, "To making dreams come true."

"Here, here," Gran added, and we clinked.

Gran and Kitty thumbed through the Las Vegas souvenir books they'd bought while I surveyed the room. Troy and I appeared to be the youngest people there. Nothing but gray and balding heads dotted the show-room — a Berber carpet of aged fans. A man in the front shook his cane along to the piped-in music.

Leaning back toward Troy, I said, "I hear Wayne does a great cover of 'Get Jiggy with It.' "

"Hey, speaking of that song," he said casu-ally, "the station's throwing a big concert. August seventh. Will Smith's going to perform. Want to come?"

"I'd love it."

"It's a date, then."

A date!

Although August 7 was ringing a bell.

I didn't have time to ponder it. An an-nouncer onstage said a hello and urged us to give a big welcome to Mr. Las Vegas himself. A cry went up in the room when the lights lit up on the stage. The crowd wriggled to attention.

It was thrilling to see Wayne Newton take command of the stage. He looked exactly as I'd remembered him from the Hollywood

Wax Museum, right down to the black hair and painted-on brows. I found myself riveted by his vocal struggling to be heard over his twelve-piece backup band. They sat in neat rows behind him — the men innocuous, the ladies overly made-up and big-breasted yet strangely wholesome. As Wayne sang and told stories about the old days of Vegas, Troy whispered things to me such as "Can you believe this guy?" "This is the hokiest thing I've ever been to," and "Oh, you smell so good. . . ."

After singing many of his big "hits," Wayne started in on a medley of patriotic songs. Gran leaned forward excitedly. "This is going to be great. A lady we met in line told us that his version of 'America the Beautiful' is a real slam-banger."

A waitress worked her way through the tables, handing out mini-flags so we could join in the fun. Kitty and Gran each took one, waving them along to the music. I couldn't help but smile, particularly as I watched Kitty. Even though this had to be painful for her, she was determined to have fun in honor of her daughter.

And with that thought, another one hit me like an anvil crashing onto my head. The force it of knocked me back in my seat. Because at that moment I remembered what my plans were for August 7.

It was Deedee's due date. The day I was going to become a mother.

And I'd completely forgotten.

"I . . . Oh my gosh, I . . ."

Troy asked, "You okay?"

I grabbed the tumbler of wine, and chugged it back. *How could I have forgotten?*

The crowd was clapping now, and — confused and not wanting to draw attention to myself while I sorted my thoughts — I clapped along. I said quietly to Troy, "August seventh . . . I just remembered. I can't make it. It's Deedee's due date."

"Little Deedee?"

"Yeah."

"She's pregnant? Jesus. I didn't even realize." After a moment he said, "So you need to be there for her?"

"I'm her labor coach." I stopped my clapping long enough to start in on the second glass of wine — I still wasn't feeling the first one. Then, resuming my clapping, I said, "And then . . . after . . . I'm going to adopt the baby."

"You're going to . . . huh?"

"Adopt the baby. Deedee's too young to be a mom, and I've always wanted a baby, so . . ." My voice trailed off once I caught Troy's face. He looked as if I'd told him a joke but he was having a problem understanding the punch line. "Anyway," I said, "that's the plan."

He breathed out a laugh, although there wasn't much humor to it. "Shit . . . a kid. You're going to have a kid in a matter of weeks. A newborn. That's . . ." He rubbed the back of his neck. "Wow."

All of a sudden, I noticed he was far away from me, practically sitting at the next table.

"It's a girl," I said, not knowing what else to say.

He nodded, his brows furrowed. "You know what's funny? All those times we talked on the phone setting things up. And hanging out all last night and today. You'd think in all that time . . . you might have mentioned it."

"I'm mentioning it now."

"That's nice of you." There was a bite to his voice I'd never heard before.

"What the — Why are you angry?"

"Hey, I'm not angry. It's great. A baby."

The rhythmic clapping of the crowd turned into applause as Wayne wrapped up his medley and then told the crowd he was going to sing a song that was a favorite of his, by a man who loved Las Vegas as much as he did. Then he launched into Elvis's "Can't Help Falling in Love."

"I can't believe you have the nerve to be pissed off," I hissed. "So I'm adopting a baby. As I recall, the standard response is congratulations."

"You're right. Excuse my lack of manners," he said curtly. "Congratulations."

"Thank you," I spat.

What was his deal? My head started to whirl from disappointment. Not to mention the cheap wine.

For a moment, we pretended to be engrossed in Wayne Newton, who was now coming out into the audience as he sang. Apparently, the divider that we sat next to was a ramp. Wayne walked along it, leaning down to shake hands with people as he sang. Tiny lights led his way to us.

"Oh, June!" Kitty cried. "He's coming this way. Let's try to shake his hand!"

Glad for the distraction, I gave Kitty a thumbs-up. I narrowed my eyes at Troy. Amazing how easily infatuation can turn to annoyance.

No matter, because the one, the only, the incomparable Wayne Newton himself stood in front of our table. In front of *me.*

What the hell — might as well make something of the evening. I thrust my hand toward him.

He didn't take it. Instead he shook his

head no, only to pause and give the crowd an "I can't help myself" shrug. The next thing I knew, he gestured for me to stand. When I did, he planted a wet, sweaty kiss on my lips. It felt as if he were one of those snakes whose jaw can open really wide, pulling me in deeper and deeper. For a moment, I feared being swallowed whole head-first into his gullet, until at last he released me.

The crowd cheered, and Wayne said, "Thank you, beautiful lady."

He picked up the next line of the song and moved on. I used a napkin to dry my face and wipe away the stage makeup that had rubbed off on me. It would take a shower and a few weeks to get rid of the aftershave that lingered.

"You're so lucky!" Gran exclaimed.

I might have felt special, except that he went on to kiss pretty much every woman in the place — even climbing off the ramp to plant one on an old gal in her wheelchair.

"It's the Walk of a Hundred Kisses. He's famous for it," Kitty said. "But you were first!"

"Good thing, too," Gran said. "I don't know if I'd want that mouth on me after seeing where it'd been."

Judging by Troy's stony expression, I was

certain that was the only kiss I was going to score for the night.

Having finished my glasses of wine, I mooched the second daiquiri, which Gran hadn't wanted. When the show finally ended and we stood to go, the room tipped around me. I stumbled. Troy caught me, but then he couldn't let go of me fast enough.

Kitty and Gran chattered as we walked out. The ride home on the motorcycle sure wasn't going to be the snuggle-fest it was on the way here. I started to wonder if Troy was so appalled by my status as mom-to-be that he was going to tow me behind his motorcycle rather than share the seat with me.

He had other plans. Leaning close, he said, "You should take the cab back with my mom and Gran. You're not in any shape to ride."

"Fine. I didn't mean to disgust you with my drunkenness."

"I don't want you to get hurt."

Too late for that. It was clear: Once I brought up a baby, he didn't want anything to do with me.

I remembered back to the game of "what if" I'd recently played with my mom, and my heart sank.

It wasn't fair. Troy had seemed so perfect.

So maybe I hadn't brought up the adoption until now. He sure wasn't up front about being a baby hater, either. It seemed the sort of thing he might have mentioned. *Hi, do you come here often? And by the way, I hate babies.*

I turned on him, suddenly furious. "What do you have against babies, anyway?"

"Come on, be fair. You have to admit this is out of left field."

"Actually, it's not that strange. People adopt all the time."

He paused, closing his eyes and pinching the bridge of his nose. Collecting himself. Then, ignoring me, he walked over to Kitty and Gran to tell them he'd meet up with us back at the hotel. He said it'd be best if I rode along with them.

Before I followed the ladies out to get in line for a cab, I felt compelled to say to Troy, "It's not as if I were asking you to be the father."

"It's nothing against you. A baby isn't anything I'm ready for right now. I mean, I've been through a lot lately. Besides, you and I haven't even —" And he stopped.

There was no need to finish. Kissed? Dated? Screwed? It didn't matter because the result was the same.

At last, I slid into acceptance. This was

going to be my life from now on, I realized. I'd better get used to it.

I woke to the sound of the shower running. And . . . ugh. My head felt stuffed with fuzz and my mouth with dust. I had to lie there for a few minutes before I could even piece together that I was in my hotel room in Las Vegas and it was morning.

How I got here, I had no idea.

Water. I needed water. Hell, I'd even take three-dollar water. I swung my legs over the side of the bed. My stomach lurched.

Bad idea.

Maybe I didn't need water quite so quickly.

That was when I noticed the slacks on the floor and the man's shirt . . . and were those boxers?

Frantically, I tried to piece together how I got upstairs and — I glanced downward — dressed in a T-shirt. No bra or underwear.

The shower stopped, and I heard male humming.

Okay, June, think.

Last night. After the concert, I'd met up with Brie and Martucci at the hotel bar. They were doing tequila shooters. Kitty and Gran had decided to call it a night. Their flight was leaving early in the morning, so they'd thanked me and invited all of us to Marissa's birthday party. After they left, Troy came down wearing jeans and a leather jacket and carrying a travel bag. He gave his hotel key card to Brie — said he was going to head home so she might as well have her own room.

The last thing I could remember was Martucci challenging me to an upside-down shooter. I don't recall if I said good-bye to Troy. Just did a back bend over the barstool. Then I watched as he walked away, upside down, and Martucci poured the tequila in my mouth until my throat burned and my eyes watered.

Martucci.

It was all coming back. Him carting me up to the room. Pulling off my top. Me, sliding off my panties.

There was a wastebasket next to the bed. I gazed into it, wondering if I'd see a used condom or a wrapper. It was empty. Which was either good news or bad news — either I didn't do anything or I did, and without protection. Right now, Martucci's sperm could be thundering through me, trying to create little Martuccis.

The bathroom door handle turned, and — why I suddenly felt the need to be modest I don't know — I pulled the sheets around me.

And out walked . . . Runner. My masseur. Huh.

He had a towel wrapped around his waist, his massive chest bare. His hair hung loose and wet down his back.

"Good morning," he said cheerfully.

"Morning."

"How're you feeling?"

"Confused."

"Yeah, that was one wild night." He picked up the shirt off the floor and tossed it on. I averted my gaze as he stepped into the boxers and then the pants. "You were really out of it."

Was it Runner who'd undressed me? It must have been, but the memory of Martucci was so distinct. The way I'd tugged on his rattail. But maybe it was Runner's ponytail. Or both of theirs. Who knew? I might have had my first one-night stand or my first orgy.

"Well," Runner said, heading for the door, "Brie ought to be out of the bathtub by now. Thanks for letting me use your shower."

Use my shower?

"We didn't sleep together, then?" I asked.

He boomed out a laugh. "I needed to shower before work. Brie was already in the tub and in no hurry to get out . . . or to share. She suggested I use this one."

"Ah, so you and *Brie* . . ."

"Helluva woman, that friend of yours. Glad I hooked up with you guys. Whooee, you sure put back the tequila fast last night. You didn't even make it to midnight before you started to pass out."

"Speaking of that," I ventured, "were you the one who brought me up here?"

He shook his head. "Nah, it was your friend. The Italian guy."

I nodded, smiling, as if that were swell news.

Runner left, and I managed to shower, pack, and meet the others for the drive home, where I immediately crawled into one of the motor home's sleeper bunks and slept. I woke up only long enough to attempt to gag down a McSomething or other.

Martucci dropped Brie off first, then took me home, which gave me time alone with him to ask what I'd been dreading but needed to know.

I moved to the passenger seat to sit next to him as he drove. He chewed on sunflower seeds, spitting the hulls into a bag on the dashboard.

"I don't know how to ask this, so I'm just going to ask it," I said.

"All right."

"Did we have sex?"

"Don't remember a thing, huh?"

"If you must know, I vividly recall you undressing me."

"Ah . . ." He sighed happily. "So do I."

"Very amusing. This was a tough weekend for me. I was extremely vulnerable. I can't believe you'd take advantage. That you'd —"

"Parker, don't get yourself in a twist. I was only messing with you. Nothing happened."

"Oh, please. Don't lie."

An image of me licking his face rose to my mind.

"I'm not lying. You were totally wasted, so I brought you up to your room. And sweetheart, you were begging for it. Practically dry-humping me. You know, you really shouldn't go so long without sex."

"And you expect me to believe you didn't take me up on it?" I was skeptical and, frankly, a little insulted.

"You may not believe this, but I have standards."

"I suppose you're going to tell me that you undressed me, but you didn't look."

"Hell, yeah, I looked. But I didn't touch. And you know why?"

I rolled my eyes. "Because you respect me."

"No . . . because you were freaking me out. Kept licking my face. Pulling on the rattail, saying it was my source of power. That I was Samson and you were going to cut off my source of power in my sleep."

"Oh."

"I was afraid you'd go after my other source of power. Pull a Lorena Bobbitt on me. I felt lucky to get out of there alive."

"Sorry," I said, feeling sheepish.

He turned back to his driving, his face wounded. "What do you have against the rattail, anyway?"

CHAPTER 22

"It's best that you found this out now," Susan said. "You don't need to waste time on a man who's going to take forever to want kids."

"August isn't exactly forever."

"Don't make excuses for him," she said, pointing a plastic fork at me. "That's how you wind up in these relationships that never go anywhere. You deserve better."

It was Monday morning, and Susan had invited me out for breakfast. We ate egg sandwiches and fruit cups at the deli up the street from work while I filled her in on the details of the weekend. Most of them, anyway. I omitted the part about nearly date raping Martucci.

I'd spent the rest of Sunday sleeping off my hangover and wishing things had gone differently with Troy. The idea of this list leading me to my true love — okay, it was corny, but I couldn't shake my disappointment. Troy had seemed like the sort of guy I could hang with, baby or not. It wasn't exactly effortless being with him — there was the matter of my feeling self-conscious over his sister — but I'd hoped we could get past that.

"Maybe this baby is the best thing to ever happen to you," Susan said. "It'll be a barometer. You'll know right away — a guy is either ready for a commitment or he's not. Period."

"But Troy had seemed so . . . right," I moped.

"They're always perfect before you get to know them. But everybody has their flaws. I could sit here for days telling you what bugs me about Chase. But blowing you off because you're going to have a baby — I'd assume that's a deal breaker."

I blew out a breath. "I'd be feeling a whole lot more high and mighty if I hadn't forgotten the baby myself."

"Oh, June. You didn't forget the baby. Leaving it on top of the car and driving away is forgetting the baby. Your mind was elsewhere for a while. It's allowed."

"Did you ever?"

"C'mon . . . pregnant with twins? I *wished* I could have thought of something else. Or slept, for that matter. But in your case, I can see how it would happen. It's not as if people are constantly coming up to you and feeling your belly." She chewed her lip. "June, I hate to say this now. It's extremely bad timing. But I'm going to say it anyway. No one — and I mean *no one* — would fault you if you were having second thoughts."

"I'm not having second thoughts."

"Are you sure? Because if you wanted to back out, it would be fine."

I steeled my shoulders. "I'm not backing out."

"Good," she said, picking up her food tray and standing to leave. "Because as we speak, there are thirty people gathered in my office with gifts for you. So if you're going to go through with it, you'll have a few nice things for the baby. If you might change your mind, don't remove any of the tags." We tipped our trays into the trash can. Susan added, "Oh, and act surprised."

Meryl streep can rest assured — her job is safe. I threw my hands to my face and squealed after they shouted, "Surprise!" but everybody figured out that Susan had clued me in.

No matter. I still scored plenty of loot.

At long last, after years of chipping in for

everybody else's weddings and babies and buying Girl Scout cookies and magazine subscriptions by the truckload, I was getting mine.

I tore into the gifts excitedly. The biggest one was a stroller that the staff had pitched in on. And not any stroller, I was informed, but the Cadillac of strollers. I hoped it came with a driver's manual.

In addition to that, I got a swing, a bathtub, blankets, an ear thermometer, towels, and several tiny outfits cuter than anything I own. The gift that astounded me the most was a T-shirt with little cars and buses on it. It was so *tiny.* I kept holding it up, marveling that a human was going to fit in it.

Later, over cake, the questions came in a barrage. What was I naming the baby? (Um . . . I haven't decided.) Was I taking time off? (Definitely some, but how long I wasn't sure.) Was I going to be in the delivery room? (Probably.) Was I nervous about it? (Yes.) Would I be breast-feeding? (That was from Martucci. I didn't bother to reply.)

At one point, Mary Jo from the vanpool department said, "This baby is being born in August, right?"

"Uh-huh."

"*This* August?"

"Of course this August. Why would you ask that?"

"It's only that it's so soon, and you don't seem very prepared."

"I'm prepared," I said defensively, knowing full well she was right. I hadn't even given an inkling of thought to a name. Something was definitely wrong about that, but I pushed the worry away.

Eventually, people started wandering back to their offices. Susan had to rush off to a meeting. I was packing up the gifts when Phyllis showed up, apologizing that a meeting with Bigwood had gone longer than expected.

"This is for you." She thrust a wrapped box at me. "I got the same thing for my grandbaby."

I didn't miss the message behind her words. "Your daughter got the letter," I said softly. "You've made up."

"Well, we're not exactly sitting around holding hands and singing 'Kumbaya,' but" — her face shone as she talked — "we've been talking. Met the husband. And their kids are cute as hell. They got this wild curly hair — I don't know where it came from. Danny is three, and Jennifer just turned a year."

"Those are pretty common names from a

girl named Sunshine."

"Sally," she corrected me. "She goes by Sally now. But get this: Her husband rides a motorcycle — how's that for a kick in the pants? A little Honda piece of crap, but still. There's hope for that girl yet if she picked a husband who rides." Phyllis gestured to the gift. "Anyway, open it."

As I tore into the wrapping paper, Phyllis asked how the list was going.

"I'm almost done. Two tasks left to go," I said, holding up a tiny Harley-Davidson leather jacket. "Oh, Phyllis, this is so cute! Thank you."

She nodded and then said, "Which ones do you have left to do?"

"Find a guy named Buddy Fitch and make him pay — that's a tough one. I'm stumped. I'm spending every night on the Internet searching. The other is that I have to change someone's life."

"That letter you wrote changed my life," Phyllis said. "So go ahead and mark that one done."

Shaking my head, I said, "Thanks, but not a chance. I only threw words on paper. Getting back with your daughter . . . you did that on your own. Anyway, I'm bringing the final adoption papers over to Deedee and her family this Saturday. I figure as soon as we sign them, it'll be official. Then I'll feel as if I can say I've changed a life."

My heart skittered as I said all that out loud.

Phyllis must have noticed because she said, "There's nothing to be nervous about. You'll do a fine job."

I sure hoped so. Little Whatever-her-name-was-going-to-be deserved the best mom possible.

Deedee paled as she watched the woman writhe nude on the screen in front of us. Maybe this childbirth class was a mistake. The adoption lawyer had recommended it because it was especially for girls giving up their babies. I promised to take Deedee every Wednesday night until she went into labor. Unfortunately, seeing what she was in for in just over a month's time, Deedee looked more frightened than I'll bet I had when I'd seen *The Birds*.

I did my best to comfort her. "The sort of woman who'd let her birth be filmed for the world to see is going to be the type to scream a lot," I whispered. "And I know for a fact that you don't have to be completely naked."

A girl whose name tag identified her as Janai leaned over. "Yeah, and I got two

378

words for that lady: bikini wax. I thought her bush was the kid's head coming out."

Another piped up, "Why is she doing it without no painkillers?"

"I say pass the Demerol and wake me when it's over," Janai added. "And I'm getting me a Brazilian wax before I go in. If a whole bunch of people are going to be staring at my snatch, I might as well make it pretty."

"Especially if it'll help take the focus off my ass," a girl agreed woefully. "I know guys like junk in the trunk, but I've got a fucking dump truck going back there."

"I hear that," someone seconded.

I could tell that Deedee wanted to participate in the exchange, but she was way out of her league. Although the other girls were teenagers, they all seemed to have more mileage on them. Still, for all their swagger — and they'd spent the first part of the session swapping stories about deadbeat boyfriends so bad that they made Troy Jones seem like Father of the Year — there was no missing that they were scared.

The birth movie ended, and the instructor opened the floor for questions. Janai raised her hand. I expected her to ask about painkillers, which was what I would have wanted to know in her shoes. But she said,

"What if there's something wrong with the baby and they don't want it?"

The instructor — and there was a woman with a tough job — then facilitated a discussion about a birth mother's rights vs. adoptive parents' rights. That segued into how to find a good lawyer and how drug use during pregnancy affects the baby's health. I whispered to Deedee, "Guess you'd better cut down on the crack cocaine, huh?" but she either didn't hear me or pretended not to.

On the drive home, Deedee was as quiet as she'd been during our first few get-togethers. I didn't push it. I had plenty on my mind myself.

There'd been a moment in the film when a girl handed her baby over to an adoptive mother. The pure joy on the woman's face as she accepted the child should have been thrilling, but it sent a shot of panic pulsing through me. I'll bet anything she had remembered the due date. That she had a name picked out. That she knew the difference between a washcloth and a burp towel. Heck, she'd probably read *What to Expect* cover to cover a dozen times.

Was there something wrong with me?

I had told Susan I wasn't having second thoughts, but what about the fact that I wasn't having *any* thoughts at all?

I'd been counting on getting more excited as the baby's due date neared. Instead, fears that I might be making a huge mistake had been creeping into my consciousness. It was getting harder and harder to squelch them, but I had to. There was a little girl about to be brought into the world who needed me. I couldn't let her down.

When I pulled up to drop Deedee off, there was an unfamiliar car in her driveway. "Looks like you have company."

She groaned. "My mom's fiancé."

I was stunned. "I didn't know your mom was getting married. You never even mentioned that she had a boyfriend."

"He's the manager at the restaurant where she works. They've been going out awhile now."

"Do you like him?"

"They French-kiss in the living room," she said by way of reply, making a gagging noise.

"How soon are they getting married?"

She shrugged. "My mom wants to do it before her thirtieth birthday for some reason. That's in December."

My jaw dropped and nearly hit the steering wheel. "Your mom is only twenty-nine?"

"Why?" She snickered. "How old did you

think she was?"

"I don't know. Older than me, I guess. She's about to be a grandma!"

"No, she's not," Deedee said quietly, and she pushed on the door handle to let herself out of the car.

What could I say? She was right. *My* mom was about to be a grandma. As I watched Deedee walk up the steps to her house, I thought about that film again.

The whole time, my eyes had been on the arms holding the baby. It occurred to me for the first time that Deedee's had been most likely on the arms handing the baby away.

It was ten o'clock by the time I got home. I changed into an oversize T-shirt and my cotton robe, then hit "play" on my answering machine while I set up the coffeemaker for the morning.

There were three messages. The first was from my mom, saying that she wanted to have a baby shower for me and would a week from Saturday work?

Then it was my brother, Bob. "June, are you home? Pick up if you're home. . . . No, huh? Okay, well, I'll try to catch you later." It was the first I'd heard from him or Charlotte since the scene at my parents' party.

Bob almost never called. In fact, make that never. Even on my birthday it was Charlotte who made the call for both of them.

As soon as I heard the start of the next message, my insides flip-flopped. "Hi, June, this is Troy. I've been trying to call, but you're not an easy woman to get on the phone. I hate to leave this in a message, but here goes. I know we talked about my coming to your meeting Friday to —"

A knock on my door distracted me. Who would be here this late? I stopped the message — I didn't need to hear Troy rejecting me again. He'd made it abundantly clear how he felt, and frankly, the knife twisting in my gut wasn't that much fun the first time around.

I hollered, "Who is it?"

"It's Bob."

My brother? Here?

I threw open the door. Bob stood there, a dimpled grin on his face, holding a duffel bag. "I tried calling, but —"

"Come on in," I said, stepping aside to give him room to pass. "Is Charlotte with you?"

"No." He glanced around my apartment. "Nice place."

I offered him a beer, poured myself a diet soda, and made small talk while he settled on my couch and I took a chair.

"So, what brings you to my neck of the woods?" I finally asked.

"I'm wondering if I can bum a spot on your couch for a few days. I'd stay with Mom and Dad, but . . ." He shrugged instead of finishing.

"Sure. You can stay here as long as you need to. I've got the spare room."

"The baby's room."

"Right now it's the storage room, so good luck fighting your way to the bed. But yeah, I plan to decorate after this weekend. What's going on — you up here for work?" His company had a Los Angeles office not far from where I worked downtown. We'd talked about how we'd do lunch when he was up here, but we'd never actually gotten around to it.

"Yes. No." He slumped back on the couch. "What I mean is that I can work out of the L.A. office, but that's not why I'm here. Charlotte and I . . . we need a break."

"You're not splitting, are you?" That would be impossible. I knew how he adored her.

To my relief he said, "Not even close. But I can't listen to her carrying on about this adoption thing anymore. I need breathing room."

Now it was my turn to slump. "This is my fault."

Instead of assuring me that wasn't the case, Bob chuckled in agreement. "Finding out you were adopting a baby did send her off the deep end. We haven't talked about anything else for the past week and a half. She wakes me up to carry on about it. I'm desperate for sleep."

Part of me felt bad for him, but I also thought he'd brought this on himself by being so stubborn. I was probably overstepping my bounds, but I said, "Do you mind if I ask you a personal question?"

"It doesn't have anything to do with my sperm count, does it?"

"No, but I'm curious: Why are you so opposed to adoption? I mean, just because a baby doesn't have your genes doesn't mean you couldn't love it."

Bob looked sucker punched. "You don't think I know that? June, I'm not the one who's against adoption. Charlotte is. I'd give my left nut for a kid. *Any* kid."

"Charlotte?"

"She's got it in her head that having a baby of our own is the only way to go," Bob explained. "And I understand where she's coming from. She didn't even know her own dad — she wants to guarantee that I feel bonded. But I don't give a crap at this point. Between her medical problems and mine, we've had a dozen doctors tell us our chances to conceive are slim to none. Most use the term *miracle* when they're talking odds. I'm sick of the hormones and the thermometers. Hell, I'm getting sick of having sex."

"I find that hard to believe."

He smiled. "Okay, maybe I'm sick of sex on a schedule. Anyway, as soon as Charlotte heard you were going to become a mother, she freaked. She's on my ass about another round of in vitro, more tests . . . and I'm done. She doesn't want to hear it, but she needs to. I'm fucking *done*."

"Well, for the record, I hope you work it out," I said. "You'd be an awesome dad."

"Thanks." He swigged down the last of his beer. "And I enjoyed your letter, by the way. I always knew you worshipped your big bro."

As I helped him make up the bed in the spare room, I saw his gaze fall on the baby gifts from the shower, which I had stacked in there. "Sorry about all this junk," I said, wishing I'd had him sleep on the couch, where at least he wouldn't be surrounded by what he deserved but for some freak reason I was getting instead.

CHAPTER 23

I shook my brother awake at three a.m.

"What the . . . ?" he grumbled. I clicked on the overhead light, and he shielded his eyes in protest.

"You should adopt the baby," I said excitedly. Everything in me felt buzzy. I hadn't slept at all.

"No shit. Haven't we already had this discussion? Yes, I hope to adopt a baby. Now turn the light off and let me go back to sleep."

"You don't understand. Not any baby. *My* baby . . . that is, I mean Deedee's baby. I think she'll go for it. You're my family, so that's practically the same as me. You'd be a great dad. And I realize that Charlotte doesn't want to adopt, but if we explain to her that this isn't some distant dream — that it's a real baby due in a month — maybe she'd change her mind."

Bob sat up in the bed, rubbing his eyes

awake. "Slow down. You've lost me here. Why would you want us to adopt your baby?"

I sat on the edge of the bed. "Because somebody needs to, and I can't do it." The words fell like bricks around me.

"You can't do it?"

I shook my head. "Or I shouldn't, anyway."

"Why?"

"I've been trying to come up with the answer to that question myself. I guess that I wanted to change somebody's life so badly that I convinced myself that my biological clock was ticking. I don't know . . . now I'm wondering if it was just gas." I gave a halfhearted smile. "Instead of getting excited as the due date gets closer, I'm more and more certain it's the biggest mistake of my life."

"You're scared. I'll bet everybody feels that way."

"If you were about to get a baby, is that how you'd feel? Scared?"

"Sure. A little."

"But mostly you'd be thrilled, right?"

"Yeah."

"I'm not. Not at all. I'm either pretending it's not going to happen, or I'm giving myself a pep talk. Trying to convince myself it's going to be all right. That I'll be fine once the baby shows up. But then tonight when I heard you talk about everything you've been through to have a baby, I couldn't pretend anymore. I'm not ready to be a mom. At least not on my own. Not this way."

Ever since I'd said good night to Bob a few hours before, my mind had been reeling. The growing feeling of unease that had started when I forgot Deedee's due date couldn't be ignored anymore. This wasn't a task that I was crossing off a list. It was a baby — a soon-to-be living, breathing baby. I'd been preparing to grit my teeth and go through with the adoption. Suddenly I realized how wrong it would be. Sure, I'd be a better parent than a fourteen-year-old girl, but not much better. Yet I couldn't leave Deedee in the lurch with only a month to go. She'd made plans with her life. Walking into her house on Saturday and saying, "I've changed my mind," was unthinkable. But telling her I'd found a better situation — a couple who I knew for certain would give her baby girl everything she deserved to have — that I could do.

"You're serious about this," Bob said.

"As a heart attack."

A smile crept across his face. "You know,

Charlotte might go for this. The thought that there's a baby who *needs* her — one who'd otherwise be stuck with a mom who's only doing it because she said she would, not because she has any real interest."

"I'm not *that* bad," I said defensively.

"Whatever. What I'm saying is, I couldn't come up with any other way to convince Charlotte to adopt, but this might work. She was good and pissed that you were getting a baby. She kept talking about how she would be so much better a mother to that baby than you could ever be. How it deserved two parents, not one who can barely manage to keep a plant alive, much less a child. This would be her chance to prove it."

I was half about to rescind my offer, insulted as I was, when I realized my brother was already dialing his cell phone.

"Sugarplum, it's me. . . . I'm fine. . . . Yes, I know I suck for taking off and it's the middle of the night, but listen . . ." And he went on to propose the idea. He'd been right — it didn't take a great deal of arm-twisting to get Charlotte to agree with this new plan. In fact, when he said the baby was due in a month, I could hear her squeal through the phone.

Over the next half hour on the phone, we

made arrangements for Bob to go back to San Diego and pick up Charlotte, who was already saying she'd be willing to relocate to Los Angeles if that's what it took. They'd come up Saturday morning and go to Deedee's with me. She'd have a chance to meet them, and if all went well, we could arrange to switch over the adoption papers right there. I could practically hear Charlotte decorating the nursery as we spoke, and I'd be willing to bet anything she had names picked out.

Before he hung up, Bob said quietly, "Char, it's so incredible. After all the waiting, this could be it."

Friday afternoon, Martucci came into my office with a box of Matchbox cars left over from a promotion we'd run last year. "What did you want these for?"

"Just in the nick of time! They're for my meeting with Bigwood at three o'clock." As I grabbed the box, I looked at him and said, "Hey, there's something different about you. What is it?"

"That's perfect the way you said that. Bigwood will eat it up. Imitation is the sincerest form of flattery, you know."

"I mean it! You look different."

He shrugged me off. "So tell me why you

wanted these cars."

I showed him the four-by-six-foot 3-D freeway map I'd spent most of the morning making. I was especially pleased with the way my clay foothills had turned out.

Martucci grimaced. "Your fifth-grade science project?"

"It's so I can demonstrate the freeway race. See, I'll take the cars and go *vroom-vroom* like this" — I took two toy cars and set them on my model — "and the one in the carpool lane will win."

Martucci was silent, which had me worried. He wasn't one to hold back.

"What?"

"Nothing."

"Tell me."

"All right. That is the stupidest thing I've ever seen."

Slumping, I groaned, "It's the best I could do. Troy Jones was supposed to help me do a live race on real freeways, but he bailed."

"Why didn't you ask me to do it?"

Good question. Why hadn't I asked? Maybe it was because he didn't have a spiffy race outfit like Troy said he'd wear.

"Oh, it would be wonderful if you could —"

"Too late. I didn't drive in today, and the motor home's off getting washed."

"Then I'm back to the science project." I sighed. "Because I'm sure not going to stand there and *talk* about my idea."

"Why not?"

"Phyllis told me that I had to wow Bigwood. She said that's what he expects — wowing."

"I agree, but a race is a race. You can describe it in a sentence — only a moron wouldn't get it. You're missing the point. A race isn't what you're selling Bigwood."

"Oh yeah? What *am* I selling?"

Martucci crossed his arms and leaned on the edge of my desk. "You."

"Then I'm doomed." When he rolled his eyes at me, I said, "I'm serious. I already tried that before — I wrote a big proposal with all kinds of ideas saying why I was so great, and he gave my job to Lizbeth."

"I doubt Bigwood ever read your proposal. Even if he did — and don't take this the wrong way — I don't blame him for skipping you over before."

"Thanks a lot!"

"It's true. Frankly, you didn't seem that excited about anything — like you were just going through the motions. I always got the impression that you were only here because you didn't have anywhere else to go."

"Well, that's not how I felt. You didn't

know me."

"Except for Susan, I don't think anybody knew you."

It was hard to have a comeback for that.

"So what you need to do," he continued, "is make Bigwood aware that June Parker is a force to be reckoned with. That you've got a track record. You've got ideas. You've got balls."

"I don't know if I can do that."

He slapped my arm. "Sure you can. Take him out for drinks — he's a bourbon man, by the way. Show him the clips of your interviews from the gas giveaway."

"You want me to remind him about that fiasco?"

"I want you to show him that you're cool under pressure."

"Well," I hedged, "I guess I could get the interview files from Brie. And she has a portable DVD player. I could pack it up and take Bigwood to the Brass Monkey."

"That's the spirit. And whatever you do, don't let him pick up the check, however hard he tries. Wrestle him to the floor if you have to. Paying is a sign of dominance."

"Got it."

"Good. But out of curiosity, why is this promotion such a big deal to you now? I'd figure with you about to be on the mommy track, you'd be laying low."

"For one thing, you're being sexist," I admonished. "A woman can have both a career and a family. Secondly" — I picked an imaginary piece of lint off my shirt so I didn't have to meet his eyes — "I'm not going to adopt the baby after all."

"Sorry, I didn't realize. Something go wrong?"

"Only that I changed my mind."

"Then it's a good thing, right? You can go back to your wild single ways."

"Yeah, well, as far as that goes, the rumor that I was going to be a mom scared off my major prospect," I said glumly. When Martucci looked at me confused, I said, "Troy. As soon as I told him that I was going to adopt a baby, he took off."

"Ah. I see."

"It's so frustrating. I felt as if the list were helping me figure out my life. I thought, *Aha!* It's a relationship and kids that have been missing. But it must not be those things — otherwise I wouldn't have let my chance for them get away."

"Come on. There are plenty more chances."

"I suppose, but I'm still bummed. Deep down, I'd hoped the list would have a bigger impact . . . that it would help me identify what I truly wanted."

"At least maybe you'll realize what you *deserve.*"

"Such as . . . ?"

"Sure as hell more than a guy who'd bolt the second you brought up the idea of a baby."

"Yeah, Susan said pretty much the same thing."

"She's right. You deserve better . . . somebody who gets you for who you are — whether you have a kid or not. Or a dozen kids, for that matter. Believe me, some men would find it very sexy all that you've been taking on."

"Aw, *garsh,* Martucci," I said. Laughing, I grabbed him in a hug. As his arms closed around me, I glanced over his shoulder, and — knock me over with a feather — who should be standing in the opening of my cubicle but Troy.

"Hey, June," he said, holding up his hand hesitantly in a wave. He was dressed in a racing jacket over a shirt and tie.

I pulled away from Martucci, flummoxed. What was Troy doing here?

"I — I thought you couldn't make it," I sputtered.

"You didn't get my message?"

He and Martucci shook hands hello while

I tried to dredge up the memory of Troy's phone call. I'd been listening to it when my brother showed up at the door. It had seemed so obvious that Troy was canceling, I'd never bothered to play the whole thing.

"It got cut off," I said, aiming as close to the truth as I dared to get. "So . . . what did it say?"

"That I'd be here today unless you called to let me know you didn't want me to come. And also" — he glanced self-consciously at Martucci — "I tried to explain why I left Vegas so fast."

"Oh."

Did Troy just say there was an explanation for his hasty retreat — or was that the sound of the two sides of my brain opening and clapping shut?

Martucci, hands in his pockets, ambled away toward the hallway, pausing by my cubicle opening. "Well, Parker, guess you're back to plan A. Good luck."

I glanced at my watch. Fifteen minutes to go until my meeting. The race would certainly be flashy — especially with Troy looking every bit the pro — but Martucci's words rang in my mind. What *was* I going for? Did I want to sell Bigwood on the idea of a race . . . or did I have the guts to pitch myself?

Turning to Troy, I said, "I feel bad making you come all this way, but I've decided on a different plan."

"No race, then?"

I shook my head.

"Oh . . . okay. Not a problem. But . . ." Again I saw his eyes shift toward Martucci. "If you've got a second, I'd like to talk about . . . a few things. . . ."

I wanted to hear what he had to say, but not with minutes to go before my presentation. I needed to find Brie and burn the files of my interviews onto a disc. I needed to eat something bready if I was going to be drinking bourbon. After that, without anyone watching, I could scurry home and play the message to find out what Troy's reason was for letting me down. Maybe it was a valid one — and if it was, well, then who knew?

"I wish I could," I said, "but right now I've got to run."

"I'll let you go, then," Troy said, and it seemed he wasn't surprised by my reaction. Even though he was standing there in his race regalia, he looked as though he'd expected it. He added worriedly, "You still coming to the party on Tuesday?"

"Wouldn't miss it," I assured him. "Martucci's coming, too . . . and Brie . . . and a few other friends who've been helping me with the list. Your mom said for me to invite as many people as I wanted, so I invited."

He laughed then and said, "Sounds good. She keeps calling it a little get-together, but it gets bigger every time I turn around. Pretty soon we're going to have to rent the Convention Center."

After Troy left, I handed Martucci his box of cars back. "Okay, I'm facing Bigwood on my own," I said. "You'd better be right about this."

"When are you going to accept the fact that I'm always right?"

Two hours and three bourbons later, I tottered back into the office. Most everyone had left for the weekend. I stopped by Susan's office, getting there as she was about to switch off her lights and leave. "I was worried I was going to miss you!" she exclaimed. "Sooooooo? How'd it go?"

"Let's just say that I astounded even myself."

I must have slurred, because she smiled. "He talked you into the third drink, huh?"

"Yes, not that it matters. I already had him eating out of my hand by that point."

"I'll bet you did. Is the job yours?"

"He says he's restructuring, so the job as

it was doesn't exist anymore, but he's definitely promoting me. He loved the race idea . . . although" — I reminded myself to give Martucci a piece of my mind later — "it took him a while to get what I was talking about. He said he wished he had a visual." Fifth-grade science project indeed.

"Well, congratulations! I'd offer to take you out for a celebratory drink, but I've got to pick the kids up — I'm already running late. You rode the bus in today, didn't you? You want a ride home?"

"No, thanks."

"You sure? We could do dinner at my house if you don't mind Burger King — I promised the boys."

"I'm sure. All I want to do is go home and veg out. This past week has been insane, and Bob and Charlotte are going to be at my place at nine o'clock tomorrow to go over a few last-minute things before we see Deedee."

"That's right. Oh, June, it's so incredible that things are working out this way."

"It's not a done deal yet," I reminded her. "Deedee still has to say yes."

"She will."

After promising Susan that I'd call if I needed anything, I went straight to Martucci's office. I was barely in the door when he said, "Hmm, I forgot to warn you that he'd try to talk you into a third drink."

Okay, I hadn't even spoken yet, so I figured I must really reek of alcohol. "Aren't you going to ask how it went?"

"With that kittenish smile you're giving me? I'm afraid you're about to tell me he made you my boss."

"We'll have to see. He's moving things around, but I'm definitely management."

"And you came to say you owe it all to me."

"I did want to say thanks. I'd give you another hug, but you know how I am once I have a few drinks. I might go after the rat-tail again."

With that, he shot me a grin and turned slightly, rubbing the back of his neck. It was neatly trimmed. Not a hairy tadpole in sight.

"It's gone!" I cried. "I knew there was something different about you. What made you do it?"

"Just decided it was time."

I didn't mention that he was about twenty years off. "Well, it suits you."

"Glad you think so."

I needed to make a dash for it if I was going to make the five-fifteen bus, but I knew I hadn't thanked Martucci for everything yet. I at least owed him that. "By the way," I said, feeling shy suddenly. "Thanks for the other night. You could have so easily taken advantage. You were serious, weren't you? I mean, that nothing happened?"

He tipped back in his chair. "Doll, if you ever got a piece of me, I don't care how much you had to drink — you wouldn't forget it."

Chapter 24

I listened to the message Troy left on my machine five times before I so much as kicked off my shoes.

The first time around, I'd heard enough to conclude he was canceling. And when he told me at the office that he'd tried to explain why he'd left Las Vegas so abruptly, I assumed it'd be a cheesy excuse along the lines of "Something suddenly came up."

The last thing I expected was what he actually said.

I hit "play" again.

"Hi, June, this is Troy. I've been trying to call, but you're not an easy woman to get on the phone. I hate to leave this in a message, but here goes. I know we talked about my coming to your meeting Friday to help with your race, and I'd understand if you don't want me to. I still plan to be there. Three o'clock. It's in my book. Give me a call if you don't want me to show, okay?

"And, shoot, how do I say this? You're probably wondering why I took off so fast Saturday night. I wanted to make sure you know that it's nothing you said or did. It's just that . . . and this is going to sound crazy . . . but all of a sudden it seemed so wrong that we were sitting there, listening to music, having fun, and making plans, and, with you about to adopt a baby, life was marching forward. I don't know why, but it pissed me off. It's not rational, but that's what it was. I guess my mom cries to deal with stuff. I punch holes through doors and drive too fast and say shitty things to nice girls. So I'm sorry about that. Anyway, I guess I'm more messed up about my sister's accident than I thought I was. I wish I met you because, I don't know, we bumped grocery carts or something. I know I'm rambling, but I wouldn't feel right if I didn't let you know that I think you're great, and if circumstances were —"

Beep.

My machine cut him off, and even though I hadn't correctly filled in the blanks of his message before, I felt I could reliably do so at this point: that if circumstances were different, we could have something together. But they aren't. So we can't.

I felt strangely at peace with it.

404

It wasn't as if he'd dumped me at the altar. We hadn't — as Troy had once stopped short of saying — so much as kissed/dated/screwed.

So perhaps the real question, I pondered as I finally got around to changing into sweats and slippers and making myself a cup of tea, was not so much why I didn't feel emotionally wrenched, but why I'd had my hopes up in the first place.

Sure, he was cute, but plenty of guys are cute. Heck, now that Martucci lost that disgusting rattail, one could say that even he . . . *Nah.* I erased the thought. Martucci would never be cute. Bunnies are cute. He'd be more likely compared with a creature that might *eat* bunnies. Anyway, the point was that a pretty face could take a guy only so far in my affections. It had to have been more than that with Troy.

When I'd run into him at the cemetery those many months ago, I'd been wallowing in depression. Doing the list had given me purpose. In a convoluted way, I had him to thank for it, even if he had no idea he'd been the impetus. It was that look he'd given me when I'd told him I was going to complete the list for his sister. In a glance, he erased my mundane past. The reflection I saw of myself in Troy's eyes was like staring in a funhouse mirror that made me appear braver and bolder than I was. Even if I knew it wasn't real, I couldn't tear my gaze away from it.

As of tomorrow, however, I wasn't going to need the illusion anymore. I was going to make something happen that just a few months ago would have seemed inconceivable. I was going to change the lives of so many people at once. My brother and Charlotte would get the baby they'd always dreamed of. A baby would have a good home. Deedee would be able to go on with her studies and attend college. And Troy, Kitty, and the entire Jones family would know that the item on the list that most spoke to them about their beloved Marissa — *Change someone's life* — had been completed with such grace.

The paperwork for the adoption sat on my coffee table. My brother and Charlotte would arrive in the morning. We'd head over to Deedee's — I'd already called to mention I needed to go over a few things.

I absently stirred sugar into my tea. The baby was going to be a girl. Maybe they'd name her June.

Knocking on the door to Deedee's house, I tried not to let myself think about how much I had riding on this moment. Next to me, I could smell the newness of Charlotte's dress and hear my brother hum under his breath to calm himself.

I'd mentally rehearsed my lines on the drive over. I'd tell Deedee how important it was for her baby to have everything, and while I had thought I was the one who could provide it, I'd been wrong. The baby deserved two parents. I'd remind Deedee of how she didn't want her baby to go to strangers, and she wouldn't have to. This was my family. I could vouch for the sort of parents they'd be. Loving. Attentive. Eager.

A man answered the door, introducing himself as Javier, Deedee's mother's fiancé. Even in the blazing July heat he wore a skullcap, but he had a wide smile and bug eyes that gave him such a jolliness, I found myself smiling back at him. "The girls will be here in a minute," he said. "Have a seat."

I made introductions, and when Maria and Deedee showed up, I made them again. Deedee sat next to her mother and Javier on the couch. Her usual oversize jersey was replaced with a tank top, which showed off her belly to full effect. Charlotte took the easy chair, and kitchen chairs were brought in to accommodate Bob and me.

"You have a lovely home," Charlotte said

to Maria.

Javier translated, and Maria said, *"Gracias."*

Small talk wasn't going to be simple with Charlotte and me unable to speak Spanish — although Bob was fluent — so I figured I'd get to the point.

"Before we sign the adoption contract," I said, "there are things we need to discuss."

Javier started talking to Maria in Spanish — I assumed to translate, but he kept going on and on. She said something back. They seemed to be in the midst of a full-on debate. Bob could understand what they were saying, however, which was why I was frightened when he buried his face in his hands and mumbled, "Oh Christ. This is bad."

"What's going on?" I whispered. Javier and Maria kept talking as if we weren't there. Deedee stared at the carpet.

Bob wiped his hands down his face and breathed out a sigh. "I need to get Charlotte out of here," he said, so quietly that I wasn't sure I'd even heard him correctly. Then he spoke aloud in Spanish. Javier and Maria stopped their conversation, looking up as guiltily as if they'd been caught French-kissing on the couch. Bob grabbed Charlotte's hand — her confusion evident

— and said, "We'll wait outside."

I really started to worry when he kissed the side of my head before leaving. Whatever they were discussing, it had to be bad.

When the door banged behind them, I finally asked, "What's going on?"

Javier cleared his throat before speaking. "We want to thank you for coming here today," he said, his voice stiff and rehearsed. "We're grateful that you were willing to adopt Deedee's baby, but we want to tell you that that won't be necessary."

Not *necessary?* I tried without success to catch Deedee's eyes.

He continued, "Maria has agreed to be my wife. We'll be starting a life together, and a family. We've talked about it, and we want to start that family by raising Deedee's baby as our own."

My speech about the importance of two parents and family dried on my tongue. I felt myself shriveling as well, as if my physical size were trying to match the insignificance I felt inside.

They were keeping the baby.

I wasn't needed.

Bob and Charlotte weren't needed.

"Deedee," I managed to say, "is this what you want?"

She nodded, still not lifting her eyes.

"She'll be able to stay in school," Javier said. "We'll need help at home, but it will be as a big sister. Not as a mother."

So much for changing someone's life. I hadn't made a difference at all. Despite my efforts, Deedee's life was progressing exactly as it would have had she never met me.

My brother and his wife, however, were worse off because of my meddling. I'd marched them to the top of the mountain and shown them what they could have: a new life, a baby in their arms. The family they'd been dreaming of. Then I'd unceremoniously marched them back down, empty-handed.

Yet a tiny flame of hope flickered. Deedee would at least need me for the labor room. Her mom could hardly handle the job, being blind and speaking only Spanish. "I'll see you Wednesday night for the childbirth class. Right?"

"I'm dropping out of the class," Deedee mumbled, the first words she'd spoken since I'd arrived. "Since I'm not giving the baby away, I can't go no more." Then she corrected herself like the A student I knew her to be: "*Any*more."

"But you still need to know what to do during labor."

She cleared her throat. "Rose at Big

Sisters found me another class. It's bilingual, so my mom can go with me. It's on Saturdays, though, so . . ."

I finished for her, "So you can't do anything with me anymore."

The last drops of hope drained away. It was over.

We fell silent. It wasn't one of those comfortable silences that people talk about — it commanded our attention like a precocious child. At last, I stood to leave. What else was there to say? Deedee's baby deserved two parents and a family, and that's exactly what it was going to get. After offering limp congratulations, I headed for the door.

"Don't hate me." Deedee uttered the words so softly, I barely heard her. I made my way out to the blazing July afternoon, where I could see Bob and Charlotte wilting in their car.

I climbed into the backseat. "I can't tell you how sorry I am."

"You made it clear there were no guarantees," Bob said. "We took a shot. It didn't work out."

Charlotte, her voice trembling, added, "I've heard about situations like this. How the birth mother changes her mind. It happens all the time."

Instead of comforting me, her words sent my emotions plummeting. Thanks to me, she'd witnessed firsthand how very wrong things could go.

They left for San Diego as soon as they dropped me back at my apartment. I headed straight for my couch and sat there, stunned.

Why had I been foolish enough to believe that I could do the list? While I was at it, why didn't I try out for the Olympic figure-skating team? Or attempt to climb Mt. Everest in my flip-flops? Disappointing as it was, it was time to face the truth: Completing Marissa's list was beyond my grasp. I couldn't do the one task that really counted. I still hadn't even found Buddy Fitch. So I'd gone without a bra for a day. Thrown away a scale. Big deal. I'd thought I could step into another woman's dreams and somehow be infused with her lust for life. All that happened was that I'd fallen short, as always.

The phone rang on and off all Saturday and into Sunday, and I let the machine pick up. I'd call them back eventually. In the meantime, it was all I could stomach to hear messages from Susan and my mom and Susan again and Susan four more times, sounding grotesquely chipper and eager to talk to me so they could hear the good news.

412

■ ■ ■ ■

On Monday, I could tell word of what had happened had made its way through the office quickly, and at first people stopped by to offer their support. Upon seeing how badly I didn't want to talk about it, they rallied around by leaving me the hell alone. Now those are friends. Susan even called Sebastian for me and let him know he could call off any last-ditch efforts to find Buddy Fitch.

I threw myself into work, the easiest way to push out the thoughts churning in my head. And there was plenty to do. Even though Bigwood said I wasn't getting Lizbeth's old job, he certainly had been saving plenty of her aborted projects to dump on me. Still, even he must have sensed something was awry, because even though I'd become the walking dead, he never once asked what was different about me.

As Troy had put it, time kept marching forward, no matter how much I wanted to curl into a ball and hide. I managed to keep myself more or less distracted all the way to the dreaded Tuesday evening when — with Marissa's birthday party due to start in a half hour — Susan and Brie came to find me in my cubicle.

"We're heading out now. You want to carpool with us?" Brie asked.

"There are a few things I need to do first. I'm taking the bus."

Susan looked at me skeptically. "You're not going to blow it off, are you? I'm prepared to drag you to the party if need be. Those people are counting on you. Nobody's going to care that you didn't finish the list."

"I promise, I'll be there. The 440 bus heads straight down Wilshire. It won't take me any time at all. In the meantime, you guys go represent."

"Represent," Brie muttered. "Will you people never quit stealing our slang?"

Turning to leave, Susan said, "We'll save you a seat."

"Near the back, please," I replied, my voice pleading.

I'd go to the party all right, but I was aiming for fashionably late and as low-profile as possible. If I didn't have a chance to talk to anyone, maybe they'd assume I'd finished the list. The thought of lying also occurred to me — and if it hadn't been for a vague unease about being struck down by lightning, that's exactly what I would have done.

Besides, it wasn't over yet. Earlier in the

day, I had remembered one of Martucci's ideas. He'd said that if the adoption fell through, I could try to change people's lives by handing out lottery tickets. If one hit, then I'd certainly changed a life.

It was pitiful, but I was going to do it anyway.

After I was sure the others had left, I snuck down to the liquor store and bought a hundred Lotto scratchers. One by one, I stopped people on the street and asked them to scratch off the ticket on the spot — and if you ever want to know about the lack of trust in our society these days, try offering something for free.

So I wouldn't be too late, I started handing out a few at a time. By seven o'clock when the party was officially under way, I'd had only two winners: ten dollars and sixty dollars. The ten-dollar winner said, "Hey, thanks, this ought to be good for a couple packs of smokes," and the sixty-dollar winner was excited, but — as her engagement ring looked as if it had cost about sixty *thousand* — I doubted that it would be exactly life-changing.

Clutching the last ticket, I headed to my bus stop. There was a woman standing there in filthy clothes and missing several teeth — precisely what I'd been hoping for. Even if she won a small amount, it could be enough to have an impact.

"Hi," I chirped. "I've got this lottery ticket to give you."

She sneered at me. "What for? Is this a trick?"

"No. Here —" And I handed it over. She started to tuck it in her cleavage, and I said, "Please scratch it off now. I need to see if it's a winner."

"I ain't got a coin."

I dug through my purse and handed her a nickel.

"Quarters work better," she said slyly.

I kept digging until I found a quarter, then held my breath as she scratched off the card.

Nothing.

Disappointment rose like bile. I must've looked stricken, because she said, "Girlie, it ain't no big deal."

"I know. But if it'd been a winner, maybe it would have made a difference in your life. I'd like to have done that."

"You want to make a difference in *my* life?"

"Desperately."

She gave me a slow once-over. "Them shoes of yours look comfy. Mine pinch my feet something awful. I'll bet anything if you gave me them shoes, that'd make a big difference."

My shoes? I was about to scoff when I thought, *What the heck.* I slipped off my shoes, a hundred-and-twenty-dollar pair I'd recently splurged on at Macy's.

She took them, and without a thank-you or so much as a word otherwise, she left. I stood at the bus stop, waiting for the bus to arrive. Maybe tomorrow, after a night's sleep, I could come up with another way to change someone's life. I decided right there that I wasn't going to give the list back until it was done. I'd go to the party and face everyone as a loser. But, hey, at least I'd tried.

The thought of which left me utterly thunderstruck.

I'd tried.

I'd failed. I'd picked myself up, dusted myself off, and *tried again.* Me!

Of course — that was it!

A horn honked nearby, tugging me from my thoughts.

"Hey!" It was Martucci, calling to me through the rolled-down passenger window of his Mercedes. "Get in, you nut job! I'll give you a ride."

I ran over and climbed into the passenger seat — and mmm, the fragrance of real Corinthian leather sure beat the smell of

417

your average city bus stop. Martucci chuckled as he shifted into gear. "I'd ask why you
were standing there in your socks, but I'm
not sure I want to know."

CHAPTER 25

20 THINGS TO DO BY MY 25TH BIRTHDAY

1. ~~Lose 100 pounds~~
2. ~~Kiss a stranger~~
3. ~~Change someone's life~~
4. ~~Wear sexy shoes~~
5. ~~Run a 5K~~
6. ~~Dare to go braless~~
7. Make Buddy Fitch pay
8. ~~Be the hottest girl at Oasis~~
9. ~~Get on TV~~
10. ~~Ride in a helicopter~~
11. ~~Pitch an idea at work~~
12. ~~Try boogie boarding~~
13. ~~Eat ice cream in public~~
14. ~~Go on a blind date~~
15. ~~Take Mom and Grandma to see Wayne Newton~~
16. ~~Get a massage~~
17. ~~Throw away my bathroom scale~~
18. ~~Watch a sunrise~~

419

The private room at Oasis was packed.
People sat at cocktail tables and stood
around holding drinks and plates of food.
When Martucci and I walked in, a woman
named Norma — I remembered her as the
Weight Watchers leader who'd given Marissa
her lifetime pin the night she died — was
near the bar, in the midst of telling a story
into a handheld microphone. The fact that
it ended with, "And from that day forward,
every woman in the group practically
stripped naked before weighing in" — followed by a roar of laughter from the crowd
— gave me an indication of the overall
mood. It was, as Kitty Jones had hoped, a
party.

We grabbed beers from a bartender near
the back and then made our way to the table
where Susan and Brie sat with Sebastian
and Kip.

"I was starting to worry you weren't coming," Susan said, pulling purses off a couple
of chairs she'd been saving. "What happened to your shoes?"

"Don't ask."

As I sat down, Troy relieved Norma of the

microphone. He was in jeans and a button-down shirt, his hair recently cut — but it didn't incite lust in me as much as it made me want to pinch his cheeks.

"Anybody else who wants to share," Troy said, "feel free to come on up." He held out the microphone.

Brie gave me a nudge. "Go up there."

A girl trotted to the microphone, buying me time. She introduced herself as a school friend of Marissa's and started to tell a story about how she and Marissa used to pass notes in algebra class.

"June doesn't have to talk if she doesn't want to," Susan said quietly to everyone at the table, as if I weren't there.

"The fact that she showed up is plenty," Sebastian agreed.

Martucci took a swig of his beer. "Of course she should talk. She's the reason they're having this party in the first place."

"I am not!" I hissed. As if I needed that kind of pressure! "They're having it because Marissa wrote a list to be completed by her twenty-fifth birthday . . . which, by the way, it isn't. Completed, that is."

Brie shook her head. "Eighteen down, two left to go. What a shame."

"Actually," I said, unable to suppress a proud smile, "only one left to go."

"You found Buddy Fitch?" Sebastian said, excited enough that he forgot to whisper. A few heads turned our way, and I shushed him.

"No, I still have to do that one."

"Then what — ? How — ? I mean, I thought . . ."

As Sebastian flustered, Brie took the opportunity to elbow me. "Your man, Troy, is looking mighty fine."

"The brother?" Kip asked. "You've got something going on with the brother?"

"That's dishy," Sebastian said with obvious interest.

"There's nothing between Troy and me."

"At least not yet," Brie taunted. "The night is young."

"Yeah," Martucci piped up, a little roughly even for him. "Now that you're not going to adopt a baby, he'll probably be interested again."

Susan grunted in disgust on my behalf. "Leave her alone."

"It's not what you think," I said, wanting to clarify, and for some reason I turned to Martucci. "He's just messed up about losing his sister — they were close. I kind of feel sorry for him."

"Did I miss something?" Susan asked. "Are you and Troy a thing?"

"Nah," I said. Troy had again taken the microphone and was holding it out for whoever might speak next. "He's a nice guy," I said, rising from the table. "But to be honest, he's not my type."

I claimed the microphone from Troy, who gave me a brief kiss on the cheek before going back to stand near his family. I blew out a breath, trying to calm my nerves, and then faced the crowd of sixty or so people. I hadn't written a speech. Sure, I'd given it plenty of times in my imagination — but when I had, it was always about finishing the list. The speech I'd mentally rehearsed over and over was one of triumph — the list a wrapped gift I'd present to a grieving family. I was going to have to wing this one.

"Hi, I'm June Parker," I said, surveying the room. I recognized faces from the funeral, although that day now seemed a lifetime ago. "As some of you may know, I was the one who was in the car accident with Marissa. What you may not know is that I discovered that Marissa had written a very special list. On it were twenty things she planned to do by her birthday . . . today." I paused, and there was a murmur from the crowd. This was news to most, I could tell.

"In honor of Marissa's memory, I set out

to complete the list. She already had crossed off two of the tasks herself. One of them was to lose a hundred pounds, a goal she reached and, as I understand, was very proud of. Luckily for me, not all the tasks were so challenging. The other one that Marissa did on her own was to wear a pair of great, sexy shoes . . ." I smiled, glancing down at my stocking feet. "Which was too bad, because I wouldn't have minded doing that one myself."

That received a few chuckles, and I gazed out into a sea of smiling, open faces. This was not going to be a tough crowd by any means; they were eager to hear how Marissa's dreams came true. I only hoped my unsuccessful attempt wouldn't disappoint them too much.

"I didn't have a chance to get to know Marissa," I continued. "The Marissa I'm familiar with is the one who wrote the list, and from it, I know she must have been an amazing person."

There were several nods to that.

Not sure what to say next, I asked, "I suppose you want to know what was on the list?"

A smattering of applause and a chorus of "Yeah!" answered me.

"Let's see . . . ," I said, starting to loosen

up. "There was trying boogie boarding. Getting a massage. Going on a blind date. Making a big donation to charity. Taking her mom and grandma" — I glanced over to where the family sat, and Kitty gave me a wink — "to see the great Wayne Newton in concert." That got an "Awwww . . ." and some applause, and I scanned my brain for the others. Even though the list had been such a huge part of the last year of my life, I was having a rough time recalling everything.

"There were more," I said, "but I want to tell you about the most important one . . . the one that I believe was even bigger to Marissa than losing the weight. She'd written on her list that she wanted to change someone's life. Those of you who were close to Marissa probably realize how that would have been dear to her heart. Everyone tells me what a giving person she was.

"So I set out to try to change someone's life — which I'm sure you can agree is no small order. I wanted to do something special, and I thought I had the right thing. I'd managed to find a way to help a family desperate for a baby to adopt one from a teenage girl who couldn't keep her baby herself. Only . . ." I realized I was getting far more personal than I'd intended to, and

I was having a difficult time choking out the words. "It didn't work out. The girl kept the baby, and the couple . . . well, they're still childless."

I caught the eye of an elderly woman who had that deer-in-the-headlights look of someone who senses a speech is about to veer into a very ugly direction. I figured I'd better cut to the chase. "And yet changing someone's life is still crossed off the list. To explain why, I'll have to tell you something I'm not exactly thrilled to admit. Because the truth is, before I started doing this list, I hadn't made much of my own life. In fact, a person who in recent months has become a very close friend — someone who has been there when I needed him and whose opinion I've grown to truly value and respect — said he always felt I was just going through the motions. As much as I hated to hear it, he was right.

"Part of the reason I did the list was so I could feel what it was like to have purpose and direction the way Marissa did. I had no idea whether I'd finish it, and I'll have to confess right now that I didn't. There's one item I still have to do. But that's the point I'm trying to make. On my way over here, I was still trying to finish the list. Even though I hadn't completed it on time, I wasn't going to give up."

The last few words came out as a squeak. Tears welled in my eyes. I heard Kitty say, "You're doing fine, sweetie."

My voice quavering, I said, "What I realized is that I didn't need to change anyone's life. Because Marissa changed *mine.* She's taught me what it means to value life. To try. To put myself out there for something that's important to me.

"I'd hoped to come here tonight to tell you about what I'd done for Marissa . . . but the best I can do is say how truly grateful I am for all she's given me. I'll never forget it. And I'll never, ever take it for granted."

With that, I set down the microphone and padded back to my seat with the crowd cheering and whooping. Susan greeted me with one of her bone-crushing hugs, and Sebastian and Kip were both sobbing.

"Best fucking speech I ever heard," Martucci said, using his thumb to wipe a tear from my face.

Brie said, snuffling, "That's it, I'm going to do me a list."

A guy bearing bagpipes who said he was in the marching corps with Marissa came to the front of the room, saying he wanted to play her favorite song, "Amazing Grace."

We listened attentively because, frankly, it's hard to have a conversation with bagpipes blaring. After he finished, and not getting any more takers on the microphone, Troy thanked people for coming. "Please stick around," he announced. "There's still a ton of food. Plus, we'll be cutting the cake soon."

The jukebox kicked on as Norma came up to the table. She was eating a piece of pie. Considering she was a Weight Watchers leader, I admired how she didn't feel the need to apologize for it.

"Well done on finishing the list," she said.

I corrected her. "*Almost* finishing it."

"Ah. Close enough. I'm sorry you never came back to the group, but you look good. Thin."

"It was the I'm-too-depressed-to-eat diet," I said.

Brie shook her head. "I wish that would happen to me. I eat when I get upset. And when I get mad. Or stressed. Or if I'm happy. I eat then, too."

Norma swallowed a bite of her pie, then said, "I hear you there. And Marissa dying so soon after she lost the weight — it was so sad. The group took it pretty hard. We had a couple meetings that were less about food and more about the process of grieving. Poor Buddy took it the hardest. He —"

I nearly choked on my drink. "Did you say Buddy?"

Sebastian glanced up. "Who said Buddy?"

"I did," Norma said, clearly startled. "I was telling June how Buddy took Marissa's death especially hard. He's in my Weight Watchers group, and he and Marissa were quite —"

Sebastian cut her off. "His name isn't Buddy Fitch by chance, is it?"

"I do believe his last name is Fitch. Why — do you know him?"

I couldn't believe it. I'd been searching everywhere for this guy, and I never thought that he might be one of the Weight Watchers group. I may have even seen him the night I went for my one and only meeting. The last thing I wanted to do was face those people again. But if I had to, I would. I'd be able to finish the list. "I want to meet him," I said. "Does he still go to the meetings?"

"Not since he reached his weight goal," she said.

"Oh no." I couldn't hide my disappointment. But they probably had records. Of course they did! I'd be able to —

"But if you want to meet him, it's no problem. He's here."

Sebastian slapped his hands on the table

so hard that it made our drinks jump. "Get outta town. Here?! In the bar?"

"Well, yes. When Kitty Jones invited me, she said to go ahead and extend an invitation to anyone I wanted."

"He's *here*," I said, stunned. Buddy Fitch was here. "Where?"

Norma gestured toward a man standing with his family. "Over there. Here, I can take you to meet him. Let me go get my —"

I didn't even wait for her to finish. Here was my chance to complete the list! Oh, I hoped he'd confess to whatever misdeed he'd visited upon poor Marissa. If not, I'd do whatever it took to drag it out of him.

"That was a great speech," he said when I approached. He was a husky man with thinning red hair and a square but friendly face.

"Thanks," I said, and then got right to the point. "Are you Buddy Fitch?"

"Me? Nah. Name's Peter Fitch."

My spirits sank, but then a kid's voice said, "I'm Buddy."

I gasped. "You're Flash!" I said right as he pointed to me and said:

"Now I remember who you are! You're the lady from the race!"

"*You're* Buddy Fitch?" How could the nice kid from the race possibly have hurt Marissa? There must be a mistake. "I need to talk to you a minute," I said, leading him away.

"You still running?" he asked, settling into a chair behind a giant potted fern where I thought we could get privacy.

I gave him a guilty look and admitted I'd done it only for the list. "Speaking of which," I said, unfolding it, "maybe you can explain something to me." I showed him #7: *Make Buddy Fitch pay.* "You have any idea why Marissa would write the one about making you pay?"

"Sure. She and I had a bet. When I joined Weight Watchers, I had thirty pounds to lose. I wanted to get on the track team, and one day when I sat next to Marissa, I told her I bet I'd never make it. She bet me I would, and we put money on it. She promised that she'd help me train."

Unbelievable. "So it was literal. Make you pay."

"She came to run with me a couple times after school before she . . . um . . . Anyhow, I didn't quit. I kept running."

"How much did you bet?"

"A dollar."

I leaned close so my eyes were level with his. "So I guess what I need to know is, did you make the track team?"

"Yep."

"In that case, Buddy Fitch" — I extended a hand, palm up — "pay up."

#7. Make Buddy Fitch pay

Soon after I brought the list back to the table and crossed off the last item, my friends gathered to leave.

"I'm so lucky to have all of you," I said, overwhelmed with emotion. It was finally sinking in that I'd finished the list. Mere minutes earlier, I'd thought I still had a long way to go. "I could have never completed the list if it hadn't been for your help."

There was much murmuring of "You're welcome" and "Glad to do it," until Martucci said, "Don't start blubbering all over me, Parker. This is a new shirt."

"Are you going to give back the list?" Susan asked.

I nodded. "That was always the plan: that I'd return it as soon as I was done. I was starting to fear that it might never happen."

"It did — and on time," Sebastian said warmly. "It must be the writer in you . . . can't miss a deadline."

Everyone left except for Martucci, who said he'd stick around to give me a ride home. I found Kitty Jones straightening a balloon bouquet. "Here you are," I said, handing her the list. "Complete." I explained about Buddy Fitch.

"He told me that he made the track team at his school because of Marissa," I said. "So that's another thing she made happen by herself."

She squeezed my arm, her voice breaking. "Now don't make me cry. I've managed to hold it together so far. I'm going to take this" — she held up the list — "and have a good, long look at it as soon as I get home."

I glanced around the crowd, which was starting to thin. "I need to get going, but I wanted to say good-bye to Troy first."

"He's over by the food table with his aunt Lorraine. She's probably grilling him about why he's not married yet. I'll bet he'd be eternally grateful if you rescued him."

She wasn't kidding. As soon as I approached, Troy said loudly, "It was a pleasure chatting with you, Aunt Lorraine, but I need to talk to June here."

"Guess what?" I said as he ushered me to a quiet end of the bar. "We found Buddy Fitch. He's here . . . and he's a kid from her Weight Watchers group. So the list's done."

"June, that's incredible."

"Anyway, I was about to leave, but I wanted to say thanks for everything."

"I didn't do much, but you know I was

glad to help any way I could."

"By the way," I boasted, "I wound up getting the promotion at work."

"I knew you would." He rubbed a hand nervously through his hair. "Look . . . about the other day when I came to your office. You told me that the phone message I left you got cut off. Which is probably for the best. I did a lot of blabbering. But the upshot was — and I know this sounds cliché — but as far as what happened in Vegas, it wasn't you. It was me."

"It's okay."

"No, it's not. I snapped at you because you were going to adopt a baby. And did I even understand you right? It sounds now like you aren't going to do it."

"I didn't really want to be a single mom — I got swept up in everything. And as for Vegas, it was no big deal. Honestly. You've been through so much; you and Marissa were so close. I can understand that you'd feel conflicted."

He shook his head and smiled. "I should have seen it coming. I remember the first time I saw you at the funeral, when you came down the line shaking hands. You had that huge black eye, and when you got to where I was, I thought, *Wow, she's hot,* and found myself peeking down your blouse to see how far the bruise went. Then I was disgusted that I'd notice something like that at my own sister's funeral."

Before I could respond — and really, what could one say to that? — a woman approached and said, "Troy, your grandma wants me to tell you that you're needed. They're about to cut the cake."

"Tell her I'll be right there." Then he turned to me. "So you'll keep in touch?"

"Are you kidding? Now that I have this new job, I'm going to need connections in all the right places."

"You got it. Anytime."

I hugged Troy good-bye and then walked back to where Martucci sat, discussing racing strategies with Buddy Fitch. "I'm ready to go when you are," I said.

As we left, I paused at the doorway to take one last look inside the room. Troy and his family gathered around the cake. Twenty-five candles had been lit, and the firelight danced on their faces as they leaned close. No one sang "Happy Birthday." I watched — drained and yet never feeling more full — as Kitty took in a deep breath. And then everyone around her helped blow out the candles in one collective *whoosh*.

CHAPTER 26

"It's strange not to have anything I *have* to do," I said to Martucci as he pulled his car in front of my apartment building. The evening was warm, and he had the moon roof open, exposing a twinkle of city lights.

"You did good."

"I just don't want to go back to my old ways."

He cut the engine. "Then don't."

"How?" As I asked it, I had to marvel. Once again, I was turning to Martucci for advice, when only months ago I could hardly stand to be in the same room with him. He'd changed in my perception from repulsive to . . . well, I wasn't sure. I liked being around him. Suddenly I was noticing things like how he smelled good . . . the rumbly growl of his voice . . . how the corners of his eyes crinkled when he smiled.

"It's easy," he said, grinning — and see? There went the crinkles. "Think about what you would have done before, which would have been nothing. Then do something."

"Very funny." I added, "The old me would leave to go inside right now."

He lifted an eyebrow. "And the new you . . . ?"

I shifted in my seat so I faced him, then I placed one hand behind his head and pulled him close in a kiss. And it was nice — warm and soft and sweet — and I kissed him again, and again, and soon I was gulping him in, and he was tugging me close, tangling his hands in my hair, and it was crazy . . . Dominic Martucci of all people! Yet for once I wasn't second-guessing myself or letting myself get lost in doubt. I knew for certain that — wherever it might go or whatever might happen — sprawled across Martucci's front seat with my tongue greedily seeking his was exactly where I wanted to be right now.

He gazed at me, brushing my hair away from my face. "For the record, Parker," he said, "this definitely qualifies as something."

"Glad you approve. I have to play it by ear now that I don't have a list."

"Mmm. I've been working on one of my own, you know."

"You have?"

"Sure. Ever since I got a preview of your

goodies in Vegas, I've spent a helluva lot of hours thinking exactly what I'd like to do to you." Laying kisses along my neck, trailing them softly down to my throat, he murmured, "It's probably best you don't have a list right now. Mine's going to keep you mighty busy."

Staring at the blank paper before me, I chewed on the tip of my pen. This was harder than I'd thought it would be.

All I'd written so far was, *June's To-Do List.*

I supposed I didn't need a list. My life was already so different from what it used to be, plus Martucci's list was proving to be quite satisfying. Still, a few goals that involved my clothes on couldn't hurt.

The first thing I'd done the Saturday after Marissa's party was pack up the gifts I'd gotten from the baby shower at work and drive to Deedee's house. Even though I knew she had the childbirth class, I figured it couldn't take the entire day. She might have wanted to cut me from her life, but it was going to take a machete to do it.

Deedee answered the door dressed in a tank top over an enormous swell of stomach, and I gaped at her. "Cripes, you swallow the Olson twins since the last time I saw you?"

"I know. I'm a big old cow, huh?"

"Nah. You're cute as ever. But that's a heck of a belly."

She furrowed her brows. "How come you're here? I thought for sure you hated me."

"Not a chance. I'll admit I was disappointed, but how could I be mad? You made the smart choice. Now are you going to make me stand out here, or will you let me in so I can give you these gifts?"

She called Maria over, and I didn't need a translator for the oohs and aahs, especially when I rolled in that Cadillac of a stroller. I'd had no qualms keeping the gifts from my co-workers. I could have put a down payment on a home with all the cash I've laid out for other people over the years. I simply let everyone know it was going to a poor blind grandma, and that was that. There was no need to mention she was twenty-nine.

As Deedee chattered on about running into her archnemesis, Theresa, the other day, I smiled to myself. I'd almost adopted a baby because I was so smitten with the idea of a little girl needing me.

Well, there was still a little girl who needed me.

Sure, she had a tendency to swear and wear too much eyeliner, but she needed me.

It was a few days after that that my brother called to tell me to check my e-mail. "I sent you a file of a page to be posted by our adoption agency. You're a writer — I wanted to see if you had any suggestions."

"You're adopting — that's great! How did that happen?"

"Hold on," he said, "I'll let the boss explain." And he put Charlotte on the line.

She told me how she and Bob had talked on their way home from Deedee's that day and how she had realized that if she could get that excited about a baby she'd known about for less than a day, there'd be no problem bonding with another. The adoption process could take a year or more, she told me, but that was nothing compared with how long they'd already waited.

"And you're not upset that you didn't get Deedee's baby?"

"I was for a bit. Then for the first time I realized that this is going to happen. Bob and I will be parents. The right one will come along. Sad as I was, I had to accept it — that wasn't our baby."

■ ■ ■ ■

Maybe I'd put *Swimming with the dolphins.*

Then again, maybe not. My mom might want to frolic among Flipper's little friends, but it wouldn't make my list.

Truth was, I'd ambled through most of my life, not putting much thought into what I'd wanted. Even for the past year, when I'd worked so hard to complete the list, it had been a list of someone else's dreams. It was time to put my own in motion.

Yet when I wrote down my first task, I surprised even myself.

After all, there were so many places to visit. So many things to do. Maybe marriage or babies. Taking up tap dancing. Reading the classics. Buying a sportier car. There were a million things I could put on my list.

But what I wrote was, *#1. Go skydiving.*

What was up with that?

I'd never had the slightest urge to skydive. In fact, I'd always thought it was about the silliest thing a person could do.

Yet suddenly the idea of making a wild leap — hurtling through the air, yet trusting that I'd know when to open my parachute so I'd have a soft landing — well, it sounded like something I might like to try.

ACKNOWLEDGMENTS

I'd like to make a little list of my own, people in my life to whom I'm indebted for all they've done to make this book possible.

A big thanks goes to Sally Kim — if there's an editor's hall of fame, she deserves to be in it — and everyone at Shaye Areheart; and to Kirsten Manges, for being a wonderful agent (and for lighting that fire under me), and Jenny Meyer for helping June to see more of the world.

My thanks also go out to the "Javiers," Candy Deemer, Kate Holt, and Sandra O'Briant, for keeping me on track; readers Kate McMains, Rose Morales, Mary Jo Reutter, and Shelly Smolinski for advice and input; Monique Raphel High, a great coach and friend; the rideshare agencies and all my rideshare pals, especially Cheryl Collier, Harlan West, Carolyn Hart, and "free gas" survivors Al Rangel, Donna Blanchard, Norma Elston-Adams, Aileen Landau,

Brenda Stevenson, Robert Lew, Sarah Zadok, and Teresa Milliken (it's a miracle any of you speak to me); Lisa Kemp Jones and Susan Smolinski for Vegas inspiration; the book club "chicks" for always asking how the writing's going; Scott Strohmaier who was there for the whining; Marcy Brown, Jerri Simpson, and families for keeping me sane through the editing process; my brothers Bob and Jim for (hopefully) being good sports (and I can think of a million reasons I'm grateful for them); and my son, Danny, who'd always pause a video game if I really, *really* needed to bounce something off him.

Last, I want to thank my parents, who not only didn't try to stop me from being a writer, but who actually encouraged it.

ABOUT THE AUTHOR

Jill Smolinski is the author of *Flip-Flopped*. She currently lives in southern California with her son. Visit her at www.jillsmolinski .com.